THE LAZA

Stuart Prebble was born in London in 1951. He read English Language and Literature at the University of Newcastle upon Tyne, then joined the BBC as a trainee journalist and worked for several years as an on-screen reporter in the North-East and on national television news. In 1981 he joined Granada Television where he now works as a Producer/ Director in current affairs.

Stuart Prebble lives in Cheshire with his wife Marilyn and their two daughters. *The Lazarus File* is his second novel, following *A Power in the Land* (Collins, 1988).

STUART PREBBLE

The Lazarus File

FONTANA/Collins

NOTE

This is a work of fiction. All the characters and institutions in this novel are wholly imaginary and are not intended to bear any resemblance to any real person, living or dead, or any company or government body

First published by Fontana Paperbacks 1989
Copyright © Stuart Prebble 1989

Printed and bound in Great Britain by
William Collins Sons & Co. Ltd, Glasgow

For my daughters,
Alex and Sam

CHAPTER ONE

The thin wail of an emergency siren pierced the city night from far away across the empty streets. An orange glow on the horizon cast streaks of light into the sky, acting as a beacon to guide Jonathan Maguire towards his destination. Above the engine noise from his rusting Citroën, the urgent call drew him on. He wondered whether the local radio had been alerted and reached across to switch on the news. A friendly Glaswegian voice was immediately familiar as that of the popular disc jockey who kept company with insomniacs.

'It's "Night-time" taking you through the wee small hours. Let's take another call now, and it's Mavis from Roxhampton. Hello Mavis, you're a regular voice these nights, what's on your mind sweetheart . . .?' Maguire dimmed the sound. The intimate Scots whisper faded into the background as Maguire concentrated on the noise which now seemed to be all around him. He looked at his watch and saw in the darkness the pale-green glow from the luminous dial: 1.30. Ten minutes ago he had been in bed. The crew would not be as quick, but Maguire always seemed to be on the scene early.

He wondered how many times he had driven fast through the night towards the scene of someone else's disaster. A routine call from the duty man on the newsdesk to the fire brigade had produced something unusual – an incident in progress. Little was known so far except that the incident involved a domestic residence and that several people were still inside. That was enough to justify the duty newsman waking Maguire; these days it did not need to be much to justify waking Maguire. Frequently the only available pictures for the early-evening news were morning-after shots of the smoking embers of another warehouse, probably burned down by the owner for the insurance money. The chance, however remote, of having a reporter on the spot of a house-fire in progress which might yield tales of heroism and tragedy, and to get good action movie, was too good to miss. Anyway Maguire was a bachelor; more important still, he was a freelance who was paid according to the number of stories he covered. Everyone on the desk knew that he was among the few who did not complain too loudly when asked to leave his bed in the middle of the night. Fifteen minutes ago he had been in another world, dreaming fantastic dreams. Now, uncertain whether he was awake or asleep, Maguire sped towards the shrill sound.

As the ageing black bullfrog-nosed car sped through the wet streets, the vivid glow from the distant flames was overlaid by regular flashes of blue light. Many emergency vehicles were closing in ahead of him. Police, fire, ambulances and press; all converged on the location of tomorrow's news. Maguire wound down the window, which stuck halfway and forced him to push it down with his left hand. The wail floated across the cool night air towards him and grew still louder. In ten minutes his growing nervousness would be stomach cramp, in ten years it would be an ulcer, but at this moment Maguire preferred to think of it as plain adrenaline.

He had little doubt that by the time he arrived on

8

the scene the action would be over. Most frequently it was. It would usually take the fire brigade fifteen minutes after getting to an incident to decide that it was worth reporting back in detail; then it could be another hour before the next of the regular calls from the newsdesk to brigade headquarters. The newsman's call for updated stories for the early radio bulletins usually woke up the duty switchboard operator. 'Nothing newsworthy,' he would say, in a tired and irritated voice. 'You put out the fires and I'll decide what's newsworthy.' Maguire had said the same thing many times. So by the time the reporter had been woken up and was on the scene, the excitement was almost always over. He would arrive just as the last hoses were being rolled away and the ambulances were disappearing into the distance.

'You should have been here an hour ago – it was pandemonium.' Maguire was never certain whether or not the firemen said it just to irritate him. If so, it was a consistently successful trick. While the newspapermen hurriedly scribbled down stories of deaths and narrow escapes for the last editions, there was nothing left to point a television camera at. Most often Maguire would ask the cameraman to shoot some routine news-footage and then go home to bed, lying there as night turned into day, unable to sleep.

This time it looked as though the situation might be very different. Everything indicated that there was still plenty going on. His destination was just a few streets away now. The grey houses of the Bentley estate were silhouetted against the orange sky. Above the gable ends of the rows of dismal terraces, sparks hissed upwards into dark oblivion. Maguire turned off the radio. The wailing siren seemed to have stopped but there was something else. He could not immediately

9

identify it. An intermittent cry, like the tortured alarm-call of a wounded animal, seemed to rise above every other sound and render them mute. This sound was unfamiliar; it was not from the sirens or the machinery. The noise of fire-fighting machines and men grew louder again as Maguire rounded the last corner; but still, far above the clamour, the now unmistakable sound of a woman screaming rent the night.

He double-parked the Citroën next to a police-car and leapt out, already running towards the blazing block of flats. Maguire broke through the line of onlookers, their bright faces illuminated by excitement and by the light from the fire. A uniformed constable approached him with whom he had a nodding acquaintance, but all the same he reached into an inside pocket and produced a plastic pass.

'I'm press. Maguire. Stadium Television.'

The smooth face of the young constable was aglow. 'All right Maguire, but don't get too close. It's a nasty one.'

Maguire did not hear him. His eyes were searching the scene for the focus of the action, and his mind was trying to sort out the terrible sounds. A familiar acrid smell filled his nostrils. These times and places always smelled the same. Maguire had tasted this smell in his mouth and in his stomach a hundred times before tonight and knew that he would experience it a hundred times more. It was the stench of wet wood burning, and of the thick, black and poisonous smoke from blazing foam-filled furniture diffused into the damp night.

In front of him the low-rise block of flats was surrounded by fire engines. A dozen canvas hoses snaked like the tentacles of some fantastic beast across overgrown gardens and into the arms of groups of firemen who were engaged in a disciplined struggle to control them. These scenes always reminded Maguire of old news footage of the Blitz. The men leaned back and supported each other to control the thrust of thousands of gallons of water, directing the jets upwards towards the roof and through the broken windows. Flames licked and burst forth from a balcony and sporadically through the shattering tiles, but no one was watching them. All attention was directed to the window of a third-storey room to one side of the main source of the fire. There, through the smoke, Maguire glimpsed the dark figure and outstretched arms of a young woman. Her head appeared through the thick folds of smoke and she screamed a scream which sliced through the darkness and the thick greasy air. Again and again the young woman screamed until she choked and screamed again, and then as the smoke engulfed her, she gasped a deep animal-like cough and seemed to fall backwards into the building, her voice momentarily stifled. Maguire felt his stomach rise inside him with the nausea of the air he breathed and the agony of the moment.

'Get a ladder in there for Chris'sake.' It was one of the young firemen, pointing urgently and helplessly to the window.

'We're trying but we can't get the damned thing close enough.'

The revving of the fire-vehicle drowned out all else as it was manoeuvred into position, crashing over the pavement and into a garden wall in the rush. Maguire looked up again. Smoke stung his eyes and tears streamed down his cheeks as he squinted through the darkness. There was more activity at the third-storey window. A confusion of flailing limbs was visible through the smoke. It seemed for a moment as though the woman was preparing to jump, but a new cloud of smoke belched from the window, obscuring Maguire's view. He looked desperately all around for the camera-crew and mentally cursed the fact that their hunger for a story never matched his own. There was no sign of them. Still the ladder was being edged into position, pushing over the concrete bollards which enclosed the gardens and crunching them under giant wheels. Maguire moved closer. For an instant the clouds of smoke cleared enough for him to see. A small child was being held out of the window. He tried hard to hear above the roar of the fire engine. Again he could hear the woman calling.

'My baby. Save her. Please save my baby.'

The voice faded once more into silence but the smoke subsided and Maguire could see the tiny child being held up by her wrists, her small brown legs pedalling wildly as if to gain a foothold in the empty air beneath her. He saw in a frozen instant the fear in her eyes as the child looked down, and suddenly Maguire knew that she was going to fall. He turned quickly around and saw at once that all the firemen were involved in moving the ladder into place. There was a second of indecision. He looked at his own hands and momentarily it seemed to him that they were not his, that they belonged to someone else. There was his notebook, a dirty blank page ready for the words he would use to describe just another tragic fire, someone else's disaster. He threw the book into the mud and ran forward, his sudden movement catching the attention of a fireman next to him.

'Hey, don't get too close!' But as he shouted the fireman saw the reason for Maguire's dash toward the house, and ran after him. Both men reached the spot below the window at the same moment. Maguire braced himself and looked directly upwards, only to see the tiny splayed-out body hurtling towards him. Instinctively he linked hands with the fireman, and a split second later the body crashed mightily on to his arms, painfully shattering the grip and falling heavily on to the ground at their feet.

Maguire felt that he could not bear to look down. His eyes filled as though with a rush of blood and heavy weights pulled down on his eyelids. A glance was enough. The child's legs and arms were spreadeagled at bizarre angles, and dark-red blood oozed copiously from a gaping wound in her skull. The cry of horror from far above his head could have been his own. The mother's scream mingled with the silent scream which was erupting from deep inside him. The swirling smoke had parted enough for the mother to see her own tragedy clearly. Maguire wanted to move forward, to shield this woman from the reality, to make it undone. He wanted the power to push back time, to reach back into the recent past and move the pieces differently, as though by moving them as he had moved them before he had been responsible for what had happened. He felt sick at his own impotence as he turned his gaze again to the shattered body of the dead child. The dark-brown eyes of the small face stared vacantly out into the night and told the world that they did not understand. Through his tears, Maguire's eyes mirrored her question, and he too could find no answer.

Two hundred yards away, a man's narrow yellow eyes blinked away wisps of smoke. Pale and effeminate features were lit by the distant glow and framed by a black balaclava. The rain had stopped and the new stillness carried the faraway sounds uninterrupted across the open space to where he stood. The Asian mother of a dead child whimpered pathetically as a fireman supported her towards her sorrow. In this dark corner, and very slowly, the enlarged head lifted and the flabby chin jutted out, fleshy cheeks cracked into ugly dimples and the yellow eyes disappeared into two puffy mounds of flesh. A remote, haunting giggle began deep inside the fat throat and vibrated upwards. For a minute the man stood still, his arms hugging himself in delight. The whimpering from the distance turned into moaning as the mother cuddled the shattered head of her dead baby, and large globules of blood splashed on to the pale-pink flowers of her well-worn nylon dressing gown. Still the fat man giggled and the fleshy pink jowls vibrated in his pleasure; until suddenly his body stiffened and abruptly one arm was brought up in a clenched fist and the palm of the other slapped across his forearm. The obscene gesture came down just as suddenly, and the figure turned sharply around and dissolved into the night.

'Did you get the pictures?'

Though pressed firmly into his clenched fists, Maguire's eyes could see the dead face of the child as clearly as though she was still lying on the ground at his feet. The abrupt voice brought him sharply back to reality. He looked up from his seat on the garden wall to see Tim Walker, his Aaton camera slung over his shoulder.

'What? The what?'

'The pictures – family pictures of the dead children. Foster is sure to want them. Didn't you get here first?'

'Children? Dead children?' Maguire stood up. Tonight, someone else's tragedy had become his own. 'Are there more than one?'

14

'Three as far as I can gather.' Walker looked over his shoulder. 'Is that right, Bill? The police did say three kids dead?' Tim was an Australian freelance news cameraman who had stopped off in Britain for a month five years ago. He had seen it all and done it all, at scenes of death and disaster and genocide all around the world. For him, three dead children were all in a night's work. He looked back at Maguire and saw that he had sunk down on to the wall. 'If you haven't got them I've a feeling you've been beaten to it by the man from the *Mail*. He's been talking to neighbours. I've seen him.'

'Have you got all the movie?' Maguire pressed the fingernails of both hands into his scalp and scratched hard, then cupped his hands together behind his head. He had forgotten his anger at the crew's late arrival and was still trying to regain his wits. 'I'm sorry I wasn't with you. Did you get much action?'

'I got here in time to see the last of the stretchers go into the ambulance and then the mother was carried in. She didn't look hurt but she was in a hell of a state.'

'Hardly surprising.' It was the soundman. Bill Tyler, a Stadium TV staffer, had been recording wild track sound of the engines leaving and had missed the first part of the exchange. 'Three kids dead in a fire and you'd be in a bit of a state.'

'Gentle Jesus.' Maguire looked around. 'Where's the guy from the *Mail*?'

Tim Walker waved in the general direction of the last remaining fire engines. 'I'll shoot some mopping up while you're negotiating. I got some good pictures of the flames if you need something to trade.'

Maguire walked past small groups of neighbours and onlookers. Some drank tea brought hurriedly from their houses and exchanged gossip about the family that had been all but obliterated this night. He looked for the man from the *Mail*.

15

CHAPTER TWO

The glorious first love scene from *La Bohème* burst forth from the six large speakers carefully positioned around the Mayfair penthouse, filling every corner of every room with music. The passionate duet floated across the antique leather chesterfields, sending perceptible vibrations through the crystal chandeliers but leaving the marble busts of Roman warriors utterly unmoved upon their plinths. Though he was now feeling a distinct chill causing goosebumps to tide across his pale soft skin, Sir John Bartholomew was determined neither to run more hot water nor to get out of his bath until Mimi had accepted Rodolfo's advances. Emerging fractionally from beneath the soapy water, his index finger conducted the singers who performed for him behind his eyelids. His lip curled at one corner, an involuntary reaction to the magnificence of Rodolfo's courtship. Two startling chords were his cue to emerge from the water, and in the sudden silence he was aware of the warble of the telephone.

Sir John Bartholomew made no attempt to hurry. The tepid water slopped generously on to the heated marble floor as he reached for his luxurious silk-lined dressing gown and put his wet feet into soft leather slippers. He pushed freckled fingers through his greying auburn hair, and padded lazily across the thick Chinese rug towards the hi-fi where he flicked a switch. The first bars of Act Two groaned gradually to a stop and into silence. The telephone was still warbling. He snatched at the receiver.

'Bartholomew.'

'Is that Sir John Bartholomew of the Mallin Harcourt Merchant Bank?' The man's voice was distant and precise. There was an accent which, though he considered himself rather an expert on the subject, Sir John Bartholomew was unable immediately to identify. His expression indicated irritation, but his voice remained composed.

'This is he. And who is speaking?'

There was a pause and then a crackle on the line. Bartholomew's irritation increased as the clear ticking of an enormous grandfather clock in the hallway marked the passing seconds. A flicker of curiosity creased the waxen white skin of his forehead and he reached forward to lift a concealed lid in the telephone table. He pressed the button marked 'record'.

'Now listen very closely.' The words were enunciated carefully and separately, as though cut out and pasted together like a blackmail note. 'You don't know me but I know you. I've got a piece of information for you.' Bartholomew was about to interrupt but something in the man's tone forestalled him. 'Watch the television at 9.30 tonight. Channel 4. You'll see something of particular interest to you. And remember when you see it that there is more to come.' There was now a tone of taunting enjoyment in the voice. 'Think about that, Sir John. Much more to come. Good night.' There followed the distinctive electronic click which instantly told Bartholomew that he had been listening to a tape recording. A thousand memories flooded into his head as he struggled to react.

'But I have an engagement.' The banker's accent was pompous and aristocratic, and his response

17

sounded indignant and lame. 'I won't be here. What's all this about?' The question was interrupted by a further sharp click followed by a tone. 'Who is this?' Bartholomew called pathetically into the dead line, and then held the receiver away from him, looking at it as though demanding an explanation. 'Damned irritating. Damned peculiar.' He slammed it down on the cradle.

Half an hour later Sir John Bartholomew was standing in front of his dressing table and straightening his tie, but the shallow cracks turning down at the corners of his eyes indicated that his mind was elsewhere. In the background Rodolfo was breaking his heart over Mimi's fatal illness, but Sir John was not sympathetic. It took two attempts to position the Windsor knot exactly as he liked it. His afternoon had been spent at a meeting to coordinate City events for this year's Lord Mayor's parade and banquet. The Jermyn Street business suit he had worn all day was hanging in the wardrobe behind him, and now he wore a much older and far more comfortable Harris tweed. As he ran two hairbrushes backwards in parallel to smooth the wispy hair on each side of his otherwise balding head, he was preoccupied by the irritating telephone call. The penthouse belonged to the bank and the number was not in the directory. How could the caller have known it, or that he was here; and what the devil was it all about? Channel 4 at 9.30. Bartholomew scarcely ever watched the television; when he did it was usually because a member of his board of directors was giving expert opinion on the state of the markets or on the Chancellor's latest piece of stupid interference in things he knew far too little about. Even then the Chairman switched off as soon as he had assured himself that his man was not making a fool of himself.

He looked at his watch. The bulky gold was uncharacteristically ostentatious for the English gentleman banker. It showed 9 p.m. He was due to have dinner, as always on a Saturday evening, at the Travellers' Club. Tonight's menu included mutton, a speciality of the chef and one of Sir John's particular favourites. The friends with whom he had dined each Saturday for twenty years, barring high-days and holidays, would be waiting. Channel 4 at 9.30. He cursed aloud and his irritation brought a bitter taste scrambling upwards from the pit of his stomach and into the back of his throat. The incident had disturbed his temperamental digestion and he now had little chance of enjoying his dinner.

Sir John Bartholomew mumbled his annoyance as he picked up his tortoiseshell-rimmed half-moon spectacles and looked around for a newspaper. A crumpled copy of the *Financial Times* lay in a waste-paper basket under the desk. He carefully unfolded it and wondered where he would find the television billing. He could instantly turn to every other regular feature of the newspaper, but not this one. He scanned ten pages before he found it. 9.30. His finger ran down the column. *Encounter*. It was one of the few television programmes of which he had heard. He adjusted his spectacles to read the details and whispered the words, his tone unambiguously derisive. 'The hard-hitting weekly news magazine programme uncovers some shady deals in the nuclear industry.' Bartholomew blew out his cheeks and exhaled noisily. The thin flesh of his grainy face was momentarily smooth before settling into its more familiar deep lines. Sitting heavily down on to the worn leather chair behind him, he adjusted his spectacles and studied the billing once again as if to extract more information from it. There was none. He closed the paper suddenly and angrily threw it on to the Chinese rug. The vague ache which had hovered ominously around and above his heart for the last half-hour now stung him sharply for the first time in several weeks, and Sir John reached for the small golden pill-box which was never far from his side and placed a tiny tablet on his tongue. Within moments the ache began to recede. Whatever happened now the relaxing evening he had planned for himself was ruined. A moment later he picked up the telephone and dialled a number he knew by heart.

'Fielding? Sir John Bartholomew. Tell the others that I'm afraid I'll be a little delayed for our regular gathering. Tell them to eat and that I'll try to join them for bridge and liqueurs.' There was a pause while the elderly doorman repeated the message at dictation speed. 'Thank you, Fielding. Goodbye.'

Bartholomew was staring blankly into the television screen as a colourful advertisement for a popular breakfast cereal he had never heard of was followed by another for a group of tyre and exhaust centres he would never have need to use. The jingles washed over him. His mind was focusing on the telephone call and the upcoming programme. He knew little about the nuclear industry and in the ordinary run of things he would have cared about it still less; but just at the moment the state of this particular industry was of very considerable importance to him.

Money. That was what Sir John Bartholomew knew about. It was what he was good at. His remarkable aptitude was still to be discovered when he left the Office at the relatively young age of thirty-eight. The clear evidence of a heart murmur on his routine ECG had been enough to be of concern to the service, but not sufficiently serious to alarm an ordinary employer in the outside world, especially not when that employer was so well disposed to men from Bartholomew's particular background. Like many of his colleagues before him, Bartholomew had joined the Mallin Harcourt Merchant Bank as a junior director, a position in which his unusual and developing talent for money quickly became conspicuous. It was the reason that he had been made Vice-Chairman at forty-eight and that at only fifty-eight he was now the Chairman of the bank.

Even if he had been innumerate, Mallin Harcourt would probably have done its best to keep a chap like Bartholomew in a respectable if perhaps relatively junior position. His friends and contacts in Whitehall and in military establishments around the world would be of enormous use to the bank. As it was, though, his acute political and financial abilities had enabled him to bypass many others who might have expected preferment ahead of him. It was a situation which had brought him widespread admiration and few friends.

Mallin Harcourt was one of the most respected names in the City of London and in the exclusive world of high finance way beyond. Along with the Chairmanship of the bank had come his knighthood. Sir John Bartholomew had joined the great and the good. The wilderness of mirrors was way behind him now, and the many public services he performed these days bore very little resemblance to the kind of services he performed for the unknowing and ungrateful British public twenty-five years ago. The few people who had ever known about the less public activities of Johnny Bartholomew in his earlier incarnation were either compromised by their own involvement in the same matters or they were dead. Either was equally secure.

These days Sir John felt completely at home in the

conservative society of exceedingly well-to-do English gentlemen bankers; but deep in the background he also remained a part of that world on the other side of the looking-glass which, once inside, no one ever completely leaves. It is a world in which traitors are seen lurking in every well-intentioned pressure-group; it is a world populated by people who know that only their constant vigilance prevents the forces of foreign ideas from engulfing our island race. All this was a part of his life of which Sir John Bartholomew spoke very little. He did not need to. His views were well known to those he wished to know them. A member of the Travellers' Club who was also a knight of the realm had usually served Queen and country in a manner which it was scarcely the done thing to boast about.

Sir John Bartholomew was a happy man; a square peg in a square hole. In addition to being at home with matters of high finance, the wider politics of the world of international finance had also come very easily to him after his life in the service. Many of the same rules applied. Much of the success or failure depended on backing instinctive judgements about people and situations. Much also depended on knowing whether or not to place trust in someone you were dealing with. Sir John had quickly formed the view that many of the same criteria were applicable. As in the service, anyone with a hint of liberal or reformist zeal about them was immediately suspect. The same person who would be likely to compromise on a national objective because of wider considerations of justice or human rights would also be the kind of person who would allow humanitarian or social considerations to get in the way of the interests of the bank's shareholders. Neither man was to be trusted. A fellow must, above all, be

22

sound; and if he was sound then one could trust him with investment of money, of national ambitions, or with one's life. If he was not, then far better off without him. Sir John Bartholomew prided himself on being a good judge of people and a good judge of situations.

Recent business had, however, taken the Chairman a little beyond the area in which he operated most comfortably. In normal circumstances it made very little difference whether the project under discussion was a multi-billion yen office development in the Ginza district of Tokyo, or an international syndicate of City gentlemen with more cash than they were able to account for establishing a string of stud farms in Virginia. It was all a question of risk and Sir John Bartholomew had a nose for a risk. Two decades ago his talent in such matters had saved his own life more than once, and the lives of others. The matter presently in hand was somewhat different. He had no aptitude for anything scientific and he knew nothing about the technical side of the nuclear power business. All he knew was that a consortium of British and American companies were working together on a plan to sell a new and controversial type of nuclear reactor to the British Energy Corporation. He also knew that the Americans had particular long-term reasons for wanting the project to be a success and therefore money was no object in the pursuit of a successful sale. That was where the bank came in. If the consortium was successful, Mallin Harcourt would put together the financial package. It would amount to several billions of dollars. The bank would stand to make a percentage of the total. A successful deal for the Americans would mean a very handsome profit for Mallin Harcourt. It was the familiar territory of balancing risk against return.

There was, however, one aspect of this particular matter which made it of special personal interest to the Chairman, and it was an aspect which he would sooner not have to discuss with the board. So Mallin Harcourt, in the person of its revered Chairman Sir John Bartholomew, was doing everything in its power to make sure everything went smoothly.

Things had been going conspicuously well, and Mallin Harcourt was in its element in such a role. The Government was, as usual, sympathetic; and the Opposition was, also as usual, vociferous but ineffective. Ripples were being smoothed, wrinkles were being ironed out, and Ministers were being handled. A very lucrative deal was on the way for the bank and Sir John Bartholomew was at the helm.

So, what was he to make of this? An anonymous telephone caller who knew his ex-directory number and made reference to a television programme famous for its investigations was deeply irritating. Sir John Bartholomew leaned across the arm of his chair to pour a second glass of Remy Martin and as he looked up, the familiar logo of Stadium Television dissolved into a fast montage of action stills and dramatic theme music which heralded the start of the *Encounter* programme. Without taking his eyes from the screen, Bartholomew flicked a switch on the remote control and behind the false door of a walnut cabinet beneath the set, a video-cassette dropped into place and began recording.

'Good evening.' The caption super-imposed across the bottom of the screen announced Peter Griffiths. So this was Peter Griffiths. Bartholomew had heard the name: Griffiths was an investigative journalist whose speciality was the City of London. Time and again the lugubrious Griffiths and his *Encounter* programme had

24

produced stories of insider dealing, insurance swindles and tax-evasions among the very rich which had embarrassed the financial world and caused uncertainty among shareholders. Uncertainty and embarrassment were two things which the merchant banking sector did not like. They adversely affected confidence, and any loss of confidence cost money and profits. That was always a cause for concern. Bartholomew had never been directly affected by such reporting, but had witnessed and shared the irritation of his friends and colleagues. 'Something ought to be done about these people.' He had often heard the sentiment uttered by exasperated clients.

'I'd like to know where the hell they get their information from. Someone must be feeding them.'

The Chairman of the bank knew only too well from his own experience how easy it is to get inside information if the investigator is sufficiently patient and resourceful. Access to an insider was always a wonderful advantage but was rarely achievable. When he heard such complaints he would usually suppress a smile and earnestly agree that it was outrageous and intolerable, and then quickly get on with the business in hand. It was only a television programme, he would reassure them; they never change anything. For once, though, Sir John Bartholomew was intent on hearing what Mr Peter Griffiths had to say.

'Tonight we look at an extraordinary story about the nuclear power business. *Encounter* has obtained secret documents which show how American Energy Industries, the biggest manufacturer of nuclear power plants in the States, is going to unusual lengths to sell a new kind of nuclear reactor to Britain. And it seems that the reason is not their appetite for British or even

European markets. Their eyes are set much further away – the Far East, and notably North Korea.'

Long thin fingers curled loosely around the large bowl of the brandy goblet now tightened and came dangerously close to shattering the glass. The words struck the usually reserved and impassive Sir John Bartholomew like a thunderbolt and he reached again, as a reflex, for the small golden pill-box. A small vein pulsed beneath the tight and almost translucent skin at his temple. Without taking his eyes from the screen, he reached for the elegant white trimphone and pressed a pre-programmed three-figure short-dial. A few seconds later the ringing tone ended in a sharp click. Bartholomew did not wait for a voice.

'Tremayne? Bartholomew. Are you watching the television? Then switch it on. Get a cassette of the programme and find out what you can. I'm in Milan tomorrow and Monday. Meet me in the office on Tuesday morning at seven-thirty.' Bartholomew replaced the receiver and concentrated. Griffiths had moved across the studio until he stood in front of a huge blown-up silhouette photograph of a sinister-looking nuclear reactor. The cameras closed in on the long and lined face.

'The nuclear non-proliferation treaty prevents American companies from exporting nuclear technology to communist countries. The United States and Britain are both signatories to that agreement, and so American Energy Industries cannot sell to North Korea directly. That's where we come in. Britain's interpretation of the NPT rules is less strict. The technology *could* go to the Far East from here, and documents which have come into our possession show that the Americans intend to launder the technology through

Britain, in order to get around their obligations under an international treaty. But they can only do that if Britain accepts that the new reactor reaches our stringent safety standards – and that is the subject of a public inquiry going on at Ringwood at the moment. Which is why the Americans are going to unprecedented lengths to make sure that the inquiry finds in their favour. This report from Jonathan Rigby.'

Sir John Bartholomew was no longer listening. He had heard enough. Now he was interested in something which had already been said and he stared at the screen as though mesmerized. The cameras panned across the Wessex countryside to the area where the British Energy Corporation proposed building the new-generation American reactor, but Bartholomew had no interest in the pretty landscapes or the earnest interviews with concerned local residents. He knew what he was waiting for, and when it came he leapt forward like an ageing lion and crouched stiffly in front of the television set, his face only inches away from the screen.

'Internal memoranda and other documents originating from American Energy Industries which have come into our possession indicate that the company is prepared to go to almost any lengths to secure approval for their reactor in Great Britain. The company has authorized its partners and representatives in the UK to spare no expense in time and money to win the arguments at the public inquiry.'

As Peter Griffiths came on screen to sum up the report and to trail the following week's programme, Sir John Bartholomew was already using the remote control to wind back the video cassette. The visual search function made the reporter walk backwards across an open field before Bartholomew found what he was looking for. He froze the frame. The picture vibrated

27

irritatingly. He scanned the screen inch by inch looking for a familiar symbol. At such close quarters he found it almost impossible to make out an image among the minute dots and between the six hundred and twenty-five black lines which divided up the screen. Then he found it. Underneath the American Energy Industries letterhead was the faint trace of an imprint of a rubber stamp. The blurred screen made it impossible to read, but the design was sufficiently familiar to Sir John Bartholomew for him to know already what he needed to know. It said 'Received Mallin Harcourt . . .' and then a date. The secret papers had come from the files of his own merchant bank, and if Stadium Television had those, what the hell else did they have?

CHAPTER THREE

'Here Tibby Tibby Tibby. Here Tibby. Nice pussy. Where are you now? Come on then. Come on.' Harriet Nuttall scuttled along in the rough grass on her hands and knees with an agility that quite belied her age. Chasing her very favourite of all cats when he had been out all night for two nights in succession was an exercise important enough to put youth into her stiff limbs; but Tibby was not to be tempted. The long white fur brushed past the stalks of brightly coloured dahlias as the animal padded by, and the oriental, almost human face turned towards the appealing voice then contemptuously ignored it. Tibby had other matters on his mind. Only when he had disappeared into the undergrowth did Miss Nuttall's movements more accurately suggest her age.

Sometimes it was only with difficulty that she could believe that this would be her twentieth year in retirement. A generation of cats had come and gone since she had given up her life's work, only to have as many of them around her feet as ever she did when she was one of the most famous cat breeders in the country. Even when it had been her livelihood, Harriet Nuttall had regarded the ten or fifteen cats of many types that she kept around the house as her friends. Customers would come to the large tumbledown house in two acres of garden which was her home and her place of work. Harriet would give them a cup of tea and would sit and talk to them for half an hour about their work, their hobbies, their children, their holidays; anything except animals. As she did so she would watch. She would look carefully to see how the customer reacted to an approaching feline; whether the affection was spontaneous and genuine. She would examine how comfortable the customer seemed with the animal and, just as important, how the animal reacted to the customer. She would try to assess whether the customer wanted one of her prized and special cats for a beloved friend of the family, or as a novelty or talking point among smart friends. Many times Harriet had turned away perfectly good paying customers because she had not liked the way one of her cats was being petted.

'I'm so sorry that you have had a wasted journey. I've no cats for sale at the moment. Good day to you.'

'But all these? You must – '

'Sorry. All my own pets, I'm afraid. None for sale at the moment and none likely to be in the near future. Try a pet shop. Good day.'

The customer might have travelled a hundred miles to buy one of Harriet Nuttall's famous cats, but it made no difference. She would scuttle the bemused would-be buyer out of the house, and then return to the cat in question and give it an extra hug and some words of encouragement.

'Now then. We wouldn't let you go to stay in a house like theirs, would we? Not at all. You're a beauty for sure, but you're not *just* an ornament are you? No. You stay with Harriet. Good pussy.'

Harriet Nuttall saved her quiet voice for her animals. With human beings she was invariably loud and forthright. Shopkeepers down in Lansbury where she bought her groceries once a week were always courteous, for she was a good customer. She would announce her requirements for all to hear, and if the shopkeeper made the smallest mistake she would point

30

it out at the same volume. Always having been alone and having fended for herself in a world which had not yet heard of women's liberation, she had developed a strident and no-nonsense manner which some now considered eccentric. They would smile and say 'Good day Miss Nuttall' as she left, and the younger women would raise their eyes to the ceiling and share a patronizing smile. Unaware and unconcerned, Harriet would roar up the hill in her black Morris 1000 back towards Lane End and unload the treats she had bought for her companions.

'No, this is not for you, Toby,' Harriet would gently scold. 'You had a very special present yesterday, didn't you? You mustn't be a greedy pussy. We don't want you to get fat, do we?' The cats would purr and Harriet would purr back at them.

Now abandoning hope of tempting Tibby indoors for another afternoon, Harriet Nuttall collected the bunch of sweet-peas she had come into the garden to pick and held them to her face to enjoy their special fragrance. The garden was well-stocked with perennials, and Michael, who helped her out one day a week, saw to it that everything was kept neat and under control. The one flower she insisted on planting herself and watching over every year was her sweet-peas. She would carefully place fifty small plants which she had grown from seed alongside the long brick wall which skirted the far end of her garden, dividing it from the small and neat blocks of housing association flats on the other side. Throughout July and August each year her house, which she sometimes thought was prone to a slightly musty feeling, would be full of dozens of tiny vases of multi-coloured flowers, and the scent made Harriet feel as though it was sunny even when it was raining outside.

31

Now it was getting towards the end of September and cooler weather was in the air. The sweet-peas were starting to look very sad, and it was especially important to enjoy them in their first brief moment of bloom. This particular bunch was going into the small terra-cotta vase she kept on the kitchen table where she did her work. Once indoors, she set down the flowers and asked Kitty kindly not to walk on her neat pile of handwritten pages. She sat in the unvarnished pine windsor chair at her kitchen table and took up her pen to write.

Humanity in general and the British public in particular have deliberately been kept ignorant of the fact that their extravagant and arbitrary consumption of electricity is creating these dangerous and unwanted pollutants. With the technology available at this time, mankind cannot guarantee safe storage and control for even a few decades in the case of high-level waste. In the case of the long-lived actinides, the problems caused are effectively for ever.

She set down her pen and read from the top of the page, her mouth forming the words under her breath. The thin vertical lines which worked downwards from her bottom lip and upwards from her top, pinched close together in furrows. She was impatient with herself. She had reminded herself time and time again and still she kept on making the same mistake. Harriet took her pen and decisively scored out the last paragraph.

'I'm preaching again. We mustn't preach, must we Dora. We mustn't preach. We must stick to the facts.' The beautiful grey-blue cat with vivid blue eyes swished its tail arrogantly and walked across the page. Harriet waited for the animal to pick its way carefully past before she began writing again.

Harriet Nuttall had become involved with nuclear energy late in life; in her seventy-fifth year to be precise. It had interrupted her otherwise tranquil and sometimes even boring retirement one cold and wet November evening when a young man wearing a grey duffle-coat and a woolly hat had knocked at her door and asked if she would sign a petition. Harriet had never signed a petition in her life, but as it was pouring with wintry rain and the young man seemed soaked through, she asked him into the house. She found that despite his rather untidy long hair and wispy beard, he had a very nice way with cats. She had given the young man a cup of tea and a piece of layer cake which she had baked that same afternoon. The petition, it turned out, was in protest against a plan to transport nuclear waste by rail through Lansbury on the way to reprocessing at Sellafield. It was being proposed that freight wagons loaded up with highly active nuclear fuel from power stations all over Britain would pass through the village. Harriet was horrified to hear from the young man that the trains would trundle past the playground of the primary school half a mile away where she herself had begun her education seventy years earlier. They would also travel over the old railway bridge at the bottom of Lane End which was at least a century old and already had weight restrictions.

So what was so bad about this nuclear waste or whatever you call it, and what does 'highly active' mean, Harriet had asked. If it leaked, said the young man, it could contaminate an area for miles around. The material on its way through Lansbury had a nuclear half-life of twenty-four thousand years. That would mean that the entire area would effectively become uninhabitable for ever. Harriet Nuttall was an intelligent and accomplished woman who had single-handedly run her own life and her own business for more than half a century. Nevertheless she had never come across the expression 'half-life' and had not the slightest idea what it meant. When the young man explained it to her in concise and sober terms, she replied that never in all her seventy-five years had she heard anything which she had found so shocking. She had immediately signed the petition and asked how she could find out more.

The young man with the nice way with cats, it turned out, also had a nice way with old spinsters and he had been glad to take her along to the weekly meeting of Friends of the Earth. Harriet had listened intently as the guest speaker had talked about the burning of plastic waste materials, the dumping of residue in the North Sea, and the effect it was having on fish. The man showed a series of lurid and disturbing colour slides of dreadfully diseased marine life, riddled with growths and genetic deformities. They made Harriet shudder in revulsion. Her cats ate a lot of fish. The more she saw, and the more she heard, the more outraged she became; but nothing angered her as much as the things she heard about nuclear power. How could we, she would ask in exasperation, be so irresponsible as to produce dangerous material which we are leaving for those who come after us to deal with? Nothing could be worth it. It was deeply offensive to everything she had been taught by her family and at school more than sixty years ago. Hers was a generation which placed great importance on personal responsibility and on sense of duty. The idea of passing on problems to unborn children and to their unborn children for generations ahead was genuinely horrifying to her, and brought out in her feelings of indignation which she had never in her life felt before, or even known that she was capable of. We would all be better living by candlelight than producing electricity by such a method, she would tell her friends and neighbours.

At one moment she made up her mind to do exactly that, as her personal protest, and as a way of avoiding paying another single penny to the people who were producing this dreadful waste material. Then she made up her mind to do much more, anything she could in fact, in whatever time she had left. She turned to the subject with the same application which had motivated her through her working life, and which had made her a great success and a famous person in her own field.

Harriet had read everything she could find on the subject and sought out more besides. It took two years of attending regular meetings, talking to as many experts as she could manage to meet and reading every relevant piece she could lay her hands on, before she plucked up courage to write something in the local Friends of the Earth newsletter. Her intelligent analysis of the economics of the Magnox process, coupled with her simple indignation and outrage, had made her article stand out from the more usual doctrinaire pieces. To her astonishment she had been approached a few days later by a representative from the 'Stop Ringwood' committee. Harriet had read a little about Ringwood but had not concerned herself directly with it because it was more than two hundred miles from Lansbury, and there were plenty of local issues which had preoccupied her. The committee had seen her article in the FOE newsletter, Stephen Ross had said. Would she consider writing something to present to the public inquiry which was considering whether to place the new style of radio-fission reactor at Ringwood?

At first Harriet had refused. She knew so little about the general subject, and nothing whatever about this new type of reactor. All the other evidence would be from experts and economists. Her views were just those of an ordinary citizen who was angry about what was going on.

'That's exactly why we want you to do it,' Ross told her in one of their increasingly frequent telephone conversations. 'All the rest of the case against will have been prepared by nuclear scientists and organized groups. Your piece could be just the view of a concerned individual. We think it would have an impact. It could be just the thing that makes the difference.'

Still reluctant, Harriet had nevertheless promised to consider the idea and had started to read everything she could find about Ringwood. The more she read, the angrier she became. There was already a nuclear power station at Ringwood. This new type of radio-fission reactor seemed to have a chequered safety record in America. What reason was there to think it would be any better here? The reverse seemed rather more likely. On preliminary examination, it seemed to Harriet that there were some contradictions in the industry's case for the reactor; they had left out some of the hidden costs of nuclear energy, distorting the comparison with more traditional methods of electricity supply. Having acquired a comprehensive knowledge of accounting through running her own business for so many years, this was exactly the sort of thing Harriet had a talent for spotting. When she gave the information to Stephen Ross he was plainly delighted, and told her that it confirmed his original view that she was just the person to write the paper he had in mind.

After several weeks of study and worry, Harriet eventually made up her mind. She telephoned Stephen

Ross to tell him that she would write a paper for the inquiry. He had been very pleased. He had given her the address of the Inquiry Secretary and told her what to do. She had then written a very polite letter asking to give her evidence. She was a private individual, she told him, representing no organization or group, and her paper would be a general appraisal of the necessity for the additional energy Ringwood would produce, with other observations about the appropriateness or otherwise of the new technology. She had waited for three weeks and then one day she had received a formal note from the Inquiry Secretary saying that he would be pleased to hear her evidence, and giving her a provisional date six months away when it would be heard by the Inspectors.

That had been four months ago. With the deadline fast approaching Harriet now used almost all her waking hours to prepare her most important paper. She had no living relatives and her only visitors were neighbours or friends, of whom she had many. Anyone who called on Harriet was harangued about the outrage which the British Electricity Corporation seemed about to perpetrate on the innocent people of Britain. The many people who liked Harriet or loved her were glad to see her so invigorated. Everyone encouraged her.

An hour had passed when Harriet became aware that the old-fashioned telephone in the entrance hall was ringing. Though she had not actually heard it, she had the feeling that it had already been ringing for some time. Still she carefully put down her pen and stood up slowly from her chair. The close work had upset the focus of her eyes, and she had to steady herself for a moment by the sink. Everyone who knew Harriet allowed the telephone to ring for a long time before giving up.

'Hello. Harriet Nuttall speaking. Who is this please?'
Harriet always treated the telephone most courteously.

'Hello Harriet. It's Stephen Ross.'

Harriet was pleased. Though the two had still not met, he had become a friend and counsellor to her, and telephoned regularly to check on progress and to offer encouragement.

'I'm so glad it's you. I've been working on my paper.'

'Good, Harriet. Look. I haven't got long. Did you see the *Encounter* programme?'

It took Harriet several moments to work out what her new friend was talking about. No, she told him, she always worked on her paper in the evenings. It was about American Nuclear Industries, he told her, and it was very useful publicity for the campaign.

'But there's something else coming up which is even more exciting. I need to speak to you about it. Can we meet?'

Harriet was startled by the anxiety in his voice. 'Yes of course. But I can't travel very far . . .'

'No, no, don't worry about that,' Ross said. 'I'll come to you. Would Sunday be all right?'

'Wait a moment.' Harriet turned to the wooden board where she pinned notes to remind herself of engagements. She consulted her calendar and then came back to the table. She always spoke very slowly on the telephone, carefully articulating every syllable. 'Sunday is a little difficult. My old foreman and his wife are coming to see me. They live in Berkshire so it's rather a long way. They usually stay to tea.'

'That's all right, Harriet,' said Ross. 'It's important but not urgent. How about the following Saturday?'

Harriet paused again before answering. 'Yes. That seems all right. Saturday the 8th? Yes. Very good. Will you come to tea?'

Stephen Ross's smile was audible. 'That will be lovely, Harriet. Thank you very much. I'll look forward to seeing you. About three o'clock on the 8th. Goodbye.'

Harriet Nuttall replaced the old-fashioned black telephone receiver on the cradle. She picked up the stub of pencil which was suspended by a piece of string next to the calendar and wrote a note about her visitor. She felt the always welcome sensation of soft fur rubbing against her leg as she wrote, and looked down. It was Tibby. She picked him up and stroked the long pure white fur lovingly. The ever-present inscrutable smile widened still further.

'Come on, Tibby. Just another half an hour on that silly old paper, and we'll all turn in for bed. There's a good pussy cat.'

CHAPTER FOUR

'Counting out of programme, on the weather, standby to alert presentation. Cue Bill's good night. Cue music, cue roller. Ten seconds to credits. Nice smile Bill, back tomorrow, well done, five to roller, four three two one. On music, on credits, thirty seconds to presentation.' The tinny music rattled from a huge speaker to one side of the mountain of monitors. 'Well done everyone,' the programme director waved sycophantically to the sound-crew beyond the double-glazing, 'well done, see you tomorrow, good night.'

From the comfort of the warm cinema seat at the back of the studio control room, Jonathan Maguire watched the production team credits roll up the screen and the image fade into the stylised raked bleachers which was the logo of Stadium Television. Maguire always thought it looked like a staircase, but he had been assured that it represented a row of seats in an auditorium, and that it must be rather stylish because an outside firm of designers had won an award for it. Still, to Maguire, it looked like a staircase. Another programme was over and all around him the director, sub-editors, secretaries and PAs were packing up to go to the bar.

'Pint, Maguire?' It seemed to Maguire that Miles Foster, the producer of *Stadium Tonight*, had spoken the same words to him after the closing credits every night for the last ninety-five years.

'I'll be there in a minute.' Maguire's reply was equally familiar to everyone. After a breathless day spent dashing from one location to the next, of sitting in airless film cutting-rooms, and then the anxiety of live 'on-air', Maguire felt the need of a few minutes of quiet time to readjust his perspective on the world before going off for the informal programme post-mortem over subsidised drinks in the company bar.

His preoccupation today had been the annual round of pay talks which were underway all week at the headquarters of the ship repair industry down at the quayside. Maguire had waited with half a dozen news-paper hacks in the cold wind and rain outside the grim offices for the whole of the day, sticking a microphone under the nose of anyone who came out, to ask for a progress report. Most of them had smiled a half-hearted smile, shrugged their shoulders, and walked straight on. One or two muttered inanities which were of no possible use. Even at its best this was going to be just another routine story, but it directly affected the families of several thousand men in the Stadium Tele-vision region so it had to be covered in the local news. Maguire had spent five years building his reputation as the evening programme's best hard newsman, and had earned himself some good contacts in both manage-ment and unions. Covering routine stories like today's was part of the price of maintaining that position.

After waiting for the whole day, and with the pro-gramme deadline fast approaching, the full-time official of the Journeyman's Union, Dennis Mason, had emerged from the offices surrounded by a phalanx of other union bosses who jostled to get close enough to him to ensure they got into the background of the camera shot. Several had confided in Maguire that their wives liked to see them looking important on the television. Out of mischief he always told the camera-man to zoom in as tight as possible on the spokesman to cut out any background.

Mason had dismissed the chorus of reporters' questions with a single gesture of his arm and had given his undivided attention to the tiny scrawled handwriting on a piece of paper in his hand. He spoke at dictation speed for the benefit of the newspaper men, but in a manner guaranteed to infuriate the broadcast media. Maguire checked over his shoulder to make sure that Tim had the camera running and that Bill was nearby with the rifle-mike.

'After full and frank discussions with the management . . .' There was a long and agonizing pause as Mason studied his script, 'my colleagues on the union executive have agreed that as of tonight there will be,' again a pause, 'no comment.' There was a long silence as the crowd of reporters wondered whether anything would follow. When it did not, they chorused again, 'Does that mean the talks have broken down, Dennis?'

'We have no comment to make, beyond saying that the talks have reached a stage where they are blocked by the intransigence of the management in slavishly sticking to the Government's pay guidelines, and the union will be consulting the membership forthwith in the customary fashion, with a view to seeking a mandate for strike action.' Mason waved his hands to dismiss the further clamour. 'Now I've told you boys, and I mean it, there's to be no comment tonight.'

Maguire studied the faces of the men surrounding Mason. Each of them was nodding his head gravely. Obviously they saw no contradiction in the two statements that had been made.

'Cut, Tim.'

Maguire had spent five minutes writing a script which the newsreader back in the studio would read over shots of the ship repair yards, and the three men climbed into the Volvo to get back to the newsroom in time to edit the piece for the main programme at six o'clock. His day's work had been summarized in a one minute and forty-five second film inject into the news bulletin. It had been preceded by a police reconstruction of the last walk of a twelve-year-old girl who had gone missing from her home in Bulstead but later turned up safe and sound, and followed by a report on the final preparations for the Miss Perfect Home competition to be held at the Exhibition Centre tomorrow.

Maguire looked around the empty newsroom and wondered why they were always such nasty, scruffy places. They always were. Even when the management installed high-tech furniture and computers, the cigarette burns soon appeared in the plastic table-tops and the laminate soon became scribbled on and stained with nicotine. Most of the time the newsroom was full of frantic activity which trod the border just this side of panic. Now the end-of-day silence was interrupted only intermittently by the chatter of the Press Association machine underneath its perspex cover behind the newsdesk. Maguire got up and walked towards the window. Outside the heavy commuter traffic was crawling along in constant drizzle, and the reflections of hundreds of red brake lights glittered on the shiny road surface. The distorted glare blurred the lights together into the stream of droplets chasing each other down the windowpane, and the tears which filled the corners of Maguire's eyes came with the thoughts which had never been far away for the last four days. The face of the little Asian girl, empty and alone, gaping out into the darkness, and the hideous screams of her mother which had seemed to be coming from both inside and outside his head. Three children dead. Three little lives. No matter that he kept on telling himself that this was just another piece of daily news that had nothing to do with him. Maguire had been unable even to begin to purge the scene from his thoughts.

It seemed to him that Tim's impressively dramatic pictures of flames leaping into the air and ambulances rushing to and from the scene had completely failed to convey the reality of what had happened. The movie had no relationship whatever with real life as he had experienced it. Not for the first time Maguire felt a sense of deep frustration with the limitations of the medium in which he worked. It had been an unusually long report by normal standards, four and a half minutes, and he had worked hard on the script, writing and re-writing it to try to get across something of what he felt; but it had not been possible. The adjectives did not fit comfortably with the spectacular pictures. He knew that the public wanted to be told how many firemen had rushed to the scene, how many fire-engines were called upon, and preferably any tales of heroism or miraculous escapes. His own feelings were impossible to express, and anyway it was irrelevant and unprofessional even to try to convey them.

The programme presenter Bill Jordan had realized that the report meant something more than usual to Maguire, and had tried hard to inject some emphasis in his voice which distinguished it from the usual ragbag of news which came and went in fifteen-second bursts. Though Bill Jordan had to spend longer in make-up every day to disguise the ravages of age and alcoholism, he was still an old professional in the business and his efforts had helped. In his heart, though, Maguire knew he had wasted his time. Three little dead children with unfamiliar-sounding Asian names would have an impact on the viewing public which would last only until the next item.

His report had earned Maguire a rare pat on the

back from the programme producer, and he had been glad to receive it.

'Maybe you should have another think about going on-screen yourself. The chance is always there if you want it.'

'Thanks Miles,' said Maguire, 'but that isn't it. I wouldn't deliver it any better than Bill – and half of my contacts wouldn't be able to be seen with me if I had a famous face.'

Foster had assured him that everyone had their ups and downs, and that Maguire was far too professional to allow himself to be down for long. Maguire was less certain. Unlike the many other tragedies he had covered in his years as a television reporter, this one would not go away, nor was it showing the glimmer of an inclination to do so. There was something else about it, something he had not been able to see. It was contained in, and encapsulated by, the mournful sobbing of the Asian mother as she cuddled the bleeding head of her dead child to her breast. It was more than hysteria, which would have been completely understandable and which Maguire felt he was within an inch of sharing that night. The woman's grief had had a disturbing quality which he found easier to sense than to define. Now that he considered it again, having turned it over and over in his mind during sleepless hours and daydreaming days, he thought he was beginning to identify it. He had seen or experienced nothing like it before, but now, as he stared out into the clear memory of orange darkness, there was a reference point somewhere in his head and at last he knew what it was. It reminded him of the frequent television news pictures of women in refugee camps in Eritrea or in Palestine, pointlessly holding their dead or dying loved ones close to them. It was the sobbing of someone who had known for a very long time that the tragedy was going to strike. The only thing they did not know was when.

Maguire forced his eyes to refocus through the blur before him and reached for the telephone. He consulted the electronic directory on the desk. His call was answered immediately.

'*Daily Mail*.'

'Newsdesk please,' said Maguire. He heard the extension ringing.

'Newsdesk.'

'Is Tony Adams there? It's Jonathan Maguire from *Stadium Tonight*.'

'Just a second, I'll call him.' The hand over the receiver at the other end only partially muffled what came next. 'Tony? That guy from the tele. Maguire. On five.'

It took Adams only a few seconds to look up what Maguire wanted to know. The woman who had given them the school-photo of the three dead children of the Sharma family was Mrs Alsop of 106 Christchurch Road on the Bentley estate. The address was a few doors from the burned-out flat. Ten minutes later Maguire was retracing the journey he had last made at 1.30 in the morning four days ago. This time the roads were congested by rush-hour traffic and there was no glow in the sky to guide him, but he knew the Bentley estate well enough. It had been the scene of many of his reports, and precious few of them had been happy ones: the youth drug scene, the problems faced by single-parent families, muggings and burglaries. As he drove his car beside the desolate blocks of low-rise flats, past boarded-up shops and wrecked cars, it was not hard to guess why the youth of the area turned to almost anything to try to escape the reality of their lot, even if it was just for a very few minutes or hours.

Maguire could hear the sound of hammering as he pulled into Christchurch Road and he looked across to see a group of council workers nailing boards of wood across the doors and windows of the gutted flat. It was surreal to visit the same location by daylight, a mundane street which had a few days earlier been the backdrop to such unspeakable tragedy. He could see trails of black smoke-stains snaking up the brickwork above each window, and a hole in the tiled roof revealing charred rafters within. The lingering faint smell of burning wood still haunted the scene.

'Another one that won't ever be lived in again.' Maguire heard the voice as he got out of the car and turned to see a middle-aged woman standing on the edge of the pavement. She wore an apron and had a scarf tied up above her head. There was no obvious explanation of what she had been doing before Maguire had drawn up, and since there was no one else about Maguire assumed she was talking to him.

'I guess not. Is it completely wrecked?'

'They say so.' The hand-rolled cigarette stuck to her bottom lip as she spoke. 'If it wasn't wrecked by the fire, then it will have been by the lads who've been in every night since. They're like buzzards they are, round here. The poor woman had only been out five minutes, and her with her bairns gone, and they were in there scavenging about for anything worth nicking. It's a bloody disgrace if you ask me.'

Maguire walked around the car and stood beside her on the pavement. He saw that her ankles were enormously swollen so that her feet appeared to have been crammed into the furry pink slippers. Both of her legs were tightly bandaged beneath thick stockings.

'You a neighbour?' he asked.

'That's right. Lived here since these were put up, fifteen years back. That was when it was a decent neighbourhood.'

'I'm looking for Mrs Alsop.'

Now the woman looked wary. 'Why, who might you be? Not the old bill or the tallyman by the look of you.'

Maguire laughed half-heartedly. 'No, not the old bill. I work for Stadium Television. I'm a reporter.'

'Oh I get it. Never seen you like, I watch the other channel. Anyway, I'm Mrs Alsop. What can I do for you?'

'It's all right, you wouldn't have seen me, I'm just a backroom boy.' Now Maguire smiled warmly and tried to make her relax. 'You loaned us the picture with the three children in. The school photo. We got it from the *Daily Mail*.'

'Yes that's right, my granddaughter's school photo it is. My husband said I was a mug. You should 'ave paid for that, and the paper should 'ave too. I'm on a pension you know, and I've got me poorly legs. I'm on the waiting list.'

Maguire assured her she would receive a payment and she seemed content.

'Does anyone know how the fire started?' he asked.

'Not for sure, not that anyone's told us. But there's plenty of rumours going about.' Maguire asked what they were. 'None worth repeating. But they was immigrants wasn't they? Not that I've got anything against them mind. Speak as you find, that's my motto, and these were as quiet and clean as anyone round here. But there's some who don't welcome them.'

'And what's that got to do with the fire?'

'Well stands to reason, doesn't it?' The woman spoke as though Maguire was dim-witted. 'They wouldn't be the first black family that's been burned out of their house round this way, not by a long chalk.'

It took Maguire a few seconds to comprehend properly what the woman had said to him. When he did, his immediate instinct was to reject the idea that anyone, however full of hatred, could have deliberately set fire to a building in which three children were sleeping. A moment later he knew that to express this opinion would be pointless and even counter-productive. He made an effort to control himself.

'No one's seriously suggesting that, are they? There's no reason to think it was deliberate?'

'No reason to think it wasn't, neither.'

Maguire thought for a few moments. 'Is there anyone around here who knows about these things? Any community group representing the immigrants?'

'I wouldn't know, son.' Now the woman seemed to be growing hostile again. She shifted her weight on to her right leg and then back again. The grimace was for Maguire's benefit. 'There's no shortage of people speaking up for them as far as I can see. But I can't help you with where to look for them. That's up to you.'

'Do you have any idea where Mrs Sharma went? Does she have friends or relations in the area?'

'How would I know? I've never spoken to the woman. Didn't even know that was her name 'til I seen it in the papers. Our Joanie's kids told me the little ones were in the school photo; otherwise we wouldn't have known.'

'But she was your neighbour, I just thought . . .'

'Only thing you can do is ask at the school, that's your best bet. Kids' teacher, Mrs Layfield, at the Bentley school. She knows the family and is always going on about minorities and that sort of stuff. She wanted to teach our kids Urdu or whatever it is these people speak in their own country. That was 'til the people round here had it stopped. Like I say, nothing against them but enough's enough like.'

Maguire now felt an urgent need to get away. He returned to the old black Citroën and pressed his foot hard down on the accelerator. The tyres screeched and he ducked his head self-consciously as he saw several passers-by turn to look. He knew that had he stayed any longer talking to Mrs Alsop he would have said something very rude. He preferred not to. The school was only a few streets away and the pupils had all gone home hours earlier. As the car pulled up on the pavement outside the gates Maguire saw a woman come out of the school building and lock the door behind her. She was walking in the direction of a rusting red Renault 5 which was the last vehicle in the car park. He leapt out and hurried towards her.

'Excuse me, can you tell me where I can find Mrs Layfield?'

The woman had been unlocking the car door and she had to push her long black hair away from her face to be able to look up at him. Once again his inquiry was being received with suspicion, but this time it was clouding the features of a stunningly attractive face. The woman brought up her hand to shield her eyes from the last rays of the setting sun behind him.

'I'm Mrs Layfield, what can I do for you?'

Maguire realized that he had not worked out what he intended to say to her. His usual self-confidence always deserted him when speaking to beautiful women.

'My name is Jonathan Maguire. I work at Stadium Television . . .'

'You don't say? What do you want?' Her abrupt

response threw him momentarily into further confusion.

'I was out the other night, at the fire at Mrs Sharma's house. I did a report for the news.'

'I know. I saw it. What has this to do with me?' Her manner was very hostile and immediately made Maguire feel even more uncomfortable. He saw that he was being taken for one of the army of journalists who spend their days grubbing around for yet another piece of titillation to add to already tragic news stories.

'Look, it's just that I was wondering whether anyone knew how the fire had started. I asked a woman who lives a few doors away from the Sharma family and she said, well she said she thought it could have been a racial attack. I just wondered whether . . .'

'And did she also tell you that Mrs Layfield is the local do-gooder, always trying to persuade the white kids and the black kids to get on together?' The brown eyes flared in instant anger, but the woman was not waiting for a reply. 'Well if she did, it's true, and I don't think that particular cause will be helped by a superficial story of nigger-bashing of the type you people specialize in.'

The vehemence of her speech took Maguire by surprise and he put up his hands as though to protect himself from the onslaught.

'Hey hey, steady. I didn't say anything about a story. At this moment I haven't got the smallest reason to think there *is* a story. I was at the scene of the fire. One of the kids fell right past me as she dropped out of the window. I watched the mother pick up her dead daughter.' Now he was becoming angry himself. 'I don't give a damn about a story, but if I can find out the reason why those three kids died I'd be bloody glad to do it. Now if you don't want to help me that's fine.

Sorry to have troubled you.' Maguire turned to go, and had walked a few steps when he heard a quiet voice behind him.

'I'm sorry.' It was so quiet he could easily have missed it. He stopped and turned back to her.

'Did you say something?'

'Yes, I said I'm sorry. I'm sorry that I was so rude.' Her head was now bowed and half-turned away towards the car. The light of the setting sun gave a hint of red to the wavy black hair. Maguire had a moment to take in her trim shape, even disguised as it was by the teacher's tweed skirt and thick cardigan. Now she looked up at him again. 'I was rude. It's been a long and very taxing day. It usually is but I'm not always this objectionable. We can't stand here and talk. There's a coffee bar round the corner where some of the kids go after school.' Now her first smile lit him up. 'It's good for my image to be seen with someone from the tele. Follow me if you like.'

Mrs Layfield got into her car. She had started the engine and was moving past him even before Maguire had collected himself sufficiently to turn back to his own. She did not seem to pause, and he had to run to ensure that she did not go out of sight before he could follow. After twisting and turning around suburban streets for two minutes, they pulled up outside a rundown café with a red strip light outside twisted into the word 'Lois's'. He was still locking up his car as she headed towards the doorway.

'Aren't you locking yours?'

'No need. All the kids round here know my car. It's more than their lives would be worth to steal it. Anyway,' her expression told Maguire that she was enjoying herself at his expense, 'it's a wreck.' Maguire's old and tired reptile of a car exhaled the air from the hydropneumatic suspension and settled down as though breathing a sigh of relief after the hurried journey.

As the couple entered the café a group of six teenage schoolchildren, four black and two white, turned and called out friendly greetings to the teacher. They then returned to a huddle and embarked on an undisguised discussion of the man she was with. Maguire smiled feebly.

'They seem friendly enough. Shouldn't they be home by now? School finished three hours ago.'

'Not for them it didn't. This group is doing extra English with me.' Maguire's face showed that he was impressed. 'They want to pass their exams, and I want them to as well. So, we do extra English.' The teacher sat down at a table by the window and called out to a homely looking fat woman behind the counter, 'Evening Lois, cup of coffee please.' She looked at him, her eyebrows inquiring.

'Make that two.' Maguire was beginning to feel more relaxed in her company. As she looked inside her handbag for her purse he noticed that she wore a narrow gold wedding ring. 'Your regular evening haunt?'

'I sometimes have a coffee with some of the boys on my way home, especially if I've just kept them in on detention. It's often easier to get things straightened out with them out of school.'

'It must be a rewarding job.'

'Not as rewarding as yours.' Her eyes flashed at him across the table so that Maguire was unsure whether they conveyed mirth or anger. 'We don't value teachers as highly as television reporters in this society. But then again, why should we? Teachers are not in the entertainment business.'

'Touché,' said Maguire. 'Though no one who has

ever seen any of my work would describe it as entertainment.' The remark made her smile again. 'Now if you can resist the temptation to bait me for just five minutes, maybe you can tell me what I want to know. And it's not for publication – not without your say-so anyway.'

The fat waitress brought two cups of coffee in old-fashioned shaded perspex cups and stood with her fists resting on her hips while Maguire fumbled with loose change. The cups reminded Maguire of his teenage days.

'These take me back a bit.'

'Some things just come around.'

'I know, I'm waiting patiently.' Her smile in response to his weak joke made Maguire feel still more at ease. The teacher poured sugar from a glass bottle with a steel spout on to her plastic spoon and slowly stirred the murky liquid. She raised her eyes and indicated across the street.

'You see that wall across there beside the supermarket?' Maguire followed her eyes and saw a brick wall which was practically obliterated by graffiti.

'I see it.'

'At the far left, you see? A circle with two chevrons through it and the initials NS. You know what that stands for?'

'Of course I do,' said Maguire. 'It stands for National Socialist Party of Great Britain. The loonies who goosestep up and down in jackboots and leather and make speeches on street corners about how wonderful it would have been if Hitler had won the war.'

'You're right and you're also wrong.' She set the spoon down on the table and looked directly at him. Despite her earnest look Maguire could not help thinking how lovely she was. 'You're right that it stands for the National Socialists and that they're madmen, but you're wrong to write them off as harmless eccentrics. These guys are active, they're very very busy, and they are recruiting fast. And the reason they are motivated around here in particular,' she turned and indicated the group of boys at the far end of the café, 'is that they don't like that.'

Maguire once again followed her eyes but could not imagine what she referred to.

'They don't like what?'

'They don't like what you see there. Black kids and white kids mixing together perfectly naturally without even noticing the difference in colour between them. Kids who've wised up enough to realize that they have got much more in common than keeps them apart. They don't like it because as far as they're concerned it undermines the purity of the master-race. And they are recruiting, Mr Maguire. They're recruiting in pubs, in betting shops, in workplaces,' her voice rose in pitch and volume with her growing indignation, 'in the dole office, and even in my bloody school.'

Maguire looked as though he was about to speak, but he stopped himself when he realized that anything he said would betray the complete inadequacy of his knowledge. In the face of her obvious earnestness and commitment he was embarrassed at his ignorance. He had not given a thought to the far right in British politics in many years, dismissing them as an ugly but ineffective irrelevance.

'Look, Mrs Layfield.' He stopped as she looked up from her coffee. He changed what he was about to say. 'It seems daft me calling you Mrs Layfield. I sound like one of your class.'

'Not many of them are so polite.' She paused as

though making a decision before speaking again. 'It's Pamela.'

'Mine's Jonathan, but I'm more comfortable with Maguire.' He sat back in his chair and thrust his hands into his jacket pockets. 'Look, Pamela, you'll have to forgive me. I had no idea. I'm a journalist who is supposed to be in touch with what's going on in the world – especially round these parts – so I'm embarrassed that I know so little. How do these people do their recruiting?'

'At the school? It's very simple. A group of yobs waits outside the school gates at the end of the day, and they harass mothers of Asian, West Indian or Jewish children. They just stand there and shout abuse at them. No one stops them.'

'What about the police?'

The teacher did not hesitate. 'Not interested. We've called them half a dozen times. They turn up half an hour later, have a word with the louts, and let them wander off. Next day they're back again. Recently they haven't even bothered to turn out when we call. The headmaster has given up. He wouldn't have called at all if I hadn't made him.' Pamela Layfield took a sip of her coffee. It was lukewarm and the floating skin momentarily attached itself to the edge of her mouth. Maguire watched her lick her lips. She put down the cup. Her eyes suggested that she was making herself angry again. 'They just stand there and do it, and believe it or not that sort of thing attracts some of the less intelligent among our number. Before you know it the kids have left school, have no job to go to, and a few of them have joined the growing mob outside the school gates. The party tells them the reason they have no work is that all the jobs have been taken by blacks.

It's very persuasive stuff when you're on the dole. It means you can blame someone else instead of yourself.'

Maguire could see that she was barely able to keep her indignation under control as she spoke. He waited for a few moments as she concentrated on slowly stirring the coffee.

'And what sort of organization do these people have?'

The question brought her out from behind her thoughts. 'I don't know much, but I have managed to talk to some of the lads who have gone along to their meetings, and even to one or two who have left the school and gone quite a long way into the party. From what they say there's absolutely no shortage of money, and apparently there are some very important people indeed running the show.'

'Names? Did they ever get any names?'

'No. To tell you the truth I haven't asked. I've had no real reason to. Anyway, I doubt if any of the lads I've spoken to have been close enough inside to be told any real secrets. They've just had talk of titled people and millionaires dangled in front of them to impress.'

Maguire's interest spiralled. 'OK, I'm impressed too. Now, what makes you think all this is relevant to the fire at the Sharma house?'

The teacher paused momentarily as though weighing up whether to confide in him further. Maguire decided to say nothing and to hope that she would make the right decision. She leaned forward across the table and for an instant he thought she was going to put her hands over his. He felt his insides melt with expectation, but she clasped her hands together around her half-empty coffee cup and spoke softly.

'I don't think it, I know it.' Her eyes were fixed on his. 'I've known these kids since they first came to the

57

school. I knew the child you saw the other night for three years, the others for less. I knew their mother too. She was a widow. Her husband died in an accident at work.' She paused and looked out of the window as she tried to decide how best to get across to him the seriousness of what she was about to say. 'Mr Maguire, she told me she had been threatened. She showed me notes which had been pushed through the letterbox, horrible notes telling her to get back to where she came from. More than once I have found the children crying in the corner of the classroom. They've been suffering from nightmares because of it.' Now she leaned back in her chair and brought her hands to her lap, fidgeting in her growing anger. 'And do you know what I told them all, Mr Maguire? I told them not to worry, I told them everything would be all right, that no one was going to harm them. That's what I told them.' Now her voice was growing louder as she lost herself in the distress of the memory. '"Stick it out", I told them. "They'll get fed up of taunting you. Bullies always do".' The attention of the boys across the café was now being drawn to their teacher's raised voice, and their boisterous conversation became subdued as they tried to listen to what she was saying. 'But I gave them very bad advice, didn't I Mr Maguire? They shouldn't have listened to me, they should have listened to the very good advice that was shoved through their letterbox at the dead of night. They should have gone home to Bangladesh shouldn't they, where they might have had a chance to be happy. Instead of that three of them are in boxes, what's left of them, and their mother is in hospital and no one has been able to get a word of sense out of her for four days.'

Pamela Layfield sat back with her hand touching her brow, the sobs coming gently until the tears ran down her cheeks and on to her raincoat. Maguire sat silently, feeling awkward and helpless, waiting for the moment to pass and hoping to find something adequate to say. After a few seconds the teacher collected herself and got up to go. He followed her to her car.

'I'm sorry to have been so stupid about this. I really want to know what happened. And this will sound even more stupid, but if someone has done this then I want something very, very bad indeed to happen to them.' She had opened her car door and Maguire held it for her. The strength of his desire for an answer to the unasked question spurred him on to ask it.

'I guess you'd better get home. Mr Layfield will be wondering where you've got to.'

She revved her engine hard and wound down the window as the car moved gently away. There was a trace of a smile on her beautiful face.

'There isn't one. Goodbye, Maguire.'

CHAPTER FIVE

Peter Tremayne pressed the frame advance button on the video backwards and forwards, trying to get a clear freeze of the letter from American Energy Industries to Mallin Harcourt. He had been well on his way to getting drunk at the end of a hard week on Saturday night when Sir John Bartholomew had telephoned so unexpectedly. By the time he had hunted around the wreckage which habitually littered his tiny bachelor flat on the top floor of what had once been a splendid mansion in Camberwell, and had managed to locate the small black and white portable television which was hidden under a damp towel and the track suit he used in the bank's gymnasium, the *Encounter* programme had been almost over. Even if he had possessed a video recorder of his own he would scarcely have been in time to catch the closing credits. Tremayne had spent the rest of the weekend trying to track down one of his friends who might have recorded the programme, but he had no success. Most of his old colleagues from Oxford who were now in merchant banking had gone off to spend the weekend in the country house of some rich débutante or other. The few he did locate had neither seen the programme nor recorded it.

'Marxist rubbish. Never watch it,' had been one of the responses. He might have been inclined to agree, but such remarks were of no help to Tremayne, who was under clear instructions to have obtained a cassette and to have made enough preliminary inquiries for him to provide some useful information for his master by the crack of dawn on Tuesday. It was one of those apparently simple instructions which he would look an idiot if he were unable to carry out, but which it was almost impossible to pull off without prior notice or good luck. Tremayne's career in merchant banking had been given a welcome and unexpected boost when he had been made personal assistant to the Chairman three months earlier, but he was still very much on trial. Bartholomew was the sort of man who would react with incredulity if his personal assistant was unable to fulfil so apparently simple an instruction.

By Sunday night Tremayne was very anxious and was even considering telephoning Stadium Television to ask for a video of their programme. In his growing panic he thought that he might pretend that he was an avid admirer of the series and was disappointed to have missed what his friends had told him had been a vintage episode. Even as he considered it he realized he would have to come up with something more plausible. Worst of all was the fact that having only seen a small part of the programme, he had only a partial idea of why the Chairman was so concerned. He had caught enough to know that it related to Ringwood and concerned the financing of the project among other matters; but he did not even know whether the Mallin Harcourt bank had been mentioned, let alone criticized. How would he be able to make the intelligent and perceptive comments which were doubtless expected of him if he had not the slightest idea what all the fuss was about? It was unfair and Peter Tremayne was not used to life being unfair to him. He began to feel desperate. If Bartholomew was considering taking legal action against the television company, then no doubt their solicitors could obtain a cassette easily enough. For the moment he had no idea whether or not this was the proposal. The only thing he was certain of was that his entire weekend had been wrecked, and he had nothing to show for it.

Tremayne had completely run out of ideas and was sitting at his desk with his head in his hands when Clive Hubbard, who was Personal Assistant to the Finance Manager and shared an office with Tremayne, breezed in at eleven o'clock.

'Christ, did you see that programme on Saturday night? I reckon the shit will be hitting the fan today. Someone's security stinks.'

Tremayne had to restrain himself from leaping across the two desks separating them and grasping Hubbard by the throat.

'You mean the *Encounter* programme? You saw it?'

'Sure I did.' Hubbard sat down heavily on his upholstered chair and reached into his briefcase. 'As a matter of fact I saw the billing and realized some people round here would be interested, so I recorded it.' Hubbard smiled smugly and produced a cassette. 'I didn't get where I am today by failing to use my initiative.'

Tremayne was filled with a mixture of repulsion at his colleague's sliminess, and gratitude bordering on adoration. He walked decisively across the office and snatched the video-cassette out of Hubbard's pudgy hand.

'If you really had even the flimsiest shred of initiative you'd have called me up over the weekend and told me about it. As my boss is senior to your boss, I am senior to you, so don't forget it.' While Tremayne had attended the right school and mixed with the right people at Oxford, Hubbard was overweight and had attended Bristol Grammar School and Kent University. Both men were in their late twenties and were going to end up in important places, but Tremayne believed he was destined to arrive there far quicker than Hubbard.

Now Tremayne had no time to waste. He watched the video recording and needed no help in grasping the nature of the problem. The producers had shown a copy of a confidential letter from American Energy Industries which obliquely referred to their plan to use the UK to circumvent the international non-proliferation treaty in selling a nuclear power plant to North Korea. Though the programme did not mention it, the letter was addressed to the Mallin Harcourt Bank. Tremayne could just make out the outline of the bank's 'received' stamp, so it was clear that the leak had come from Mallin's.

Two hours later Tremayne had ascertained that two photocopies of the letter from the Americans had been made after its arrival at the bank's headquarters nine months earlier. The letter had been sent to the Chairman of the bank, Sir John Bartholomew, and the original was still in the locked filing cabinet of his secretary's office. Tremayne reckoned he could assume that it was secure against someone taking and making a further copy.

One photocopy had been made and given to the bank's Senior Projects Director, Philip Maynard. It had been marked with a red number 1 in the top right-hand corner, as was bank policy for sensitive documents which needed to be copied. It too had been locked in a filing cabinet and Peter Tremayne now held it in his hand. The television picture had cut off the top edges of the letter so it was impossible to see whether it had a number in the corner. Tremayne was examining the remarks in thin pencil which Maynard had scrawled in the margin, and trying to compare them with the letter on the television screen. The freeze frame would not keep still or clear long enough to make the job easy. He could not be sure, but he did not think that the letter on the screen had been copied from the one he now held.

That left only one further copy, also kept in a locked cabinet, in the office of the General Secretariat. There were two keys to the cabinet, one kept by the Office Manager, Piers Johnson, the other by the Company Secretary, Moss Stephenson. Tremayne felt he was getting closer. In another hour and a half Peter Tremayne would have the answer, or at least enough of it to satisfy Sir John Bartholomew the next morning.

The night porter warily opened one of the enormous double doors of the bank to admit Peter Tremayne at precisely 7.15 a.m. on Tuesday.

'The Chairman is already here, Mr Tremayne. He said you were to go in the moment you got here.'

Tremayne swore under his breath. He had hoped to be waiting for Sir John when he arrived. 'You have to get up very early in the morning, Roberts, to be one jump ahead of our Chairman. Hold this.' He handed Roberts his briefcase and umbrella while he slipped off his raincoat. The night porter was nearly old enough to be Tremayne's grandfather, but neither man felt any discomfort at the patronizing manner of the younger.

Tremayne set off at his fastest walk, and came close to slipping on the freshly polished marble staircase with its elaborate oak banisters which led to the bank's executive offices with their enviable view over St Paul's Cathedral. He walked straight past his own office, which overlooked a narrow back alleyway, and in the early-morning quiet his shoes clicked noisily on the stone floor. Tremayne never failed to be impressed by

the long rows of dark but splendid portraits of former
directors of the bank, dominated as they were by the
intimidating figures of Mr Mallin and Mr Harcourt who
had jointly founded the bank in 1878, each apparently
trying to outglare the other across the corridor. In his
happier moments, Tremayne allowed himself to imagine what his own portrait would look like when it was
placed in the hall of fame. He had no doubt that the
day would come, the only question was how soon. That
day would be hastened if he managed to make a
continuing good impression on Sir John Bartholomew.
He often admitted to friends at his club that he would
willingly commit murder in order to do so, and he was
not always totally drunk when he said it.

The huge double doors at the end of the hall stood
ajar and Tremayne was several yards away when he
heard his master's voice.

'Come straight in, Peter.'

'Morning, Sir John.' Aware that the Chairman of the
bank liked to waste as little time as possible on
everyday courtesies, Tremayne went directly to the
chair facing the enormous walnut desk and reached
into his briefcase for his notes.

'Speak,' said Bartholomew.

'Well sir, no reaction has yet reached us from
American Energy Industries or anyone else about the
programme. My guess is that it is quite unlikely that
any of their senior people will have seen the programme on transmission. Their attention will no doubt
have been drawn to it on Sunday or yesterday, and
they will have had some trouble getting hold of a copy.
It isn't easy.' Tremayne resisted the temptation to refer
more specifically to his own remarkable achievement
in obtaining one. 'Even if they *have* seen the programme they are unlikely to have noticed the

"received" stamp on the letter straight away. It's very faint and we have only spotted it because we were looking for it. They will therefore be holding their own internal inquiry to try to find the leak. Only, in my view, if that draws a blank are they likely to embark on the train of thought we have already embarked on. As you know, the programme included reference to a number of secret documents which were quoted from and shown only in stylized graphic form on the screen. I have to tell you that all of the information in the programme could, I only say could, have come from documents presently under lock and key in this bank.' Tremayne paused very briefly to allow the import of his remark to register. 'The letter from the Americans to us was the only original document shown. That may mean that they have only seen the others and do not have them in their possession. Or it could mean that there was something about them which would identify their source even more clearly than the letter.'

Bartholomew was looking down and scribbling on a pad of paper in front of him. Tremayne was unsure whether his Chairman was immersed in what he was saying and taking copious notes, or whether he was bored and doodling. He continued.

'We can guess that if the Americans have not already done so, they will notice our "received" stamp on the letter shown on the programme within the next day or so. They will then realize that the leak has come from here. When they do, their reaction will be the same as ours – namely that if these documents haven't been secure, what the hell else has been taken away and copied.'

'As usual, Peter, you have gone to the nub of the problem.' Bartholomew leaned back heavily and threw his pad on the desk in front of him. Tremayne glanced down at an elaborate drawing of a vase of drooping flowers. The Chairman was still speaking. 'Our difficulty at this moment is this. Do we assume that the Americans will eventually reach the conclusion you describe, and therefore pre-empt their wrath by going to them now and saying that we suspect a breach of our security? Or do we wait and hope that they do not realize that we are the source of the leak? Evaluate.'

Tremayne paused only momentarily. He had given this question considerable thought overnight, but guessed that his boss would be more impressed if he appeared to be analysing the situation as he went along. In merchant banking, instant and accurate analysis of risks was very important indeed, and those who could do so reliably inevitably rose quickly to the top.

'Well, sir, the risk is that if we don't tell them and they realize that the leak has come from here, they might start telling other people before they told us. In that way our other clients would get to hear. If some of our customers started to think that we were unable to keep their secrets there would be people throwing themselves under taxis in Threadneedle Street. On the other hand, if we tell them now, we can give the impression that the whole thing is under control, and that we have contained the situation – so preventing the spread of alarm and loss of confidence.'

'How do we know that the Americans haven't worked it out already and begun spreading the word without telling us?'

'Last night's share-price was up three points. If anything like that was circulating it would have plummeted.'

'Good. Good thinking.' It was the nearest thing to a compliment Sir John Bartholomew had ever given Tremayne and the younger man pursed his lips in satisfaction. 'Make a note for me to have lunch today with the head of American Energy Industries' London office. Fitzwilliam his name is. We'll meet at my club. Americans always like that. Now, what about the leak?'

'There were three copies of that letter. The original and two photostats. The original is under lock and key in your secretary's office. I take it that Mrs Blake is . . .?'

'Not a shadow of a doubt. She's been with me for twenty years. Go on.'

'The first photocopy went to the Senior Projects Manager. The television picture was too tight to show any of the indelible mark. Fortunately Maynard scribbled some notes in the margin of it at an early meeting and there is no sign of them on the television copy. They could have been clever and erased them, but for the moment I have assumed that it wasn't his copy.'

Bartholomew grunted in a way which Tremayne took to be at least provisional agreement.

'The second photocopy was in the office of the General Secretariat. It was marked 2 as is normal practice, but that doesn't help us. It also was locked in a cabinet, one to which only Piers Johnson and Moss Stephenson have keys. Both have been with the bank for more than ten years. Johnson has his mortgage from the company, children at private school, is very heavily committed financially, but has an absolutely clean bill of health politically.'

'And Stephenson? Why don't I know him?'

'Fairly recent sideways move from the New York office. He was slightly disgruntled at leaving the Big Apple but is thought to have settled down. He's in his early forties. The only "if" about his record was a spell in the Young Liberals after he left university.'

'Which one?'

Tremayne looked at his notes. 'Cambridge.'

'Might have known it. They breed traitors there.' A fellow Oxford man, Tremayne smiled an ingratiating smile. Bartholomew got up and walked towards the window. He looked out at the slowly building traffic as if to try to spot the nasty rumour emerging from the underground stations and spreading around the City like a plague. 'This could do us appalling damage if word gets out. Damned television company. We can't even sue or complain about the breach of confidentiality without drawing attention to our own security problem. Blast them.' He turned back to face Tremayne. 'Anything else?'

'Just one other thing you need to know. We've had one man leave from the General Secretariat in the last eighteen months, a man called Stephen Ross. He joined us five years ago from the Foreign Office. We head-hunted him as a matter of fact. He was a high-flier and both Johnson and Stephenson thought very well of him. Then in February last year, for no apparent reason, he upped and left. No reason given. No other job to go to that we know of, and no one has asked us for a reference.'

'And would he have had access to the filing cabinet?'

'He shouldn't have, but when pressed Johnson said he might have from time to time.'

'Does Ross speak with an accent?'

It was an inquiry Tremayne had not anticipated and he had no idea of the reason for it. He fumbled through his papers as he tried to think of a reason why he did not know the answer to this apparently obvious question.

'Says here he was born in mid-Wales, if that's any help.'

Bartholomew winced and then decided. 'It is of enormous help. Ross is our man.' He walked quickly round to the huge armchair and sat down heavily, leaving Tremayne to wonder how Bartholomew had clinched the decision that it was Ross. 'Make a note for Johnson and Stephenson to receive a formal reprimand for sloppy security and to have this year's salary increase suspended. Ross is our man. Get on to our vetting people and find out what they know about him. Meanwhile get back to that file and find out what other papers could have gone missing. If any papers from the Lazarus file are in that damned cabinet and have gone astray, we may as well close the doors of the bank this afternoon and you and I will have to shoot ourselves. That's all for now.'

Tremayne had no idea what the Lazarus file was, but Bartholomew's manner suggested that it was something he should know by heart, so he decided not to confess his ignorance. Bartholomew was immersed in his papers when Tremayne silently closed the double doors behind him. A minute later Tremayne flung open the door of his own office and launched himself into his leather chair, putting both feet on to the desk. Hubbard was unpacking his briefcase and making a pile on his desk which included a packet of sandwiches and a Thermos flask.

'You look bloody pleased with yourself,' he said. 'Who's died?'

'No one has died, Mr Hubbard,' said Tremayne. 'I am pleased with myself for the very excellent reason that it is only eight o'clock in the morning and already I have greatly impressed the mighty one. I have given him advice and he has taken it. I have addressed a problem and he is using my intelligence to solve it.'

Hubbard slouched in his chair. 'I, on the other hand,

have a pile of invoices from our computerized database, and have been told to check every inquiry costing over fifteen pounds and find out who made it and how they justify it.'

'Poor Mr Hubbard,' said Tremayne without a trace of sympathy. 'By the way, what is the Lazarus file?'

Hubbard looked up, all trace of mirth having disappeared from his expression. 'I don't think we're even supposed to mention that file by name. It's the report by Professor Jacob Lazarus of Stanford University.'

'On what?'

'You haven't been doing your homework, have you? There is some irony here, Tremayne. You are supposed to know about the Lazarus file and don't; I'm not supposed to know about it and do. Fortunately my boss is sufficiently careless for me to be able to read his files.'

'Don't give me that crock of shit, Hubbard, just tell me what the report is about.'

'It's a report for which American Energy Industries, jointly with our good selves, paid a sum which is said to exceed a quarter of a million pounds. And you won't find it mentioned in the audited accounts.'

Tremayne whistled through his teeth. 'And it tells us how to turn base metals into gold?'

Hubbard spoke with all the pleasure of one who holds a delightful secret and therefore holds power. 'Much more profitable than mere alchemy.' He relished Tremayne's agony, but dared not bait him for too long. He spoke slowly. 'Professor Lazarus is probably the world's foremost expert on safety procedures in nuclear power. His report tells us how we can install a series of safety devices in a nuclear power plant which will give an impression of being expensive to the point of making the project nearly unviable. What is brilliant about his

71

work is that while these systems look and sound expensive to develop and install, they are in reality very cheap indeed. These devices will be budgeted for in tens of millions of pounds in the bill presented by the American Energy Industries to the British Energy Corporation, but will in reality cost peanuts.'

'And as we are putting up the finance for the project, we get a share of the additional profits?'

'As always in matters of immorally gained profit, Mr Tremayne, you have a razor-sharp mind. But there is only one drawback to these rather impressive-sounding safety devices, which accounts for their remarkable cheapness.'

'And what is that, pray?'

'They don't work.'

Ten minutes later Peter Tremayne was flicking urgently through the filing cabinet in General Secretariat. Obviously the Lazarus file should not be anywhere near General Secretariat, but if a copy of it had been put here, and it had been photostated, the consequences would be as bad as Sir John had predicted.

He went to the section marked L and did an exhaustive search, painstakingly looking through every individual file. There was no file marked Lazarus. Experience had taught him also to look further afield, so he searched under J and K to see whether the file had been misplaced. Once again there was no sign. He checked M. There were only five files and Lazarus was not among them. He checked N. The index said there were twenty-six separate files. Twenty-three, twenty-four, twenty-five, twenty-six. Tremayne's fingers froze as his eyes settled and his brain tried to tell him he was hallucinating; but there could be no mistake. There was an extra file. It was in a slim buff folder, rather smaller than the others around it, and had been replaced at a slight angle, as though whoever had put it there had been in a hurry. Tremayne took it out and turned it over. The single word 'Lazarus' had been printed on the top corner. He shoved the file under his arm and pushed the drawer closed with a crash which made a dozen people in the open plan office of the General Secretariat look up in irritation.

Sir John Bartholomew received the news with evident composure, only placing the tips of his fingers into the pocket of his waistcoat and extracting a small metal box. Without apparent haste, the Chairman placed the box on the desk and opened the lid, putting two small white tablets from it on to his tongue. He replaced the lid and walked around the huge desk three times before sitting down and leaning forward, his head resting in his hands.

'That will be all, Tremayne.'

Tremayne was on his way to the door when Bartholomew called him back.

'There is just one thing. I think this is a job for a specialist. Telephone my friend Mr Davis and ask him if he will kindly call on me.'

CHAPTER SIX

'Want to see any more, Maguire? It all seems to be much of the same.' The canned voice came from a cheap intercom which was set into the laminated surface of a large desk. Maguire leaned forward and flicked open the talkback switch.

'Just a few more, Geoff, if it's OK with you.' He flicked the switch closed.

'No problem.'

Maguire was once again sitting all alone in a darkened room. The dozen plush cinema seats around him were empty. He waited in silence until the gloom was suddenly broken by a regular flash of light on the screen as the film leader ran through the projector. 6,5,4,3,2,1. The numbers burst flashes of light which filled the room and then the film began. A few seconds were sufficient to confirm that the projectionist had been right. He was looking once again at silent news footage, the camera panning back and forth around the burned-out ruins of what had recently been someone's house. Black walls, charred furniture, smouldering upholstery, and everything drenched in water from the firemen's hoses. Maguire noticed how, in almost every item, the cameraman's eye seemed to fall on a small child's abandoned toy, the smashed doll or scorched teddy-bear pathetically symbolizing the injured child. He made a mental note to try to avoid the temptation to use the visual cliché in future, and immediately knew that he probably would not be able to do so.

The light from the screen was sufficient to enable

him to read the index card relating to this item. It was the sixth piece out of ten which the film library had classified under 'house-fires' in the last six months. 'Aftermath of house fire,' the card said, '6 appliances called to blaze at private dwelling in Burfield. Asian family forced to flee in middle of night. Interview with Chief Insp. Bob Harris on scene. Reporter Chris Furley.'

Just then the thin whirr of the projector was drowned by the tinny voice of a police inspector giving an interview. It was the morning after and this was obviously a man who had been asleep in his bed as his subordinates dealt with the ugly side of the job. Now it fell to him to reap the public glory. Maguire knew Chief Inspector Bob Harris only too well.

'The family was lucky to escape without injury, and I would like to pay tribute once again to the officers of the fire service and to my own men for their courage and efficiency in dealing with what could easily have become a very nasty incident indeed.'

Maguire wondered why all senior policemen habitually put on transparently false upper-class accents when they spoke in public. The more senior they became, he reflected, the more they became social climbers. Chief Inspectors went to plays by Noël Coward, Chief Constables to the ballet.

'Is there any indication as to the cause of the fire, Chief Inspector?' The voice of his colleague Chris Furley renewed Maguire's concentration.

'No, it's early days yet.' The officer's words were being enunciated with meticulous care, a style cultivated by many years of giving evidence from the witness box. 'We will of course be conducting a thorough investigation, but in my experience these things are often caused by a chip-pan fire, an unextinguished

75

cigarette, something of that sort; and this would be a good opportunity if I may take it of warning the public to be extra careful to ensure against fire hazards, especially when turning in for the night.'

Maguire could imagine the local newspaper headlines as clearly as Bob Harris imagined them when he spoke. *ANOTHER FIRE TRAGEDY: police urge public to extra vigilance.* Maguire had little doubt that the story would have featured Chief Inspector Bob Harris to full advantage.

'But this is the fifth Asian family to be burned out of their homes in as many weeks in your police area, all of them in circumstances which so far remain unexplained.' The question came from Chris Furley. 'Do you not suspect the possibility of a coordinated campaign of racial attacks?'

'No, not at all.' The vehemence of the policeman's response took Maguire by surprise. No doubt there was a risk that the emphasis of the headlines might be shifting away from an innocuous warning to take extra care, towards spotlighting the inability of the police to solve the many recent cases of arson attacks. 'There are possible explanations for all of the fires you refer to other than arson by someone outside the family. Furthermore, there is no direct evidence at all to suggest any racial motive for these incidents. Of course we know nothing concrete about this one as yet. It would be reckless and, if I may say so, irresponsible, to start talking about racially motivated attacks at this stage.'

Maguire was now looking at the lined and tired face of his colleague Chris Furley talking to the camera, against a background of firemen damping down the scene.

'So once again police are reaffirming their belief that

the recent spate of fires at the homes of Asian families is merely coincidental. Meanwhile leaders of the Asian community are claiming that in every case the families involved have received anonymous threats, and they are increasingly concerned that a coordinated campaign of racist attacks is under way. This is Chris Furley reporting for *Stadium Tonight*.'

Ten minutes later Maguire was carrying a cup of tea towards a table in the staff canteen where Chris Furley was sitting alone, reading the *Daily Mirror*.

'I've just been looking at a piece you did in May about a fire at the house of an Asian family.'

Chris Furley was fifty-two years old and had spent the first twenty-five years of his journalistic life in newspapers, before coming into television as a reporter five years ago. He was contentedly plodding out the last few years before he could take early retirement, and was perfectly happy to do 'aftermath' stories while younger and more vigorous reporters like Maguire got out of their beds in the middle of the night.

'Which one was that?' Furley sipped his tea without looking up. 'I've done half a dozen.'

'Gupta family I think. You did an interview with Bob Harris who seemed very anxious to write it off as an accident.'

'Was he? I can't remember.' Furley remained immersed in the newspaper. 'He wasn't so keen to do so a week later.'

'How come?'

'Because they charged the father with arson.'

Maguire put down his tea in a hurry, but not quickly enough to prevent it from slopping into the saucer.

'They did *what*?'

The reaction made Furley look up and put his tea and newspaper on the table in front of him. 'Yeah,

77

they charged the old man; they reckon he had fallen out with the wife and had wanted the insurance money on the house. Apparently he'd increased the premium two months earlier. He's awaiting trial for it right now.'

Maguire curled down the corners of his mouth in an expression which was familiar to his friends. It meant he was hearing a story which he did not believe.

'So they still don't think there's a racist campaign going on then?'

'Good God no, they'll do anything to refute the idea. Harris has been hinting to the press that all these Asian guys burned down their own places.' Furley smirked unattractively. 'He must think it's an old tribal custom or something.'

'Have you talked to any of the Asian community leaders? They've got one or two who don't usually mind sticking their necks out, haven't they?'

'None of them are talking on the record; they don't want to say anything on camera because they're afraid of becoming targets themselves, but off the record they're bloody sure that there's an organized group after them. They say that all the families received threats – of the rather charming "nigger go home" variety – and were then burned out. They compared the letters that were pushed through the doors and some of them were in the same writing.'

'Why haven't we done a story on it?'

Furley shrugged his shoulders. 'These guys won't come out in the open with the allegation, the police dismiss it out of hand, and I'm too old for campaigning.' Furley was now giving the impression that he had said all he wanted to on the subject. He picked up his newspaper with one hand and his teacup in the other.

'Do you mind if I talk about this stuff to the guys on *Encounter*, Chris?'

Furley looked over his newspaper and his tired eyes smiled. 'Sure, you go ahead. You've got a career to carve out. Mine's more or less behind me. Be my guest.'

Maguire was unhappy with the implication about his motives, but decided to let it go. He finished his tea in silence and put down the cup abruptly.

'See you around, Chris.'

Furley waved the hand holding the teacup vaguely in the air without looking up, and continued reading his newspaper.

Back in the newsroom Maguire flicked through the pages of the local telephone directory. Layfield. Despite what she had said about there being no Mr Layfield, Maguire somehow doubted that she would be listed under her own initial. He was delighted to find that he was wrong. Layfield, Mrs P. 82 Cottisham Road, Bentley. So Mrs Layfield lived close to the school. It was lunchtime and though it was a longshot, Maguire dialled the number. He was about to give up when the phone clicked.

'Pamela Layfield.'

'Hello Pamela,' Maguire had never really become used to calling teachers by their first name. 'It's Jonathan Maguire. I wondered if I'd catch you at home.'

'Hi. I'm dashing back to school. I just popped home to pick up some marking I forgot this morning. What can I do for you?' Her voice was cheerful and friendly.

Maguire was surprised to find that she sounded pleased to hear from him and momentarily considered asking her to dinner. On fast reflection he thought it a little too soon.

'I was talking to Chris Furley who works here and he tells me that the police have been spreading the suggestion that the fathers of these families started the fires themselves. Have you heard that said?'

There was a silence and for an instant Maguire was anxious in case the teacher thought that he shared the suspicion. He was about to speak again when she answered.

'Sure I've heard it, they've even charged Mr Gupta with arson and attempting to defraud the insurance company. No doubt they would have charged Sarita Sharma's father if she had been lucky enough to have one still around. Perhaps even the police will draw the line at accusing the mother.'

'Let's hope so. Furley also tells me that all the families had received threatening notes and that some of them match each other. Do you know anything about that?'

Again there was a pause. Maguire knew that this perceptive and intelligent woman still had not made up her mind whether or not to trust him completely. Experience had taught him that in such circumstances assurances were of little use. Either she would make up her own mind to put her faith in him, or she would not.

'I don't. I know about the notes to the Sharma family; I told you about them the other day, but I don't know anything about matching handwriting.' Maguire was disappointed. 'But I have a way of finding out. Where can I reach you?' Now he smiled again.

'Perhaps I can pop round to your house? Is the address in the phone book right?'

'Yes, but don't come here. Come to the school. I'll call you when I have something. I've got to dash. Bye for now.' She was gone. Maguire was disappointed that she had discouraged him from visiting her house. He very badly wanted to get to know Pamela Layfield better, but he sensed that it would be counterproduc-

tive to push too hard. She had said she would call him.
He knew he would have to try to be patient.

A few minutes later Maguire was walking up the
gloomy spiral staircase leading to the annexe which
housed the team of journalists who worked on the
Encounter programme. While every other Stadium
Television programme shared offices along modern and
well-lit corridors, the *Encounter* team inhabited rooms
off a half-lit cul-de-sac in the oldest part of the complex
of diverse buildings which constituted the Stadium
Television studios. There were fifteen journalists working on the programme and Maguire believed that they
deliberately discouraged visitors in order to perpetuate
the mystique which surrounded them. The only one of
them Maguire knew even remotely was Peter Griffiths.
He had started his professional life as a journalist on
Stadium Tonight before graduating to *Encounter*.

Maguire knew that these were the people at the
sharp end of his business, who spent their lives digging
deeply into areas which powerful people wanted left
untouched. No one was sure whether the journalists
here had become so uniquely unsociable and unpleasant through working on a programme which delved
into so many dark corners, or whether they worked on
the programme because they were so made. Whichever
way round it was, none of the *Encounter* team was the
sort of person the average journalist wanted to share a
social drink with, and no one from *Encounter* would
have been remotely interested in socializing with other
journalists from within the company. Maguire
approached his present business with considerable
trepidation.

The doors along this corridor were painted iron grey

and had wire-reinforced glass in a top section, giving the whole place the atmosphere of a cell-block. 'Or a hospital for the criminally insane,' Maguire muttered to himself as he walked as quietly as possible along the narrow corridor. In the rest of the building people kept their doors open, and some even smiled at colleagues passing by. Only this airless department had doors with pieces of card taped over the glass, so that it was impossible without opening them to tell whether people were in or out. Eventually he found the door with Griffiths' name on it and knocked. There was a long silence and Maguire was just about to give up for the day when he heard a half-mumbled reply.

'Come.'

Maguire walked into an office which looked as though it had been ransacked. There was a bicycle standing against the wall with one wheel missing, and next to it a plastic bowl full of dirty water containing a half-inflated innertube. The cycle's brake handle had gouged a deep groove through the grey vinyl wallpaper and into the plaster wall. A wooden chair facing the desk was completely covered with what looked like soiled clothes, and there were several pairs of muddy boots of various types on the floor. The windows were barely visible behind the piled-up box-files on the ledge, and on the desk several mounds of papers a foot high all but concealed Peter Griffiths. Only the clouds of smoke which floated upwards from behind the debris confirmed his presence.

Maguire moved further into the room and it took several moments to examine the wreckage around him. Griffiths was sitting with his head in his hands studying some papers. Maguire's eyes traced the cloud of grey smoke to its source: a battered old pipe which lay on its side on the desk, having fallen from an overflowing ashtray. When Griffiths looked up, Maguire saw that the mousey-coloured hair on each side of his balding head was standing on end and his long face and the dark rings beneath his dark eyes suggested that he badly needed some sleep.

'Hi. You're Maguire.' It was an announcement. 'Sit down do. What is it?' Maguire looked around for somewhere to sit. There was nowhere. Griffiths saw the problem and reached over the piles of paper and swept the dirty clothes from the chair on to the floor. Griffiths' accent was decidedly more upper-class than when he spoke on the television. He did not sound welcoming. 'Sorry. I haven't been home for a week, and I usually get the girls in wardrobe to do my laundry.' He scratched his head as though trying to remember the explanation, then stopped. 'But I forgot. I say, it doesn't smell in here does it?' Maguire thought there was a faint smell of stale sweat but decided it would be better not to say so. 'Only I wouldn't be surprised if it did, and frankly few things can be more offensive. Smoke if you want to. It might help. What can I do for you?'

Maguire knew that all of these characters were eccentric in some way. They had to be in order to be still up and working at 2.30 in the morning when all sane people were in their beds. It was the approach which had given *Encounter* such an awesome reputation in just five years since Stadium Television had won the franchise to broadcast in the region. Maguire's pause for thought had been long enough for him to forfeit Griffiths' attention, which was now directed again at his files.

'I was wondering whether you have considered doing a programme about racial attacks.' Griffiths did not look up but Maguire could tell from a small movement

83

of his eyes that he was listening. He decided to plough on. 'There've been quite a few round here in the last few months, and it seems that there's some evidence of a coordinated campaign.'

'By whom?' Griffiths had still not looked up from his papers.

'One person I've spoken to thinks it's the far right, the National Socialist Party. I thought they were a bit of a joke but apparently they're actively recruiting in local schools.'

'Says who?' Maguire was beginning to understand how these people got their reputation for charmlessness, but he was determined not to be intimidated.

'Says a local school-teacher I've been speaking to. She teaches in a school where three Asian kids were recently burned to death in a fire at their home. The police keep dismissing the incidents as coincidence. They're even suggesting that it's the fathers doing it for the insurance – ' Maguire was interrupted in full flow.

'But the families have all received threatening notes telling them to get out or else, and some of them are in the same handwriting.' Griffiths looked up from the papers he had been studying and, without speaking, handed one of them across the piled-up documents to Maguire. It was a rumpled piece of A4 with huge letters scrawled across it in pencil. Maguire read it aloud.

'"Get back to where you come from nigger, or we'll burn you out."' Maguire took a few seconds to decide what to say next. 'I seem to have made a bit of a fool of myself.'

'Not a bit of it, old man.' Griffiths allowed his chair to tilt forward and plucked the paper out of Maguire's hand. 'Glad to see you're on the ball. I hope you haven't been asking awkward questions and queering our pitch?' He picked up the pipe and began noisily to scrape out the bowl with a small penknife.

'Not at all, I've spoken to no one except a neighbour and the teacher I mentioned.'

'Mrs Layfield?'

Maguire was astonished. 'Yes, how the hell did you know?'

'She's got a reputation locally of being on the side of justice and virtue. We haven't spoken to her yet. We're treading carefully because we don't want anyone to know we're on the scene. We've been looking at the NS for several weeks. Their organization was obliquely referred to in some secret papers we recently got hold of. Apparently they have strong support in this area, and a headquarters somewhere down in Rosminster, just south of Lansbury. It's out of your patch so you might not know it.' Now Griffiths stood up and walked towards the window. He leaned over the stacked-up files, rubbed away a patch of dirt from the windowpane and wiped his hand on the seat of his jeans. Then he turned again to Maguire. 'As a matter of fact, old man, you could help us if you had a mind to.'

Maguire knew that too much obvious keenness was not the trade mark of journalists on this team, but nonetheless found it hard to disguise his enthusiasm. 'I'd be glad to. I was at the scene of one of the fires last week and a little Asian girl died at my feet. I'd be very happy to help in any way I can.'

'Well at the moment the police are being bloody stupid, mainly because, with the greatest possible respect to you good people in the newsroom, they think they can get away with it. If we appear on the scene the temperature rises, slightly more intelligent policemen start looking at the problem, and they start covering things up more effectively – or rather they don't say or do quite so many stupid things.'

'You mean they're less likely to be charging the fathers of the families, for example.'

'Got it in one.' Griffiths smiled for the first time and quickly turned his back as if embarrassed to have done so. Now he was looking out through a small clear circle on the windowpane. 'Of course, what we really need is a man on the inside of this organization.'

Half an hour later Maguire was knocking on the door of the producer of *Stadium Tonight*, Miles Foster. The request for permission to take time off from the programme was turned down.

'Sorry, Miles. Griffiths said that I had to ask you to call him if you weren't able to release me.' Foster picked up the telephone. Five minutes later Maguire had been given three months' leave of absence from the evening news.

CHAPTER SEVEN

The pin-striped three-piece suit seemed to cling to every fold of the inflated frame of the man emerging from the underground station at Bank, making him appear even shorter than his five feet six inches. A starched white collar had been fastened haphazardly. It pinched tight, constricting still further the already thick bands of flesh around his neck. A shabby bowler hat perched precariously on top of the man's head might have added a comic touch, except that the expression which arranged the milky and unhappy features seemed to allow no possibility of mirth; and the military clean shave over flabby skin would have given the impression of a baby face, except for the deep lines of age which ran from the nostrils to the corners of the mouth, and furrowed the large, polished forehead.

The fat man gasped for breath as he struggled to climb the last few steps to the pavement. Stubby fingers clung tight to the handle of the black leather briefcase. A group of four brightly dressed teenage girls carrying 'Chelsea Girl' and 'Top Shop' carrier-bags paused to chat and momentarily obstructed the fat man's path. Anticipating the obstacle, he briskly lifted the briefcase level with his podgy chest and used it as a battering ram to force his way through, knocking two of the teenagers aside and causing another to drop her plastic bag. The girl cried out in distress as a flimsy white lace blouse spilled out on to the wet pavement at his feet. The fat man made no attempt to avoid it, only grunting a complaint as it clung to the highly polished toecap of his left shoe. After a few steps he kicked it away and strode on without looking back.

Three minutes later the fat man, sweating profusely despite the cool October weather, climbed the three steps to the grand marble entrance of Mallin Harcourt.

'Send him in straight away.' Sir John Bartholomew's voice echoed from the intercom around the small outer office.

In a rare careless slip from her usual unimpeachable discretion, the Chairman's secretary allowed her expression to indicate surprise. Mrs Blake would have sworn a courtroom oath that she knew all of Sir John Bartholomew's close associates, but she had certainly never seen or heard of any Mr Davis. She would have remembered if she had. Mrs Blake had slightly bridled when he presented himself in her office, obviously expecting to be permitted to see Sir John immediately. There was nothing in the appointments diary and the Chairman never, absolutely never, saw anyone without an appointment. But the obnoxious fat man had persisted and, fully expecting her boss to be equally irritated by the intrusion, she had reluctantly agreed to disturb him. Now the squat man was smiling broadly and handing her his hat. She offered to take his briefcase too, but Mr Davis clung to it with a gesture which fleetingly reminded Mrs Blake of her young niece's spoiled child with a new toy.

'Sir John will see you directly,' she said with no attempt at pleasantness. 'This way, Mr Davis.'

Sir John had come to the door to greet his guest and Mrs Blake's distress was further compounded when she saw the apparent enthusiasm with which the tall and distinguished Sir John shook the hand of this odd-looking little fat man. Sir John was quick to wave her away.

'Could we have some tea, Mrs Blake? Wait five minutes and then send in Mr Tremayne.' She was on her way out of the door when he stopped her. 'Oh and Mrs Blake? No note in the appointments diary and please don't mention my visitor to anyone other than Tremayne.' Sir John's tone was unusually abrupt, and Mrs Blake was enjoying her day less and less.

'Very good, sir.' Mrs Blake was an old-fashioned secretary who understood that her first duty was loyalty to her boss. However eccentric the request or offensive the guest, her boss's instructions would be obeyed without question. She checked her watch to ensure that it would be exactly five minutes before she called Peter Tremayne, and went through a door from her own office to the small kitchen to make tea. Her hand strayed over the Wedgwood china, and in an instant she decided on a small gesture to register her private pique. She would give them the second-best tea service. Sir John alone would notice, and that was enough.

Inside the Chairman's office Sir John sat on the black leather chesterfield, and his guest sank into a generously proportioned armchair. The fat man's grey flannel suit perfectly matched the shade of the upholstery, and for an instant it seemed as though Mr Davis and his chair were one, an enormous bulk, meeting the floor at four equal corners. The fat head popping from the tight collar looked as though it was fighting for breath and gave the impression of a man drowning in his own flesh. If the image flashed into the mind of Sir John Bartholomew, he displayed the masterful discretion which had sustained his entire professional life. No observer could have imagined that Mr Davis was anything other than a very warmly welcome guest.

'Are you well, Davis?'

'Wonderfully well, thank you Sir John.' Davis's voice

was unexpectedly high-pitched. On their previous meeting his former master had been plain Mr Bartholomew, habitually referred to by Davis as 'Mr B'. Now the usual overblown deference was to be strained still further. 'And your good self . . . er, sir?'

'I'm well. And more to the point,' the Chairman leaned a little forward and lowered his voice, 'how is our little team?'

Davis smiled a broad smile. 'Flourishing, Sir John, flourishing. I've brought the monthly activities report for the committee. They will, I think, be reassured that their funds are being put to good use.'

'Yes, I'm sure they are.' The Chairman placed his left hand over his chest. 'I'm only sorry the old ticker doesn't permit me to join you these days. Doctors say I have to watch it, that's all. How's recruiting?'

'Steady. We have to be very careful.' Davis's voice betrayed his love of the conspiracy. He enjoyed every word uttered about the shared secret. 'We have to be discriminating these days about who we take in. You understand.' The Chairman sat back in his seat.

'Perfectly. Now then Davis,' Bartholomew's tone was noticeably more brisk. 'You will recall that we have usually taken the elementary precaution of meeting outside the office; but the matter I wish to discuss with you today is so important, and so urgent, that unusual measures are justified.' Every word the Chairman spoke further increased Davis's already scarcely concealed enjoyment. 'In a few minutes we'll be joined by my PA Peter Tremayne so I just want to say this before he comes in. He is a very promising young man, but he's not – ' though not even momentarily lost for the right expression, the Chairman paused, ' – he's not one of us. I mean that in the sense that he knows little

or nothing of my own history beyond a vague aware-
ness that I worked for the Office, and he knows nothing
whatever about our other mutual enthusiasm.' Bartholomew's tone left little doubt that he was completely in
earnest. Davis renewed his efforts to disguise his
pleasure. 'There may come a time when I will wish to
introduce him into that area, but that time is not yet.
So as far as he is concerned, you are simply a reliable
private inquiry agent whom we have had occasion to
use for minor discreet inquiries in the past. Clear
enough?'

Davis smiled until his eyes disappeared. He understood completely. It was exactly the kind of minor
subterfuge which made any meeting just that little bit
more interesting. He had already been waiting with
eager anticipation to know the reason for his summons,
and his former boss's earnest tone heightened his
curiosity still further. The other added attraction was
that this would be paid work, and previous experience
of working for the Mallin Harcourt Bank suggested
that it was likely to be very highly-paid work at that.
Mr Davis managed to provide himself with many
opportunities for indulging his appetite for subterfuge,
but rarely was the pleasure enhanced by the prospect
of substantial financial rewards. He was enjoying
himself.

With characteristic efficiency Mrs Blake neatly managed to coincide the tea with the arrival of Tremayne,
and a knock on the office door announced the arrival
of both. Like Mrs Blake before him, Tremayne's self-
possession abandoned him for a second and he allowed
his face to register a flicker of surprise. Davis was
mentioned in Sir John's personal contacts book under
I for 'Inquiries'. Having acquired sketchy details of Sir
John's previous employment, Tremayne had fully

expected some mysterious and intriguing figure out of an espionage novel. The person now wrestling with his own bulk in an attempt to lean forward to meet his outstretched hand seemed to be anything but.

'Davis, this is my personal assistant, Peter Tremayne. Tremayne, this is Mr Davis. He's a former colleague of mine who has performed very valuable services for the bank on a number of occasions.'

Davis smiled and nodded his enormous head in deference, further crushing the bands of flesh between chin and collar. Bartholomew's remarks surprised Tremayne still further, but this time he did not allow a trace of it to show. He had looked for a file on Davis and found none, and the record of payments on the computer made no mention of him.

'Now let's get down to business.' Tremayne recognized the end of the courtesies and produced a small leather-bound notebook from his pocket. A frown from Davis drew Bartholomew's attention back to his assistant. 'No need to take notes today, Peter, Mr Davis isn't really here. This meeting is not taking place. Clear?' Bartholomew spoke in a tone more usually reserved for very young children or the senile. Tremayne indicated that he understood and pocketed the notebook. Davis relaxed again and Bartholomew continued.

'Our problem concerns a man called Stephen Ross. Peter will give you a file to take away with you, Davis. Ross left us recently in slightly unusual, although not necessarily suspicious, circumstances.' Davis was now drinking his tea noisily, but if he noticed it Sir John Bartholomew showed no sign. 'Last week the *Encounter* programme . . .' now he paused to ensure that Davis had registered the significance of the point, '. . . on Stadium Television carried a report which contained a reference to some private papers which we believe were stolen from this bank. They relate to matters to do with the nuclear industry with which the bank is presently involved. For reasons I need hardly go into, the loss of these papers is very damaging to us. What is even worse, these papers were in the same cabinet as another file which we have reason to believe may also have been copied, and if this is the case, then it is a matter of the most critical importance to the bank, and I might say also to me personally.' Sir John Bartholomew fixed his expression directly on his visitor. 'If that document were to come to light it would be, to put it at its mildest, erm, most unfortunate.'

Davis put down his teacup and wiped his mouth with the back of his hand. 'And I take it that this man Ross had access to the cabinet?'

'We believe so, yes,' said Tremayne.

Davis now addressed himself to Bartholomew in a tone which seemed to Tremayne to be almost admonitory. 'Very bad security.'

'Quite so. Very serious. We have taken steps.'

Davis nodded. 'Where's Ross now?'

'We don't know,' said Tremayne. 'He left us without another job to go to as far as we know and we have received no request for a reference. We have recently asked our vetting people to run him through the computer, which of course they did before when we took him on. An item which seemed innocuous at the time now takes on greater significance.' This information was new to Sir John and his interest was visibly heightened. 'He's a member of Friends of the Earth. And in the last few months since he left us he has also joined the Stop Ringwood campaign. Apparently he is giving evidence to the public inquiry.'

'Damn him to hell.' Sir John's voice was louder than

Peter Tremayne had heard it at any time in three months. 'For Christ's sake, Peter! When did you know this?'

'Just ten minutes ago, Sir John.' Both Davis and Tremayne were surprised by the strength of the Chairman's outburst.

Bartholomew put down his teacup and sat forward. Once again he addressed Davis directly, effectively excluding Tremayne from the conversation. Tremayne had never before heard him so serious.

'Davis. We have to find young Master Ross. We have to find out what he knows, and we have to find out who else he has told it to. We have to ensure that Stadium Television does not already have this file, and we have to retrieve all copies. We also have to ensure that its contents go no further.' Now the Chairman of the bank was speaking very slowly and enunciating every syllable carefully so that there could be no possibility of misunderstanding. 'Nothing could be more important than the security of this document. Any steps, any action is justified to ensure it. I take it that this is clear.'

'It could scarcely be clearer, Sir John. We will begin immediately.' Davis struggled to his feet.

CHAPTER EIGHT

Harriet Nuttall woke at 6 a.m. on Saturday as usual and immediately got out of bed. Her first job was to feed her cats. Two of the present contingent slept on her bed, another in one of three large cat-baskets in the kitchen, and three more wandered the house and garden looking for adventure, preferring to catch up on their sleep during the day. Harriet tried hard not to have favourites, but she could not resist her special affection for Tibby and Dora who slept on her bed at night. Tibby had a luxuriously long white fur coat and a face with all the charm of an oriental child. Dora was a Russian blue; sleek grey fur with a small and knowing face, and sharp and vivid blue eyes. She was the fifth cat Harriet had owned which she had called Dora. It had been her mother's name and it was a name she always gave to one of her favourite cats. Harriet liked to make a particular fuss of these two in the morning as she put on her housecoat and slippers, but she took care never to express any particular affection in front of the other cats. At mealtimes no one could have put a knife between the difference in treatment each of them received. Fresh fish, steamed at home, or raw meat, and a saucer each of milk.

Today, though, Harriet Nuttall had something else on her mind. It was Saturday 8 October and a note on her wall-calendar reminded her that she was due to receive an important visitor. She did not really need reminding because she had been looking forward to the appointment since it had been arranged ten days earlier. Mr Ross had telephoned last night to confirm that he would be setting off from his home around mid-morning and would expect to arrive some time after two o'clock. An unusually violent thunderstorm had been raging over Lansbury at the time and Ross had been forced to shout in order for Harriet to hear him clearly. Both of them had been irritated by the unusual interference on the telephone line, but neither had remarked on it.

Though she had never met him, Stephen Ross had become a very important part of Harriet Nuttall's life. It had been he who had provided her with a focus for her instinctively strong feelings about nuclear energy. While earlier she had thrown herself fully into every new aspect of the campaign that had come to her attention, he it was who had persuaded her to concentrate her energies on one major project. If the anti-nuclear movement could turn back the Ringwood development, he had told her, it would be an enormous boost for every other campaign in the wider conservation movement.

Everyone in the anti-nuclear movement had been surprised that the British Energy Corporation had thrown its weight so unambiguously behind the new American design, and that it had apparently spared no expense in propaganda to promote the case. For them to have done so implied criticism of the British designs which were, they had so often boasted, enormously successful. If that were so, why was it necessary to spend tens of millions of pounds buying in American technology, while our own industry went deeper into decline? If it were not so, Ross had pointed out, then the industry had lied in its extravagant claims for the British technology in the past; and if they had lied then, what reason was there to think that they were not lying now? These were among the questions the objectors were asking loud and often at the public inquiry, which was now in its fifth month and seemed likely to go on for another six.

If the anti-nuclear movement could turn back Ringwood, Ross had told Harriet, it would be such a tremendous triumph that the swell of public opinion could carry with it many other successes. It was a David and Goliath contest in which a victory would be likely to bring public attention and sympathy for the courageous but under-resourced enthusiasts who had taken on the giant. Harriet was now in the vanguard, that was how Stephen Ross had put it to her, in the vanguard of the most important area of the whole anti-nuclear campaign. It all seemed a very radical departure from her relatively uncontroversial life as a champion cat-breeder; it was just the sort of change that she had needed to give her a new lease of life.

All of the major conservation groups were mounting huge campaigns to oppose Ringwood at the inquiry. Local residents' organizations in Wessex were also spending large sums and marshalling opposition. The National Union of Mineworkers had sponsored expensive surveys and research by expert scientists, and so it went on. Every paper but one on the opposition side of the hearings was being commissioned and paid for by some large organization, and that one was the paper Harriet Nuttall was now preparing. Stephen Ross had said that it would be a major publicity coup when she turned up as a lone individual to give her evidence against the multinational corporations on the other side. The newspapers and television would give particular coverage to her paper, and if it spoke with the words of an ordinary concerned individual, it might ring a note of truth among the wider public. Then,

Stephen Ross had said, Harriet Nuttall would have made an impact far beyond any she could make by the well-meaning but eventually ineffectual local campaigns which consumed so much effort.

After feeding her cats and drinking her first two cups of tea of the day, Harriet dressed herself and decided to do two hours' work on her paper before going to the shops to get something special to give Stephen Ross after his journey. As far as Harriet was concerned, he deserved very special treatment. He had telephoned her once or sometimes twice each week since she had agreed to do the paper, to see how she was getting on with it and to answer any questions which might have arisen. She would give him details of anything she needed to know and could not find out locally, and he would undertake to get the information for her. He did so unfailingly, and would usually have the answers for her by the next telephone call. He would also add a few words of encouragement and keep her up-to-date with other news in the small and friendly world of the anti-nuclear movement. No doubt he had felt that after all these telephone calls it was time for the two of them to meet so that he could see for himself how her work was proceeding.

At the end of her morning's work Harriet arranged her papers neatly on her desk in order that her visitor would think her efficient and well-organized. She very much wanted him to be impressed; she wanted him to feel that all the time and effort he had lavished on a little old lady of whom few people had ever heard had been justified. At ten o'clock she put on her hat and coat as she always did, even though it was a fine day outside, and with a parting word to the cats to behave themselves while she was out, she closed the door behind her. Harriet did not lock her front door. It had never been necessary in Lansbury in all the seventy-five years she had lived there. At this time of life it would never have occurred to her to start.

The old Morris crawled hesitantly out of the gates. Harriet always waited for a very comfortable gap in the traffic before pulling out on to the busy highway which led down into Lansbury. She was aware that other drivers tended to get frustrated sitting behind her, but when she was leaving her own house she could afford to take her time. There was no one around to see or become impatient with her caution, except the man standing at the bus-stop opposite, and he was clearly quite engrossed in his newspaper. The lane she wanted to join was quite clear now, but the bus coming the other way would force the cars behind it to stop or to overtake on her side of the road. She decided to wait while the bus took on its passengers so that all directions were quite clear. A few moments later as the bus edged noisily away, Harriet fleetingly wondered why the man reading the newspaper had not boarded it. She was in an exceptionally good mood because she was looking forward to seeing her visitor. She changed into second gear and the car roared on towards the shops.

Harriet met a number of her friends and neighbours in the town, but she had no time to stop and chat. She visited the supermarket and bought four cans of beer, just in case they should be required. Then she went on to her favourite bakery. An hour later Harriet was back and preparing the house and a special tea for her visitor. It was Michael's day to do the garden and she was pleased to see that everything looked very smart. She went out to pick several large handfuls of the very last of her sweet-peas, and delighted in placing them around the house.

'Now you've got to be on your best behaviour, Tibby,' she gently scolded her best friend. 'We've got a special visitor coming today and you've got to be well-behaved for him. Yes you have.' Harriet Nuttall had never married or had any children and she knew perfectly well that she treated her cats as a substitute. She also had little doubt that this was what her friends and neighbours said of her, and if she had once minded about it, nowadays she cared not one little bit.

As the clock ticked towards 3 p.m., Harriet had a final look around to ensure that everything was neat and tidy. Michael had finished his work, the cats had all been fussed over. She flicked her duster over the telephone table in the hall and went into the kitchen to check that her papers were neat and tidy.

'Goodness gracious me.' Harriet stopped abruptly where she stood and her hand went to cover her mouth. 'What on earth has happened here?' At her feet, Tibby arched his back and miaowed loudly. The urgent tone of Harriet's voice was unfamiliar and made him apprehensive. The feeling of fur rubbing against her calf provided Harriet with the glimmer of an explanation for what confronted her. 'Tibby, you naughty pussy, what have you been up to?' Now the snow-white cat was walking across the dozen or so sheets of A4 paper covered in handwriting which were strewn across the floor. It seemed almost as good as a confession. Harriet stooped to rescue them and began to collect them, together with the untidy pile of papers scattered over the table-top. 'Was this you, Tibby, or one of the others? This is work, you know, not play. You're very naughty cats.' As she collected her precious papers together a gust of wind outside blew the kitchen curtain back so that it fluttered over the table, further scattering the loose papers.

'Well bless my soul,' said Harriet. 'Who's left that window open?' She moved towards it and absent-mindedly wiped the smear of dirt she saw on the window-ledge. 'That must have been Michael,' she explained to Tibby. 'Now why did he do that, I wonder? He could have blown my papers right out of the window.' Having struggled for several moments to pull down the heavy sash, Harriet turned, now full of concern, and picked up Tibby. 'There there, I'm so sorry. I blamed you, didn't I? I'm sorry. It must have been that naughty Michael, mustn't it, and I told you off. I'll have to tick him off next week, won't I? There's a good boy.' Her monologue was interrupted by a tapping at the door and a man's voice called out.

'Miss Nuttall? Are you at home?'

Tibby sprang to the floor and Harriet rushed out to the front door. 'Mr Ross?'

Her visitor was already in. He was a young man of perhaps thirty, with a thick head of fair curly hair and smiling blue eyes.

'Miss Nuttall? I'm Stephen Ross. I'm delighted to meet you at last.'

Two streets away, in an old and battered white transit van, two perspex discs were revolving in parallel, pushing and pulling quarter-inch magnetic tape through a series of rubber-tipped wheels and across a steel-covered band. The Nagra recorder was small enough to be secreted in an inside pocket of an overcoat, but was now snapped into a prepared position so that metallic contacts fitted snugly into the special inserts. A thin wire from the right-hand side snaked across the formica work-top inside the van, towards the timber framework and then upwards towards the drilled hole

101

which secured the electric aerial. No one ever seemed to take notice of a dirty white plumber's van with its unusually elaborate aerials and blacked-out rear windows. On the dull steel front panel of the tiny machine, a complicated series of switches and knobs gave way to a small transparent cover protecting a white dial. After much checking of cables and many adjustments, at last the dial flickered sporadically into action, and then hovered happily in the black area, just occasionally nudging the red. From the other side of the recording machine another thin wire led to a pair of headphones which were now placed across the balding top of a fat head. Between the oversized felt speaker-covers, a wide grin flickered across wet lips.

'So how is your job at the bank, Mr Ross?'

'You have insisted I call you Harriet, so please do call me Stephen.' Stephen Ross had made the same plea three times in the past half-hour, but Harriet was so used to calling her visitor 'Mr Ross' in their frequent telephone conversations that she could not yet bring herself to call him by his Christian name. 'As a matter of fact I left the bank some months ago. I decided to devote all my time and energies to this project, and I've been managing to pay the rent by doing bits and pieces of journalism.' Harriet offered him another piece of the cream cake she had bought from her favourite baker this morning. He accepted. 'Well, perhaps just one more piece.'

'That must be nice. But surely – your career in the bank? Was it wise to give it up?' Harriet knew that a career meant so much more than a mere job, and though she knew very little about young men, she knew enough to know that a career was very important for them. Journalism on the other hand sounded a most precarious existence.

'Probably not wise, Harriet, but if we always do what is wise, we will seldom do what we want.' Stephen Ross's eyes twinkled pleasantly and Harriet Nuttall felt herself liking her young visitor more and more. 'I'm pleased that your paper is going well. I'm so looking forward to reading it.'

Harriet put a single finger in the air to indicate to him that he should wait and then put her best china teacup on the table. Soon she was back, holding a thin sheaf of white paper in her two hands as though it was precious porcelain. From where he sat Stephen Ross could see that every inch of the paper was covered in black ink, applied in tiny, beautiful handwriting.

'I'm about halfway through. It would take you forty-five minutes to read it if you would like to.' Harriet hesitated as if fearing that she might be putting him to too much trouble. She placed the papers on the table in front of him. 'I'd value your opinion. It's just that you always have such good thoughts about – '

'Harriet, please, I'd be delighted. Shall I just sit here . . . ?'

Harriet clenched her hands and her eyes lit up with her excitement and pleasure. This was just what she had wanted.

'I'll go and make some more tea. I won't disturb you until you're finished.'

An hour later Stephen Ross found Harriet sitting in her kitchen, her head supported in both hands, staring out of the window. He had walked right up behind her without disturbing her thoughts. Now he wondered how to draw her attention without risking giving her a fright. He carefully tiptoed the few steps back towards the door and coughed deliberately. She turned around suddenly.

'Oh, have you finished? What time is it?' Her momentary alarm was immediately controlled.

Stephen looked at the old-fashioned kitchen clock with its second hand struggling around the dial as though on its last gasp.

'It's half-past four, Harriet. Yes, I've finished the paper. I think . . .' he paused and Harriet got to her feet, her eyes appealing for honesty but at the same time hoping for kindness. 'I think it is exactly what I always hoped it would be. It's important, it's powerful, and it's persuasive.' He said the words with a note of triumph, as though glad to have a share in her achievement.

'Of course there's so much more to do . . .' said Harriet, her businesslike manner disguising her delight in his verdict.

'Yes,' Ross interrupted her, 'and I have some ideas about how you might continue which I think you might find interesting. Shall we take a walk in the garden?'

Two streets away the lines of pleasure which creased the bloated face of the man who was now sweating profusely in the transit van turned into a frown. He watched the thin needle flicker as the signal faded down the hallway and out of the house into oblivion.

Harriet walked unsteadily past the tidy flower-beds and Stephen wondered whether to take her arm. Then he realized she would prefer to manage alone.

He smiled warmly. 'Harriet. You may remember

that I asked you on the telephone whether you had seen a television programme two weeks ago. Unfortunately you missed it. It was the *Encounter* programme and it was all about how American Energy Industries want to use Britain to help them get around the nuclear non-proliferation treaty.'

Harriet said she was sorry to have missed the programme. She had a television but could not have said with any certainty when she had last switched it on.

'The journalists who made that programme did so with the help of some documents. It doesn't matter how they got hold of them, suffice it to say that there are some other papers in the same batch that contain information which, if published, would be even more damaging to the other side's case. The television people don't have them just yet, but they know that we have something even more interesting, and would like us to hand them over. As things stand at the moment, though, we have slightly different plans. Are you with me so far?'

Harriet said that she was, just. She was excited by the information but also confused. What could all this possibly have to do with her?

'Harriet, what I am about to say will come as something of a surprise.' The pair had by now reached the furthest end of Harriet's garden, and Stephen Ross glanced appreciatively at the few remaining buds on the dwindling rows of sweet-peas and sniffed the scented air. They sat on an old wooden bench which Michael the gardener had rescued from the local railway station when the branch line had closed down. 'It's not an exaggeration to say that when this information reaches the public inquiry at Ringwood, the effect will be so devastating that the hearing will have to close. The industry's case will collapse.' He was speaking slowly so that the information would sink in. 'They will be proven to be fraudulent, to be cavalier with safety standards, and to be intending to dupe the public.' Harriet was now sitting quite quietly, looking at him, without uttering a word. 'We will have won, Harriet, and the whole thing will turn into an undiluted victory for us – for the entire anti-nuclear movement.'

Harriet Nuttall was so surprised that she did not even react when one of her cats jumped up from the moss-covered pathway on to her lap, purring loudly. Stephen Ross reached across and stroked the cat's ears while waiting for her to respond. At last she spoke.

'Then what you have come to tell me is . . . my paper is . . . all of my work . . . it's a complete waste of time. Is that it?' There was no trace of emotion in her voice, just an emptiness, almost as though she were in shock.

'Harriet, you will have to forgive me. I came here to give you good news today, but I could not give it to you until I had read your paper. I'm sorry to have been so cautious, but I had to make sure that you were exactly the right person to do the job I have in mind. Having read it, I am sure that you are.'

Now Harriet had sufficiently collected herself to acknowledge the cat on her lap. It was Dora, and she began stroking her gently under the chin. Another cat was now rubbing its fur against her leg and a third threatened to climb up next to Dora.

'What exactly do you have in mind?'

'Harriet, all of the organizations which are opposing the Ringwood development are hopelessly infiltrated by the nuclear industry.' A frown of incomprehension crossed Harriet's face. Stephen Ross saw it and explained. 'So much is riding on this for them that we know they have sent spies into our organizations long ago to find out what we were likely to say at the inquiry. In some cases we even know who they are.'

Harriet was an independent woman who had spent her entire life in business. She now felt that in all that time she had learned nothing about how the world really worked. She was shocked and genuinely indignant.

'Then I don't understand. If you know who these . . . er, spies are, why don't you expose them, get rid of them? How can you stand to have them around you?'

Stephen Ross smiled. 'If we got rid of them they would be replaced by people we don't know. At least this way we can keep the most sensitive things away from them. But this is the point.' He was now more serious again. 'This matter is so sensitive, so secret, that we cannot risk having it developed inside one of our own groups. The stakes are so high that if the industry had a clue we were pursuing this area, they would go to any lengths to prevent us. That is why I have given my friends within the movement only a sketchy idea of what I am telling you in full, and no more. The work has to be done by someone outside our organization; someone intelligent and knowledge-able enough to fully understand and express the impli-cations of these secret papers, but someone outside our usual team – someone who has complete discretion.' Harriet watched his lips and followed his words care-fully with her eyes and ears, but still had no idea where all this was leading. 'It's vital that the other side has not the slightest idea that this matter is going to emerge at the hearing until it is too late for them to stop it. Until that is . . .' Now he hesitated, but Stephen Ross was certain that this dignified and intelligent old woman had the breadth of vision and the courage to cope with what he was going to say. 'Until a little old lady whom they had completely written off as a harmless irritant should turn up, with the press and television cameras there and listening, and start reading.'

On her lap, Harriet's second favourite cat could not understand why the luxurious tickling under its chin had stopped. Dora stood up, stretched languorously, and leapt on to the path.

CHAPTER NINE

'May I speak to Mrs Layfield please?'

Jonathan Maguire had driven the Citroën along the narrow roadway separating the playground from the main school building and had done his best to look relaxed as a half-inflated leather football had bounced noisily on to the car roof and off again on to the path ahead. He braked hard while a gaggle of rowdy fifteen-year-olds grabbed the ball from in front of his wheels and ran away shouting apologies without even the remotest pretence of regret. Now he faced the over-sized and daunting figure of the school secretary, who was interrupting her lunch of watercress on granary bread sandwiches to answer his inquiry. She was consulting a complicated time-table in front of her.

'Mrs Layfield has a free lesson immediately after lunch,' the secretary spoke with her mouth full, 'so she may not be here. She's got 3B at three o'clock, so no doubt she'll be back by then.' A crumb of wholemeal clung to the secretary's lower lip as she at last emptied her mouth.

'Oh.' Maguire was staring at the clinging crumb and was unaware for the moment that the secretary was casting a critical eye over him in return. 'Well I do need to speak to her.' The secretary folded her arms across her bosom and half smiled in useless sympathy. She was clearly going to no further effort unless he gave her good reason and Maguire was desperate for an idea which did not betray his real mission. 'I'm her brother.'

'Oh well, why didn't you say?' The secretary now smiled broadly and was clearly pleased to have the answer to her unspoken question. 'Let me try the staffroom for you.' She picked up the telephone and dialled. 'Mr Hopper? Is Mrs Layfield there? She is? Could you tell her that someone is here to see her.' Another pause. 'It's her brother.' She put the receiver back on the cradle. 'She's just coming.'

'Thanks. I'll wait outside.'

Maguire closed the door behind him and stood in the corridor. Almost immediately he could hear the clip-clop of heeled shoes on a hard tiled floor echoing from some distance away. He pushed his hands through his hair and straightened his tie as the footsteps came closer. At last he saw a pair of ankles appear at the top of the stairs ahead of him, then the legs and the neat pleated skirt and pullover of Pamela Layfield. He could see that her bushy black hair was tied up on top of her head, and as she came nearer he could see the puzzled and slightly irritated expression on her face.

'Hello, Maguire. Did I get the right message? Someone said my brother was here.'

'Just a ruse to thwart authority. Hope you don't mind.'

The teacher laughed and Maguire smiled with her.

'On the contrary; it's a very good idea. These people are always trying to get me paired off.' The thought removed the pleasure from Maguire's face and fleetingly he wondered again about Pamela Layfield's husband. She was an unusually attractive woman. Maguire guessed that she was a few years older than himself; thirty-three perhaps, or thirty-five. He had a private theory that all women, irrespective of their looks, had a special time of their own. It lasted a few months or a few years if they were lucky. For some it came around

110

nineteen or twenty; others had not quite come to terms with themselves by then and took longer to discover who they were. Though she was obviously a naturally lovely woman, he guessed that Pamela Layfield had never been quite as attractive as she was right at this time of her life.

'Can we go somewhere to talk?'

The teacher looked at her watch.

'I've got a free hour. I was going to do some marking in the staffroom but I think we had better go to my house. This had better be good, Maguire.'

He was aware that Pamela Layfield had still not fully made up her mind whether to trust him. He knew he was pressing his luck. 'It is, I promise.' His half-smile was an appeal and it brought a broader one in return.

Moments later Maguire was again trying to keep up with Pamela Layfield as her car sped through the streets of the Bentley estate. Five minutes away from the school she pulled up sharply outside a small and unprepossessing mid-terrace council house. Without looking back at Maguire she marched down the path and was rummaging in her handbag for the house-key. Maguire locked his car quickly and followed her into the house. The main living-room was directly inside the front door. The teacher told him to make himself at home while she put on the kettle, and Maguire took the opportunity to look around. It was a neat and unpretentious room, with few ornaments and no photographs. There were a dozen or more paintings scattered apparently at random and covering every empty space on the plain emulsioned walls. The mixture of styles and skills led Maguire to guess they were the work of pupils at the school. The room was dominated by a huge bookcase stacked with hundreds of scruffy and well-thumbed paperbacks. Pamela Layfield returned from the kitchen.

'Kettle's on. Now what's going on?'

Maguire turned to face her, and her expression told him not to test her patience much further. 'I'll come straight to the point.'

'That would be my advice.' Once again her tone was abrupt, as it had been on their first meeting.

Maguire sat on the edge of the settee. 'I have been asked to infiltrate the National Socialist Party to get some information for a television programme we want to make about them. I have come to you because plainly I need help. I haven't a clue where to begin, and you know more about these people than I could learn in a month working on my own.' The teacher's uncompromising expression had not altered and Maguire blundered on. 'The people I'm working with are the best there are around, and frankly I'm feeling a bit out of my depth. If they knew I was approaching you with all this information, they'd probably go up the wall. As it is, I don't see I've got much choice if I'm to make any impression on them with what I can do.'

Still the teacher had not reacted. After a moment of hesitation Maguire continued, 'I'll need all the information you can find out for me about how, where and when they operate, and I'll also need to discover a way into their organization. Most of all, I need everything done with the greatest possible discretion so that not a soul has a clue you are inquiring.'

She remained silent and looked at him for many moments. Finally she spoke, pronouncing what sounded like her final verdict on the scheme. 'You'll never get away with it.'

'Why not?'

She was exasperated, and her tone implied that the reasons were so obvious a fool could spot them. 'You'll just never get away with it. They'll recognize your voice from the interviewing you do on the television. There will be someone there you've met in the course of your job. Your accent is too educated. There are a thousand reasons why it won't work and not a single convincing one why it should. They're mad, but they're not stupid.'

'I'm not completely stupid either.' Maguire spoke softly, trying to placate her. 'And the *Encounter* people, they've done this kind of thing before, many times they tell me. We'll work out a plausible background. It'll take days, maybe weeks to work it out and get it right before we embark on it. These things aren't done just off the cuff.'

She was silent again, and for a moment Maguire imagined that she was trying to think of another reason why the idea wouldn't work. She leaned against the doorframe with her arms folded as though for self-protection. Maguire heard the electric kettle boil and click off and still she made no move. At last she seemed to have something to say, but was reluctant to say it.

'There's something else. What is it?' She looked tempted but remained silent. 'Go on say it, whatever it is.'

'It's far too bloody dangerous, that's what. Too dangerous for you. It's all right for the *Encounter* people to say they've done this kind of thing before; it won't be them out there, will it? The bloody *Encounter* people will be sat in cars or offices while you stick your head in a noose and wait for someone to pull the trapdoor.' She blurted it out and even as she spoke she sounded angry with herself for doing so. Her voice seemed to plead for understanding. 'You're playing games and these people aren't. Can't you see it? They're burning down houses with people in them, they don't even care about the consequences; and you're thinking of going in among them pretending to be something you plainly aren't, and expecting to get away with it.' Now she sounded angry again. 'You must be bloody mad, and I must be mad sitting here even discussing it with you.'

Maguire was taken aback, but his surprise was mixed with some pleasure that she was obviously so concerned. He waited a moment before speaking.

'Look Pamela, I'm not thinking of going into their offices dressed like this and trying to interview them. I'll only meet them in controlled circumstances. All we want is enough inside information so that we can film one of their outings. As things are we don't even know where their real base is.' The teacher stood still, listening, but refusing to look up at Maguire. 'I know it won't be easy; I'm not underestimating the difficulties, but I reckon I can get away with it for long enough to get the little bit of information that I want.' He was looking directly at her but she did not lift her gaze to meet his. 'If the scene gets even remotely heavy I'll be off like a jack-rabbit. I'm not the courageous type. Honest.' Still she did not move, but she brought up her eyes to look steadily back at him. 'Will you help me?'

The teacher walked across to the mantelpiece where an ugly electric fire was stuck into the wall. She had her back to him for several moments before she turned to speak. 'Oh Christ. I must be crazy.' For a further moment she seemed to be wrestling with her own judgement and then she seemed to lose. 'What is it exactly you want me to do?'

'Thank you.' Spontaneously, Maguire walked

towards her and took her hand. She did not respond but made no move to avoid him. There was a moment of awkwardness as neither seemed to know quite what to do next. Maguire released her hand and stepped back. 'Now what did you find out about the notes?'

The teacher walked across to the armchair where she had left her bag and took out an education committee exercise book. She opened it and started to read. Maguire watched her face closely as she told him how she had established that local Asian groups believed the notes to be written in the same handwriting. It was difficult to produce evidence now because the police had the notes, and in many cases no copies had been kept. The prosecution of Mr Gupta was going ahead even though he had been sent one of these notes. Efforts had been made to retrieve the note, but so far the police were being obstructive.

Maguire thought for a moment. 'What about the men you told me about, the ones who wait at the gate at the end of school?'

'There's usually three or four louts. They're there a couple of days a week. They dress in very scruffy clothes, often with black leather wristbands and belts with studs – you've seen the kind of thing. They're as stupid as they come, and it's obvious that they're acting under instructions.'

'How so?'

'Well, they're too stupid even to produce the racist rubbish they distribute. It's bigoted nonsense, but at least the spelling is correct.' Maguire smiled to himself at the teacher's observation. Pamela did not notice. 'And there's something else I've remembered since we last talked. One time, a few months ago, there was a larger than usual group outside the school so I stopped my car a few hundred yards away and walked back to have a closer look. I noticed that a couple of them kept walking across to a car parked in a side-road opposite the school. I walked round the block so that I could approach it from the other direction and I saw that there was a man sitting in the front seat with the window halfway down. He seemed to be talking to the louts. Maybe he was egging them on, or giving them orders about what to shout next.'

'And you accuse me of taking chances. What did he look like?'

Pamela looked at Maguire as though she had suddenly brought to mind something she had been struggling to remember. 'I know what it was. He was fat. He was very fat.'

CHAPTER TEN

'Who in God's name is Harriet Nuttall?' Sir John Bartholomew slammed a clenched fist down on the black and white photograph which lay on his desk. The thud echoed around the wood-panelled office. 'What do we know about her? Is she the one?'

Peter Tremayne shifted uncomfortably on the upright wooden chair opposite the Chairman's huge and carefully polished walnut desk and looked to Davis for support. To his surprise he saw that the investigator appeared totally unmoved by Sir John's anger, and merely gazed steadily back at him, apparently waiting for the outburst to be concluded. When it seemed certain that it was, he spoke, his voice unusually soft and composed.

'There's no reason whatever to think that Harriet Nuttall is in any way connected to the matter of the missing file. Let us examine the limited information available to us. All that we know for certain is that our target has visited her and has apparently encouraged her in the matter of a harmless paper she is preparing for the Ringwood inquiry.'

Tremayne looked back to his master. Sir John was leaning forward slightly in his effort to hear. In doing so he was having to concentrate hard, and his attitude seemed quite different from his previous irritable demeanour. In his determination to catch what Davis was saying, his anger had apparently evaporated. Tremayne turned again to Davis and watched him. I've been underestimating you, Mr Davis, thought Tremayne; you are nowhere near being the stupid oaf you look. Davis had managed to handle the Chairman with an ease which Tremayne had not seen achieved by anyone else, and that included the most astute members of the board of directors of the Mallin Harcourt Merchant Bank.

'In normal circumstances,' Davis was articulating every word very softly but very precisely, 'what we know about Miss Nuttall would simply merit a file note and a decision to continue occasional monitoring.'

'But these are not normal circumstances – ?' Sir John Bartholomew's intervention was a question, by now almost a plea that Davis should confirm his own view. Tremayne was astonished by his boss's apparently subservient attitude.

'These, as you so rightly say, Sir John, are not ordinary circumstances, and this is far from being a routine matter. Therefore,' he glanced at Tremayne with a look which made the young man feel even more apprehensive, 'therefore we will put one of our operatives to the task of keeping the apparently harmless Miss Nuttall under careful surveillance. She, I might add, is the third such person now under a twenty-four-hour watch, not including our Mr Ross.' Davis turned back to look calmly at Sir John. 'I take it that there is no cash limit to our direct expenses?'

'None whatever. I have made that clear. No limits.' Suddenly the Chairman seemed to be back in charge. He picked up the photograph of the frail old woman, who had been caught in an awkward bow, halfway through straightening herself from petting a cat in her garden. 'Nothing could have greater priority.' Despite its import, his last sentence sounded rather lame. 'What about the tape?

Tremayne looked up from his notebook across the desk at the Chairman and was surprised to find that the great man was staring directly back at him, his eyebrows raised in inquiry. He turned to Davis for aid, but with discomfort he realized that the question was being addressed to him and to him only.

'The tape?'

'Yes the tape.' Sir John's voice was impatient. 'The tape of Stephen Ross speaking by telephone to Harriet Nuttall. I want to hear it. Where is it?'

'Oh, that tape. I don't, that is I'm not completely sure. Had I known . . .' He turned again to Davis. 'Have you, Mr Davis . . . ?' His sentence trailed away as he saw that Davis was embarking on the Herculean task of shuffling himself forward in his chair. He was holding a small plastic cassette, which he placed at the very edge of the Chairman's desk. Tremayne leapt across to move it to within easy reach of his boss. Moments later Sir John had snapped it into a tape player on the desk next to the telephone and pressed the start button.

'That's all right, Harriet. It's important but not urgent. How about the following Saturday?' The recording of the telephone conversation was loud and clear. The Chairman listened carefully and then his mouth formed an inverted U and he nodded gently as though satisfied by what he had heard. He snapped the cassette out of the machine and whipped open a small drawer in his desk, producing another plastic cassette. He slid it into the machine and switched on. 'Now listen very carefully. You don't know me but I know you. I've got a piece of information for you.' Exchanged glances around the room confirmed that there could be no mistake. It was the same voice.

'And where, pray, did that come from?' Davis's words carried a weight of irritation.

'An anonymous phone call I received at my flat on the night of the original *Encounter* programme, suggesting I watch it. It was obviously our friend Mr Ross. But why did he call?'

'It's a good question,' said Davis. 'But a better question would be why you chose not to tell me about it. It's an important clue which could have helped me to positively identify our man. It could have saved precious time.'

Tremayne swallowed hard and waited for the reaction. He had never heard anyone speak to the Chairman in such a tone, let alone anyone who fell into the general category of hired help. What he heard next added yet another surprise to an unusual series of them.

'Sorry Davis. I just wanted to be sure in my own mind before we reached the point of no return.' Suddenly something in the Chairman's voice sounded weary, as though this was the moment at which he knew he was embarking on a course which would lead to, at best, distasteful consequences. 'Now at least we know exactly where we are and who we're dealing with. We know what we have to do, and we know that nothing can be allowed to stop us.'

'Very good.' Davis's manner became brisk and businesslike once more, quite unaffected by Sir John's apparent unease. 'Now, if there's nothing else, I have a great deal to do. I will of course report developments and in any event I will update you not later than Friday afternoon.'

The two visitors got up and Tremayne pushed both chairs back so that they squared up neatly to the desk.

CHAPTER ELEVEN

The rolling green and yellow fields, bounded by patchy hedges and by lonely clumps of trees, were little more than a blur through the mud-strewn windows of the red Ford Sierra which sped too quickly down the narrow back lanes towards Lansbury.

The particular route taken by this car was usually the exclusive preserve of a few local people with an intimate knowledge of the area, but on the front passenger seat lay an Ordnance Survey map and the leather-gloved fingers of the driver's left hand traced its course, the index finger snaking a route alongside a very thin blue line which divided the farms of Graham Moss and Frank Lawson. Two fingers of the man's right hand were curled tightly around a spoke of the steering wheel, moving it deftly up and down to take the car unerringly through the many bends and over the gradients.

Two inches above and to the right of where the tracing finger now rested, the map showed a small copse which bore the name Poacher's Wood. A public right of way led across the edge of a large field towards the wood, and beyond it the path continued until it met again with a narrow country road perhaps a mile and a half distant. A thin grey line with intermittent dashes crossing its path indicated a disused railway line just ahead. A few seconds later the car, splashed and covered with mud up to its waist and with dirty rain above, reached the top of a hump-backed mound in the road, the momentum forcing it to continue fleetingly upwards, before settling back down on its suspension. At the summit the driver's neck stretched forward, and faraway grey eyes scanned the horizon for any indication of Poacher's Wood. There was no sign of it. The car hurtled too quickly into the next valley. At the bottom of the dip the road was covered by a muddy puddle. For an instant a heavy brown leather brogue hovered over the brake, but then almost immediately it returned and pushed down hard once again on the accelerator. The tyres hit the rippling surface of the flood and two enormous sheets of water spurted outwards on both sides. Momentarily the driving wheels of the car lost their grip on the road and the car threatened to be thrown out of control. A hard jerk on the steering wheel nearly tore it from the gloved hands which were now both gripping it tightly, and a wave of grey steam ballooned out on either side of the car as the water hit the hot exhaust and immediately evaporated. The sound of roaring laughter from within was drowned by the squeal of the engine.

As the wheels gripped again the car shot forwards, up and up the short steep bank to the next rise. The driver's left hand strayed again to the map, straightening the paper against the seat, and a glance confirmed that the wood should be almost parallel to the road. Over the hill and a thirty-degree bend, and it would be just on the right-hand side of the road. Moments before the summit, the driver's mirror allowed a panoramic view across miles of winding road behind. There was not a discernible movement anywhere. The driver braked hard and the car swerved across the narrow lane to come to an abrupt halt in the gateway to an open field which lay between the road and Poacher's

Wood. The driver's door was open before the car had properly stopped, and Richard Crozier stepped smartly out.

Weak rays of sunlight tried in vain to pierce the thick layers of cloud stretching from horizon to horizon in all directions, but were nevertheless strong enough to cause the creases at the corners of Crozier's narrow eyes to deepen further into a web of interconnecting lines which spread halfway down his smoothly shaven cheeks. His pale eyes scanned the distance, checking the perimeters of the sparse wood which lay two hundred and fifty yards away across the field. The gateway was in one corner, and a narrow brook ran alongside the hedgerow which led to a far corner and the clump of trees.

Quickly looking in each direction, Crozier put both hands on the top rung of the rough wooden gate and deftly sprang over. He landed softly in the mud at the other side and set off immediately along the edge of the field. After only a few yards he realized that the spot was by no means perfect for his purpose. He cursed aloud. While the hedgerow was high enough to mask him completely from the Lansbury side of the field, the gradient of the ground was not sufficiently steep to shield him from the view of any approaching car on the road he had just travelled. After a hundred yards, Crozier stopped and looked back. The tall hedge between the field and the road was high enough so that no car driver would be able to look over it to where he stood; but a tractor driver or someone on a bicycle or on foot would get a clear view. Crozier wondered whether to abandon his expedition here and now, but thought on reflection that he would continue his check, just in case he was unable to find anything better later on.

To any casual passer-by, the tall slim figure striding

confidently along the edge of the field towards Poacher's Wood would have looked as though he belonged to the countryside. There was something military about the manner in which the man carried himself, and the cloth cap and tweed jacket were self-consciously of the type worn by the well-to-do landowning classes. This was perhaps a retired army captain turned part-time farmer, using his service pension to subsidise his income from the land. It was only on more detailed inspection that the man's face might have given pause. It was not the craggy, weathered face of a man who has spent any great part of his life or made his living from the land. Instead the sallow complexion was that of a man who had spent all but one hour out of every twenty-four for the last five years indoors; but Richard Crozier's unusual self-confidence would have hidden the fact from anyone but the most experienced prison officer.

Now he was a few yards away from the edge of the wood, and even from where he stood Crozier could see that the long lines of trees, with shallow terracing between them, were exactly what he had hoped for. Thick beds of brown leaves formed a mushy carpet across the whole area.

Crozier turned over the options in his mind. The location was by no means perfect but it was at least worth knowing about in case of some unforeseen exigency. Preparation, meticulous preparation for every eventuality, no matter how remote: it was part of the discipline he had drummed into himself day upon day, week after week, month after month for the past five years.

The criminal history of the man now striding across the open countryside back towards the car had begun at the age of twelve with his first conviction for petty theft from a sweet-shop. It had proceeded to more serious shoplifting at the age of fourteen, to his first custodial sentence for criminal damage at the age of sixteen, and on and on through fraud, grievous bodily harm and indecent assault. The result was that he had now reached his forty-second year without any formal education, and without ever having had a proper job. Despite these disadvantages, Richard Crozier had seen enough and learned enough to pass himself off in many business or social circles in which others with more orthodox backgrounds would have found themselves floundering. Since childhood, large parts of which he had spent shut by a permanently angry father in a dark and cold bedroom, Crozier had been an avid reader; and the books which were to be found in the libraries of the many institutions and prisons where he had spent time had provided him with a smattering of knowledge on a wide range of subjects. While other inmates could not have been persuaded to read anything more demanding than westerns or bland adventure stories if they read anything at all, Richard Crozier read about the history of the Boer War, or the life cycle of the Indian elephant. So eccentric had been his behaviour in this respect in comparison to others around him that some inmates had briefly made the mistake of failing to take him completely seriously. It was a mistake few of them got the chance to repeat.

Despite his lack of direct experience or worldliness, the widely various information he had picked up through his reading meant that Crozier could tell a good story, and could hold a small audience on a wide range of surprising subjects. His listeners in the prison recreation room, or at better times in the bar of the local pub, were frequently amazed at the vivid descriptions of his adventures in far-off countries. Few who heard him would have guessed that the stories were woven from the threads of knowledge found on the pages of books from the prison bookshelves, and that the nearest to foreign parts ever visited by Richard Crozier was Parkhurst prison on the Isle of Wight. None of them would have guessed that this apparently urbane and cosmopolitan figure was in reality someone who had never experienced the fulfilment of a satisfying human relationship of any sort.

His wide if superficial knowledge and his unusual application had not been sufficient to redeem him in the eyes of his schoolteachers. The frequent, relatively minor brushes with the law outside school had made them angry and exasperated. Several of the teachers made genuine efforts to get through to him, to make contact with something beyond the tough exterior. Their time and effort were wasted. It was frustrating for them to be able to see so clearly the frail and vulnerable boy inside the much-abused and hardened shell, but to be so utterly unable to reach in. At last even the most persistent of them gave up in despair.

Throughout his teens and early manhood Richard Crozier had been an outsider, and after leaving school at the first opportunity, he had quickly become an outlaw – one of the many who simply never managed to reconcile his own way of looking at the world with the way the world saw itself. Richard Crozier was a misfit, and he had been a misfit all his life.

Until the age of thirty, all of Richard Crozier's many convictions had been for dishonesty and violence. Then something had happened which had awakened a new and, for the authorities, still more disturbing aspect of his personality. One dark and damp evening in a noisy and shabby public house in a suburb of Derby, Richard Crozier had met a woman. His experience with women had been limited, and anyway confined to the relatively short periods he had spent out of custody. He had had no mother that he could remember and no sisters, and Crozier's view of the opposite sex had been shaped by long periods of confinement in the company of men. The women he had met in the brief interim periods between jail sentences had not pleased him.

This particular woman seemed to be different. She told him that her name was Elizabeth; she said the name in full like that, Elizabeth. She was a few years older than Crozier. She had dyed blonde hair, but it was tied above her head in a manner which seemed to Crozier to mark her out as slightly distinct from the other women who habitually hung around such public houses. Sometimes, in desperation for something resembling genuine human warmth and feeling, however remotely, Crozier had availed himself of the services of these women. Always on such occasions he failed to buy for himself even the semblance of the unknown and indefinable thing he sought, and he felt disgusted with them and with himself. Such experiences compounded his contempt for women.

This woman, though, was not like the others. She seemed to him to have something which Crozier felt he recognized as style, and he had also been attracted to her for her apparently refined accent and her affected manners. He had not met such a woman before. Unlike so many of the other women he had met in the intervals between his prison sentences, Elizabeth seemed to Crozier to be a proper lady, someone worthy of respect. He had responded by trying to behave towards her as he imagined a gentleman should behave. It was a novelty, and an exciting one. He had asked if she would meet him on the following night and she had agreed. He had been delighted and had spent nearly all the money he had on a new suit and a new shirt and tie. He could not afford new shoes but managed to persuade the manager of the hostel to lend him shoe-cleaning equipment to disguise the dreadful state of the pair he had been issued by the prison. It was not easy in the hostel to get ready to meet a proper lady, but he had taken a great deal of trouble to look his best and had bought flowers on his way to meet her. It was the first time in his life that he had ever done anything remotely like it.

On their first date Richard Crozier and Elizabeth had simply gone to a quiet hotel and had a few drinks. She had encouraged him to talk, and he had been at his most garrulous and animated. When the bar closed he had walked beside her, back to the modest but decent-looking boarding house where she told him she lived. Crozier had said a very formal good night to her on the doorstep, and she had frowned slightly as though puzzled that he did not attempt to accompany her inside. He had happily walked five miles back to his hostel.

On the second night they had gone to an inexpensive restaurant where Crozier had felt uncomfortable because of his ignorance of table manners, or of how to deal with the waiter. The man was patronizing and made him feel awkward and angry. Once again he had walked her to her door and left her politely at the step.

Crozier had asked Elizabeth out for a third night in succession and she had declined, saying that she needed to stay at home to wash her hair. He had assumed that she was turning him down because she was disappointed by his lack of proper education or manners. He had become angry and irrational. It was another rejection in a long series of rejections which had come along throughout his life, every time he had tried to become a part of something outside himself.

That evening he had walked through the streets in driving rain and thought about her. If only he could make her understand. He could try to talk to her, try to tell her some of the crazy things which went on inside his head; not the superficial rubbish he habitually used to impress anyone he met, but something of himself. He felt that at last he had found someone who could understand him; if only he could have the chance to explain. It was a chance, perhaps his first and only chance, to have a relationship with someone which would really mean something.

At last Crozier made up his mind to go to her lodgings. He did not want to risk being turned away before he had a chance to say his piece, so he decided to surprise her. It had not been difficult to prize open the door to her room gently and quietly with a screwdriver. He had gone in, and had found her in her bed, in the throes of noisy and apparently passionate sex with a man he had never seen before.

Elizabeth had screamed and the man had grabbed the bedclothes to cover himself. Crozier demanded an explanation, and had failed to understand when she had called him stupid and talked about her business. At last she became angry and began to raise her voice; he had tried to persuade her to calm down. In the meantime the man quickly gathered his belongings and slipped out of the room. Now the woman was screaming at him and Crozier pulled her down on the bed and tried to placate her by holding her tightly and kissing her. She had screamed loudly and he had begun to panic. By the time the police arrived some half an hour later, the woman was lying naked and unconscious on the floor of her room, and Crozier was kneeling over her, weeping his apologies.

Elizabeth had tried not to make things too bad for him in court, where Crozier was surprised to find that she was well known; but the mixture of the grim circumstances and his previous record brought him a sentence of two years and a humiliating rebuke from the judge. In prison, Crozier had been dubbed a sex-attacker. It was only partially correct, but that time had been the worst of his life, and he had emerged from it depressed and alone.

On his third night of freedom Crozier found himself in another depressing pub, this time in Nottingham. The weather was cold and wet and the only thing Crozier had to look forward to was a long evening staring at blank walls in the hostel where the probation people had told him to stay. He had gone into the first pub he could find and had spent all of his cash on three pints of beer. The long abstinence from alcohol meant that he was soon very drunk, and was contemplating the last few drops in the bottom of the glass when he noticed a small, stout man standing at the bar. The man caught his eye because he was wearing a military-style camel coat and a bowler hat. It was an incongruous outfit for such a shabby pub. Also, the man seemed to be taking a particular interest in him. He had plainly been drinking heavily and now began to abuse a group of young black men who were sitting quietly and playing cards at a corner table. The man seemed to be addressing his complaints particularly to Crozier.

'Bloody spades. Look at them.' Three of the youths ignored the remark, but one of them looked up, clearly very angry.

'The Jack, you've got the Jack of Spades in your

hand, why don't you play it?' The three discouraged the fourth youth from reacting and the fat man turned to Crozier and sniggered. The card game continued. Crozier made the last dregs of his beer last for a few minutes longer, and several times the fat man caught his eye before finally he approached and offered to buy him a drink. Crozier's first instinct was to decline, but then he considered the alternative and decided to accept.

The stout drunk introduced himself as 'The Captain' and began to acquaint Crozier with his views of the world. He assured Crozier in a loud voice that the only reason why people like himself had been unable to get a decent job and earn a proper wage in this country was the immigration of tens of thousands of these 'niggers'. The man had turned back to the young blacks as he shouted out the offensive word. The same youth who had reacted earlier started to rise from his chair but the others grabbed his arm, urging him to stay cool.

Crozier explained how he also felt that life had cheated him, and now, after several more glasses of beer, it seemed perfectly clear to him that it was for the same reason. The blacks, the Pakis, the Jews, had taken what rightfully belonged to the native-born British and it was time to take it back. As he listened to the other man's theories, Crozier began to feel quite sure that at last he knew the real reason why he had never properly fitted into anything he had tried to become involved in.

At closing time the two men said noisy goodbyes and undertook to meet again on the following evening. Crozier was sitting over the last drops from the bottle of beer the Captain had bought him when he heard a scuffle and shouting outside. He looked over to the table where the youths had been playing cards and saw that it was empty. Picking up his beer bottle from the counter he turned towards the door and without pausing in his stride, smashed the top from the bottle, sending an explosion of splinters across the floor. The scene outside was what he had expected. The four black youths had set on his new friend and were now kicking him as he lay on the ground. Without hesitation Crozier laid into them, punching one with all his weight in the solar plexus, and then bringing his closed hand up hard under the chin of the youth who had reacted most angrily to the earlier abuse. He heard the thin scream and saw the dark eyes widen in horror as the razor-sharp glass pierced the tight skin below his chin, and carried on upwards tearing the flesh from the side of his face. Immediately the others stopped in their tracks and for a second stood back, aghast at what they saw happening. The hysterical cry of the wounded teenager split the night. Crozier stood his ground holding out the broken bottle like a threat as others came to their friend's aid and carried him away, still shrieking as they vanished into the darkness.

The Captain had not been badly hurt after all and Crozier had helped him back to his flat where both men continued drinking. The flat was a cold and shabby basement, with damp walls covered by many bizarre and intimidating posters which screamed racist slogans into the half-light. For a moment it had occurred to Crozier that this man might be one of those homosexuals he had come across so frequently in prison, and he determined to keep enough wits about him to discourage any advances. He need not have worried. The two men both fell asleep where they sat. On the following day Crozier was taken to his first meeting of the National Socialist Party of Great Britain. As the Captain retailed the previous night's experience, twenty men sitting in rows of fold-up wooden chairs listened with rapt attention. At the end of the story there were loud cheers and Crozier knew that he had never experienced anything as enjoyable as the looks of admiration which gleamed in their faces.

Crozier listened intently as the Captain addressed the party members about the government's recent decision to allow in several new batches of Vietnamese refugees. 'Boat-people': the Captain had used the term as though it was a profanity. These were yet another group, he said, who would be taking houses which rightfully belonged to the working-class homeless of Britain, and who would be taking jobs which should be filled by Britain's indigenous unemployed. The Captain outlined plans to find out where the first immigrants were to be housed, and to visit them. The words were greeted with dark laughter all around him which Crozier failed properly to understand, but joined in just the same.

Crozier had never at any time taken much interest in politics or politicians, but now he felt that everything he was hearing made good sense. He joined in warmly as the audience applauded every sentence of the speech. He was invited to come back to further meetings, and he gratefully accepted. Now, for the first time in his life, he had found something of which it seemed he could become fully a part. He had found a group of people who did not appear to look down at him because of his lack of education or for his prison record, neither did they recoil at his occasional strange moods or his quick temper. Rather they provided a rationale which explained to him why he felt alienated from his own society, his own kind. His new friends sought to channel his temper towards the real enemy, the people who had brought this once great nation to the brink of penury, depriving Britons of their birthright.

The National Socialists did not just talk about their beliefs, they assured him, they also acted to put them into effect. Repatriation of all immigrants was a major plank of their campaign, and since no mainstream British politician had the courage to stand up for what everyone in their hearts really believed in, the British people would have to make clear to these immigrants that they were not welcome in this country.

The Captain, he was told by one of the party members, was so called because he had been a Captain in British Special Forces in Palestine after the last war. The strange little fat man who seemed to hold his drink so badly turned out to be the ideological leader of the local organization, and after several weeks he had ordered that Crozier be taken out on one of the party's expeditions. Security was taken very seriously and no one would tell him where he was going until he was on his way. It had been strange and exciting for him to embark on a so-called secret mission, with sealed orders which only the leader of the group knew. He reported, as instructed, to the scruffy lock-up garage where the group held meetings and watched as the white transit van which one of the members used in his plumbing business during the daytime was loaded up with crates of bottles smelling strongly of petrol. Ten men appeared wearing black balaclava helmets and carrying baseball bats, and climbed into the back of the van. As the Captain gestured him to join them in the van and then threw a heavy dustsheet over their heads, Crozier knew that he had never experienced anything so exhilarating in his life.

The van drove for an hour. No one spoke until finally the driver announced that they were nearing their destination. Crozier lifted his head from beneath the sheet to try to see out of the tinted glass in the back-doors of the van. There were bright lights which stung his eyes and the writing above the shops was in unfamiliar characters.

'Watford,' said the driver suddenly. 'Our target is just round the next corner.' A few seconds later the van stopped abruptly and the man nearest the doors reached over to open them. All around him men leapt out into the street and Crozier immediately saw a group of West Indian youths standing next to two motorbikes at the side of the road. They were outside what looked like a night-club, from which the loud music of a reggae band wafted out into the heavy night air. While the black youths were still wondering what was happening, the ten men from the van ran across to them, yelling and waving the baseball bats in the air as they went.

Too late the youths realized what was going on and several were struck and then beaten bloodily to the ground as they tried to make their escape. One of the attackers lifted his foot and levered over one of the motorcycles, which went clattering down loudly on to its side. Behind him came another, who quickly lifted a tinted glass bottle into the air and smashed it down on top of the motorcycle. Immediately an explosion of yellow flame enveloped the machine creating a plume of acrid smoke.

Now the adrenaline was flowing and Crozier wanted to be a part of the action. The Captain picked up a bottle from a crate at the back of the van and beckoned him to follow. They ran towards the door of the club, where several black youths were standing ready to defend themselves against the men with the baseball bats. The fat man gestured Crozier to hang back as the other men laid about them with the bats. Then the Captain produced a lighter from his pocket. Seconds later the rag protruding from the bottle was burning and giving off thick smoke which made Crozier cough painfully. The Captain ran forward awkwardly around the mêlée of bodies and threw the bottle hard down the stairs leading into the basement club. At once the night was illuminated with the flash of a huge explosion, which forced Crozier to stagger backwards away from the force of the blast. Seconds later they were all running and then the van was screaming into the night. All around him the men were whooping with delight, already gabbling out their own experiences in excited voices.

'We whopped the black bastards,' shouted the Captain. 'Now perhaps they'll go back to Jamaica or whatever bloody hell-hole it is that they come from.' Crozier had never seen the Captain like this, his bright flabby face illuminated with pleasure. That had been the moment when Richard Crozier had found himself, discovered his own raison d'être. Now he felt part of something real, something which had meaning. Now he really belonged.

There had been many other expeditions, sometimes just daubing paint, sometimes pushing petrol-soaked rags through letterboxes then dropping a match, other times full-scale attacks. Crozier felt he was really living for the first time that he could remember. It had been nearly two years before the Captain had sent him on an expedition to burn down a house belonging to a Pakistani grocer. It turned out that the police had been tipped off and were waiting. Crozier had pitched into them while the others had made their escape, and for his trouble he had been arrested and sentenced to five years' imprisonment for arson. There was no mention

136

in the trial of any racial motive. The Captain had directed that no party member should visit him in prison, but had sent a friendly message to him via a sympathetic prison officer, assuring him that he would receive a regular payment into his bank and that his friends would still be waiting to look after him when he was freed.

Crozier had immediately sunk into a slough of depression, and after an ugly altercation with a West Indian prisoner which had resulted in him receiving a badly gashed forehead, Crozier had been confined to the hospital wing. There he remained for several weeks, becoming more and more depressed by the cessation of his exciting new life.

At last he had been approached by a well-intentioned and zealous prison visitor who had taken a particular interest in him and had persuaded the prison governor that he might not be completely beyond rehabilitation. The visitor was a middle-aged woman JP called Mrs Fleming. She had been impressed during their conversation by his wide knowledge, and had spent many hours trying to persuade him to take sufficient interest in a single subject to be able to take some examinations. Crozier had rejected every subject she had suggested, but had finally and grudgingly alighted on military history. It was a choice which opened up a whole new world to him. At first reluctantly, and then with growing enthusiasm, he had read enormous books about great battles, about traditional regiments and their uniforms, and about celebrated Generals. Then he managed to persuade the gullible Mrs Fleming to bring him books about techniques of personal survival and surveillance. He smuggled out a message to the Captain and by return, via the same sympathetic prison officer, he received manuals provided for the Special

Air Service on techniques of hand to hand combat and guerrilla warfare. He consumed them all eagerly. The new-found confidence which this knowledge brought him also enabled him to weave a new and complicated fabric of fiction about his history with which he would regale fellow prison inmates.

Crozier began to tell long and complicated stories about his own military exploits. Favourite among the tales were accounts of the many occasions when he had undergone exhaustive and rigorous military training, his narratives always emphasizing the need for careful preparation, resourcefulness and complete ruthlessness. His audience would react with admiration as he described in detail the personal survival programmes to which he had been subjected. Left alone on a remote and inhospitable island off the coast of Scotland, with no food, water or shelter, and the knowledge that in three weeks' time a platoon of army commandos would land and hunt you down and kill you if they could. Your job was first of all to survive, and then to devise methods by which you would not only elude your highly trained and determined opponents, but lure them into traps which would neutralize or eliminate them one by one.

Fellow prisoners who crowded round the wooden tables would gulp muddy cocoa and listen intently as Crozier related how at least one and sometimes several of the newest recruits would inevitably be killed on such exercises. Their dependents would be told that they had lost their lives 'on active service' and left to believe that their husbands, brothers or sons had died a hero's death in a secret operation in Ulster or some more exotic location in a far-off corner of the world. He himself, he was sorry to have to admit, had occasionally been responsible for such deaths. He regretted it but he was not ashamed to tell them. There had been no choice. These were not games, but matters of life or death. Crozier would pause and stare long and hard into his enamel cup as his listeners reacted with a mixture of horror and fascination. Eventually, when he felt sure that his story was achieving its full effect, he would continue. That was the way it was. No one who volunteered for this kind of work could be under any illusion. This was not playing around, but was the real thing. Death was part of the process.

In Richard Crozier's fantasy world, night-time raids on a family of defenceless Jews in Leeds became a behind-enemy-lines assault on the Argentinians at Bluff Cove. A squalid attack on the house of a fatherless Asian family in Bradford became a dawn raid on an INLA unit at Crossmaglen.

Crozier told the stories so well and so often that the prison psychiatrist felt it necessary to return to the medical records to check. Every visible indication available to the experts suggested that what Crozier was saying was the truth, and yet the record showed unambiguously that every single word of it was a lie. For the last twenty-five years, since the age of sixteen, Crozier's life had been spent in and out of borstals, remand homes and prisons. He had served a series of custodial sentences ranging from six months to three years. In the unlikely event that someone of his character could have slipped through the army's recruiting net, there had been no available time for him even to join up, let alone go on survival training.

Despite the deep disquiet expressed by the prison doctors, at last Crozier's sentence was up and he was free again. He especially enjoyed meeting Mrs Fleming for the last time and telling her that she was an ugly and frustrated old woman and that he had enjoyed taking her completely for a ride.

The Captain was as good as his word. The National Socialist Party held a special celebration when he was released and the Captain made a speech welcoming Crozier back and congratulating him on his bravery in preventing the others from being arrested. Four men who had been with him on that night patted him warmly on the back and made him feel one of them again. The Captain had been especially pleased to hear news of Crozier's newly-acquired expertise in military matters. During his absence the party had regrouped and reorganized along military lines and Crozier was told he would henceforth hold the rank of Lieutenant. After the celebration the Captain had taken him to one side and given him what he said was a very important job in which his new skills would come in very useful.

Now Crozier was on a proper mission of his own. He did not know who this old woman was, but he knew that it was vitally important that the organization should find out everything about her. Though the job was clearly nothing directly to do with their political objectives, Davis had said that the party would earn substantial funds which would help them to carry out the real work. Everything the old woman did, and everyone she met, needed to be known and noted. The surveillance had to be secret, and that was what Crozier now thought himself to be an expert in. There was nothing illegal or dangerous about the mission he was being asked to undertake just yet, but Crozier had had plenty of time to make preparations over the last three years, and one of them was always to have a contingency plan to cover every eventuality. That was what he was doing right now.

Crozier retraced his steps across the heavy ground towards his car. In the distance he heard the noise of a powerful engine approaching, and instantly he stopped still, not crouching down but standing his ground. He saw a momentary blue flash as the low-slung sports car whisked past an open gate half a mile up the road, and immediately disappeared once again behind the hedge. The roar of the engine reached a crescendo and then subsided without the car reappearing. It confirmed Crozier's observation that he was safely out of sight of anyone in an ordinary vehicle.

Crozier had learned a hard and costly lesson. Five years, and all because he had made the mistake of relying on others, instead of looking after his own survival. It was a mistake he would never make again. Richard Crozier did not mind taking orders from the Captain, but he would never again rely on him to make his plans for escape in case of the unexpected. His studies over the last three years had given him every possible resource available to the urban commando. One certain thing was that Richard Crozier did not intend to spend any more of his life in prison.

Ten minutes later the red Ford car was once again speeding down narrow country lanes until, five miles further on, it came to a junction with a major road, and turned left towards Lansbury.

CHAPTER TWELVE

Pamela Layfield lay in her bed and looked through a mist of tears at the photograph of her dead husband. The picture had been taken on a blindingly sunny day by a cheap camera with a fixed lens and automatic focus. She had been laughing so much when she had taken it that the image was blurred by her movement. It was not the best photograph she had of Tom Layfield, but it was the one which brought her the happiest memories, and so it was the one she chose to have next to her as she slept.

Each morning when Pamela awoke she would lie quiet and still for a few moments looking at the photograph. Sometimes her arm would stray across to the side of the bed where, had it been three years earlier, Tom would have been snoring gently while deliberately ignoring her warnings that he would be late for work. She might run the flat palm of her hand softly over the warm clean linen where, had it been three years earlier, his head would have been and, half-closing her eyes and allowing her consciousness to wander recklessly, she could imagine for a moment that her hand touched his neck. If she allowed herself to sink further into the trance, she could almost hear his soft growl of pleasure as he began to respond to her.

Now, as always on such occasions, Pamela remembered the last time. The November morning when he had refused to react to her repeated warning that he would be late for his work. Though she always woke before him, she preferred him to get out of bed before her. Anyway, if he was to get to work on time he had to leave the house at least an hour before she did. The company for which he was presently working as a surveyor was building at a site at least forty-five minutes' drive from the house, and he was supposed to be there at eight-thirty.

It was just at the point on that last morning when she thought she would have to get up before him that he had at last opened his eyes and looked at her. She had been keeping him up to date with the time at five-minute intervals for the previous half-hour, and occasionally giving him a gentle nudge. Her efforts had been rewarded only with friendly growls of 'Just another minute'. Then as Pamela prepared to get out of bed, Tom awoke and touched her. The look of love in his soft brown eyes had warmed her as it always did and he had wanted to make love with her. No, she had said, it was far too late.

'Oh come on, be a sport.' He was laughing at her in a way she found irresistible, but it really was too late.

'No no, too late too late.' She had put on her playful high-pitched voice and covered her nakedness with her dressing-gown. 'Maybe tonight if you're good.'

'Oh I'll be good,' he had said, and then noticed the clock. 'Christ almighty, why didn't you tell me the time?' The flying pillow had narrowly missed the back of his head as he disappeared into the bathroom.

That disappearing back had been the last Pamela had ever seen of Tom Layfield alive. She had left the house before him and set off for the school. At eleven o'clock the school secretary had come with grim face into her classroom and had told her that she was wanted on the telephone. Staff shortages meant that there was no teacher to look after the class, and this was the notorious 4B. She had given them dire warnings to behave themselves but had felt little optimism that a riot could be prevented.

'This is Pamela Layfield.' She pressed the receiver hard to her ear to focus her attention away from what might be happening back in 4B.

'Is that Mrs Pamela Layfield, wife of a Mr Tom Layfield?' The woman's voice on the other end of the telephone had been formal but also hesitant. Pamela's concern about 4B had begun to give way to another worry.

'Yes it is. What is it? Who are you please?'

'I'm WPC Rita Hargreaves from Grange estate police.' There was a long pause and Mrs Layfield struggled to think of something to express her urgent need to hear what was coming next. The inevitable words followed. 'I'm afraid there's been an accident.' Suddenly the teacher knew, and she felt that she wanted to reach down into the telephone receiver to put her hand across the mouth that spoke to her, as though to stop the words from actually being said would stop whatever had happened from having happened. Her head began to shake slowly from side to side as she waited for what followed. 'It's your husband, Mrs Layfield.' She knew, she knew so well what was coming. She knew it and it seemed inescapable, and yet she wanted to stop it. It was just like a scene from a film. She had seen so many of them, and WPC Rita Hargreaves must have seen them too because she was saying it just like they always said it in the movies, and for the life of her Pamela Layfield knew that she was also reacting just as they did in the movies. 'I'm afraid he has fallen from a scaffold at the building site where he's been working.'

'Which hospital is he in?' In that moment Pamela

Layfield knew that if she could just establish quickly that he was hurt but not too badly and was in a casualty department, before the WPC could say what she was about to say, she could stop what was true from being true. She spoke again, more urgently. 'He'll be hurt. I'll need to get someone to look after my class so that I can visit him. Which hospital is he in?'

'I'm afraid it's more serious than that, Mrs Layfield.'

The shaking of her head became more violent and hysteria flooded her. 'No, no no no no no.' The whispered words grew in volume so that at last they would drown out what was coming. The movie script said that it must, and so it must.

'I'm afraid that your husband is dead, Mrs Layfield.'

She felt a touch on her arm and turned to see the headmaster, Mr Potter, and the school secretary beside her, their eyes full of concern. They knew. This policewoman had told them already so that they would be there beside her. Her efforts to stop the words from being said were wasted, because they had already been spoken.

'*No!*' The scream had gone on and on and echoed through corridors and down stairways, and it had commanded the attention of every boy in the school, including those now rioting in 4B. The silence that followed lasted fully a minute before the alarming school bell signalled the end of the morning lessons and the end of Pamela Layfield's two years of marriage.

She had gone home after the funeral, quietly, alone, and had walked around in a dream, folding her husband's dirty shirts which were still draped over the chairs in the bedroom, and picking up his socks which had been carelessly aimed at the laundry basket from across the room. Carefully she placed everything into four black plastic bags and deposited them in the bottom of the wardrobe. Only the yellow plastic safety helmet which he was supposed to have been wearing, but which anyway would not have saved his life, rested on the top of one of the bags, keeping it closed.

Now Pamela Layfield lay in her bed and wept frequent tears for her dead husband and loved him and also hated him for leaving her so very alone in such a big and horrible world without a real friend or lover to take care of her when it all became too bad. She loved him and hated him for the fact that she now had to be so strong and independent and self-sufficient. She loved him and hated him because every man who noticed a 35-year-old woman assumed that she was divorced like so many others, and every man thought that 35-year-old divorced women were a pushover. She loved him and hated him because she had to concentrate unceasingly and channel all her time and energy into the things she believed in, in order to keep away the unwanted thoughts and the unwanted men. And she loved him and hated him for always being there on her bedside table in the mornings, laughing at her on the other side of the lens and on the other side of life and death, and for the fact that she still loved him every bit as much this morning as she had on that morning, and that her love showed no signs of getting less.

Pamela Layfield gently and almost imperceptibly shook her head at her husband as if to tell him off for leaving her so alone, and just to show him that she was angry with him she turned over to face the other way. She struggled hard to think of other things, and the thoughts which came into her mind, trying to push the others out, were of Jonathan Maguire.

Now that she had begun to get to know him a little, it was hard to remember what impression Maguire had

146

made on her when he had first introduced himself as a news reporter from the television. She remembered that she had been in a terrible mood on that day, and that she had been unusually rude to him. It embarrassed her now to remember it. She thought again about the café, and about how nervous he had seemed with her. He was young, perhaps a bit younger than herself. She felt slightly uncomfortable with the fact.

Pamela imagined that a young and rather handsome television reporter would be likely to have a busy social life, and it had surprised and rather pleased her to see that Maguire so transparently found her attractive. She had enjoyed pretending not to notice his very obvious attentions. Pamela had avoided having very much to do with any men since Tom. It had not been a struggle; she found most of the men around her at the school inconsequential. She had begun to regard that part of her life as closed. Now for the first time it seemed as though it had awakened just a little. Pamela smiled when she remembered that Maguire was another man who obviously thought that she was a divorcee, and she was surprised when she realized that this time she had managed to vanquish the tears so quickly. She wondered if she would ever tell him the truth, and immediately knew that she would. She wondered too what would be his reaction.

Now young Mr Maguire, who had only just begun to edge a little distance into her affections, was intent on doing something stupid and dangerous. She had not wanted him to do it but she had been unable to tell him the true reason. That was partly because she did not quite know what it was herself. His obvious disregard for his own safety had made her reluctant to get involved with him any further than the tiny bit she had already allowed. There was no room in her for any more pain.

Her thoughts became confused as Pamela tried to sort out and analyse her responses to what was happening. She felt enthusiastic about the possibility of striking back against the vile creatures who were tormenting people she cared for. That was why she had allowed herself to be carried along into agreeing to help. Yet she felt deeply uncomfortable about Maguire and the position he was putting himself in. Once again she reinforced her determination to keep Maguire at arm's length; to fulfil the promise to help him with the project, but to keep him at a distance from her emotions. Even as she made her resolution she thought of the shallow lines around his smiling eyes and she knew that her determination was unlikely to last.

'Do I really need this, Mr Maguire?' Her question was answered only by the silence. She flung back the bed covers and headed for the bathroom to start a new day.

CHAPTER THIRTEEN

Maguire sat and revved the engine of the Citroën hard. Sometimes when he stopped to think about the appalling way he behaved towards the old car, he wondered why it remained so cooperative. The engine gave a high-pitched whine of protest and at last, like an old dog getting up reluctantly to go for an evening walk, the hydropneumatic suspension edged the car upwards. When the vehicle had reached its driving height, Maguire forced the stiffening gear lever mercilessly into first, and began to manoeuvre the ungainly black monster out of the Stadium Television car-park.

The words of Peter Griffiths remained in his mind as he edged beneath the security barrier and out among the busy traffic. Griffiths had run through his cover story with him for hour after hour over recent days until Maguire whispered it to himself in the bath, as he slipped into sleep, as he dreamed, and as he awoke alone on ever colder and damper autumn mornings. In these clothes, which had been carefully chosen for him by the Stadium Television wardrobe department, he was Gerry Marland, an out of work dockyard foreman from the Isle of Dogs who had left London after his marriage had broken up and come to this area in search of a job and a new life. Griffiths had encouraged Maguire to invent most of the story himself so that it would come from somewhere within his own knowledge, and thereby be easier to remember. In fact Maguire had based it on a man he had known as a child. Gerry Marland had lived a few doors away from his own family; his daughter Claire had been Maguire's first girlfriend at the age of twelve, and memories like that never completely die.

He remembered Gerry Marland as a large and loud man who always came home from work earlier than his own father and who played street-games with the local children. Maguire's father had always worked in an office and generally returned home late, and though he would never have admitted it aloud, Maguire had been jealous that Claire's father was not his own. Mr Marland had three daughters but no sons, and had more or less adopted Maguire as a substitute for the son he had wanted but never had. He would tell the boy long and detailed stories of life on the docks, and of the many colourful and larger than life characters bred by the dockers' way of life. The man had even taken Maguire to work with him on several days during the school holidays, and the sight of all those different boats coming in from many exotic and distant parts of the world had enchanted him so thoroughly that he had gone home and told his parents that he too wanted to be a dockworker, 'just like Uncle Gerry'. That was the day that his parents had started gently to discourage the relationship and Mr Marland, probably aware of what was happening, had allowed the gap to widen. Eventually Maguire's family said goodbye to the neighbourhood and Maguire said goodbye to two of his first loves, and he had never quite forgotten either.

As he drove through the slow commuter traffic, Maguire once again went through the discipline of inventing random questions of the type that might be asked by an inquisitive stranger, and then busking the answers his new character would be likely to give. He had learned about the exercise from Peter Griffiths, who had assured him that he had done this kind of thing several times before, and that it was far from easy. To come up with spontaneous answers to routine questions was not so difficult, but it was less simple to remember whatever story you had told and to stick to it when the same subject came up on a subsequent occasion. The *Encounter* team had read the many and various guides for the urban terrorist which were readily available in every military surplus and survival shop. Such books provide training and information for the many groups of lunatics who channel their inadequacies into half-baked ideologies. Asking a suspect person to go over the same ground repeatedly was a basic and widely-known technique to find out whether or not they were telling the truth. The simple trial would certainly be familiar to the National Socialist Party, which had successfully foiled various attempts at infiltration by journalists over many years.

'For Christ's sake don't be complacent.' Griffiths had been unmistakably in earnest. 'Remember that once you are in there you're on your own. The price of failure will be high, and could be very high indeed for you. Remember what these characters are capable of. You've seen it for yourself. There's no room for the smallest slip-up, the slightest mistake.'

Maguire had said he understood and had done his very best to take the matter seriously. He knew enough about the relevant geography and working practices to be able to carry off the story. The only real problem would arise if he should have the bad luck to run into someone else who had worked in the same docks. If that happened he would have no choice but to get out as quickly as he could.

'We'll shadow you very carefully, but don't be surprised if you don't see us. It won't mean that we aren't there. If we see you cut and run we'll be alongside you

151

like a shot – if that happens, watch out for us. We'll pick you up fast and be away.'

Maguire felt apprehensive about what lay ahead of him. He had never done anything remotely like this before and it was exciting but at the same time unnerving. He felt confident that he was working with professionals, and now he glanced intermittently in his mirror to check whether the *Encounter* people were with him. He could not see them but it did not occur to him that they were not somewhere near. He half-heartedly whistled a hollow tune as he drove. It did not help.

Half a mile from the school Maguire turned the car into a narrow cobbled lane behind a fish and chip shop and parked. This was one of the advantages of having an old and unusual-looking car – the local joy-riders would not be seen dead in it. He gave it a friendly pat on the roof as he locked the door, placing the key carefully on top of the nearside rear tyre. He thrust his hands in the pockets of the worn donkey jacket provided by the wardrobe department and headed towards the school.

It was a dull and depressing afternoon, and a glance at his watch checked the time at 3.55. He was just about on schedule. He resisted the temptation to look around for anyone following him until in the distance he could see the wrought-iron railings surrounding the school. Pamela Layfield had told him that Friday was the day that the group which gathered at the school gates was likely to be at its largest and sure enough there now came into view a huddle of eight or ten men standing on the pavement opposite the school entrance. Pamela had also said that she would watch him from an upstairs classroom, and he knew that he must avoid trying to spot her.

On the street outside the gate was a larger number of mothers, standing in twos and threes. Maguire could see that several of the groups were Asians in colourful dresses and veils and there were also several West Indian women wearing western clothing. He turned up the collar of his jacket, hunched his shoulders and pushed his hands deeper into his pockets.

'Here I go, God help me,' he whispered to himself, and gently whistled the same tuneless dirge.

Maguire could hear his heart beating. As he walked the last twenty yards towards the group of men he could distinguish the distant ringing of the school bell, and almost instantly the double doors into the main building were flung open and schoolchildren began filing out. None of the men looked in his direction. Then, just as Maguire drew level with the group on the pavement, he heard the first shout. It was a coarse and aggressive local accent.

'Hey fellas, can you smell something? Isn't that the smell of curry stinking the place out? Where's it coming from?'

Maguire stopped abruptly a few yards from the men. He was shocked. His immediate instinct was to walk directly towards the man who had shouted and simply break open his head. He fought to control himself, but his inability to react spontaneously made him flush with anger. He realized that his failure to intervene aligned him with the group in front of him, and the thought revolted him. Maguire suddenly knew that the whole pretence was going to be far harder than he had anticipated. He had employed all his effort in mastering his story, but had spent little or no time considering what his personal feelings and reactions would be. Across the road he could see that the mothers, black and white, were studiously ignoring the abuse.

'Yeah,' shouted another of the men. 'The good British air is being polluted by the rotten stink of curry. Why don't they go home and stink out their own country?'

The first group of schoolchildren had reached the gates. Immediately Maguire saw that two boys near the front wore turbans and another pair, aged about fourteen, were West Indians. He continued to watch as the mothers hurriedly checked that their children's coat buttons were properly fastened before whisking them around to head away home. Even from his distant vantage point Maguire could see looks of fear in the young faces. Wide white eyes looked anywhere but across the road at the men who were hurling insults.

Two of the men standing nearest to Maguire noticed that he had stopped behind their group. He renewed his effort to adopt what he hoped would seem a casual interest in what was going on. Despite himself he could feel his face flushing with a mix of nausea and anger and for a few seconds he felt on the brink of losing his nerve. Momentarily he considered walking away and abandoning the whole plan. The two men were in their early twenties and were standing at the back of the group. Both had very tightly cropped hair; one seemed to have a small cross tattooed on his forehead. Those standing at the front of the group were too preoccupied with their taunts to take any notice of Maguire.

'Got a problem, mate?' asked the man with the tattoo. The tone was not especially hostile.

'No problem. I'm just wondering whether those little sods are going to leave school and get a job before I can get one.' Maguire had been brought up in a working-class part of south London and had little trouble speaking in an authentic accent. He had not shaved for three days and he wondered whether his appearance was sufficiently convincing to withstand close scrutiny.

'You're not from round here then?'

'Nah, down south but there's nothing down there in my line.'

'What line's that then?' asked the man with the tattoo.

'Docker. But I'm not fussy.'

'There's not much round here. Too many of those black scum taking our jobs.'

Maguire took a deep breath. Despite the cold wind he was still sweating profusely, and for a moment it seemed as though his eyes were misting over. It was either the perspiration or simple panic. He glanced across the road and saw that there was now a steady stream of schoolchildren emerging from the main gate, in approximately equal numbers of coloured and white. He wondered whether Pamela was still watching him from the school and he carefully avoided looking at the upper windows. Instead his eyes flickered down the road until he saw an apparently empty red Volkswagen parked at the kerbside. He reckoned that it would contain the *Encounter* crew and immediately felt a little happier.

'I hope you blokes do something a bit more constructive than shouting at these niggers.'

Now two more of the group were turning their attention away from the jeering and were beginning to take an interest in Maguire. One man was older, with black greasy hair with a slight curl, and very hard blue eyes.

'What would you suggest?' His accent gave the impression that he was more educated than the first two.

'I could think of a few things I'd like to do,' said

Maguire, 'but not many of them are legal in this country just yet.' He paused while the older man looked at him. Once again Maguire felt the cold sweat, and wondered whether he had taken the preparations sufficiently seriously and would be clever enough to get away with this plan. In his pockets, Maguire's finger-nails were pressed hard into his palms. He needed to handle this very cautiously. He was afraid he had overplayed it.

'Well, it may be that we have a meeting of minds.' The older man half-closed his penetrating eyes, as though still making up his mind. When he spoke again his voice was more businesslike, suggesting that he had made a decision. 'Anyway, we're off for a cup of tea. Why don't you come along, if you've nothing better on?'

'No, I've nothing else on, except walking the streets.'

The older man attracted the attention of the rest of the group and indicated that they were moving off. Several turned for a parting shout at the dwindling groups of mothers and children across the road. Maguire was aware that the older man took aside the tattooed man who had first approached him and whispered something quietly. The younger man nodded and Maguire saw that he allowed the rest of the men to walk past him, so that he was the last of the group. As he walked along with them, Maguire noticed that the tattooed man was frequently glancing behind. There was no sign of anyone following.

The group walked for twenty minutes, speaking little, around the poor suburban streets near to the school. Maguire noticed that they would frequently turn off the pavement to walk down side alleys which were only wide enough for pedestrians. Once or twice they seemed to double back on themselves, and all the time the man with the small tattoo on his forehead hung back, glancing over his shoulder at regular intervals. Maguire began to understand how the National Socialists had avoided having their organization penetrated in the past.

'Some might think it's a bit strange for a fella to leave London and come to an area like this to look for work.' It was the man with the greasy black hair.

'I've got a sister in Rosminster. I came up to stay with her when me and the missis parted company three weeks back. But she's got her own life to lead, and anyway we never could stand each other, so I'm looking for a place as well as a job.'

'I know Rosminster quite well. What part is it your sister's in?'

The inquiry was obviously more than just casual and Maguire began to be glad that he had taken Peter Griffiths' advice seriously. Maguire had chosen Rosminster because he had an aunt who had lived there for many years. The house next door to hers had recently become vacant while the owners visited abroad. Maguire had made a note of the address, but he would avoid giving precise details unless it was absolutely necessary.

'St John's Terrace, about a mile from the railway station. Do you know it?'

The man shook his head decisively and kept on walking. Moments later the group turned sharply yet again, and emerged into a yard which seemed to be behind a row of shops. Along one side was a row of lock-up garages. At the very end of the row the man with the greasy hair unlocked a heavy padlock on the garage in the corner and the group went in.

The front of the building had been on the same lines as all the other garages and Maguire expected this one to be more or less the same size. When the door was pulled open he wondered how he had been deceived. The inside of this building was at least ten times as big as an ordinary garage. The level line of fronts disguised the reality, so that the scale of the interior came as a complete surprise. No one on the outside would have been able to guess that this could be a meeting place, or anything other than a large lock-up. Aware that several of the men were keeping an eye on him, Maguire tried to disguise his reactions. The room had a small platform at one end and three rows of fold-up wooden chairs lined up neatly facing it. The concrete walls had been lined with wooden boards, and almost every inch was covered with posters and leaflets. Maguire stood to one side as three of the men went to a makeshift counter at one end of the hut and produced a large kettle and enamel teapot.

'Quite something, isn't it?' It was the man with black curly hair who now held out his hand. Maguire reached out and shook it firmly.

'My name's Gerry Marland.'

'Frank Thompson, but here they call me the Sergeant. What do you think of our little gathering place?' Maguire said he was impressed. 'You wouldn't know we were here, and not many people from outside our little group do. There are quite a few people who would give a lot to know the location of this place, so er, we'll be expecting you to be discreet.'

The man was now very close to Maguire and appeared to be examining him minutely. Maguire wondered once again about his chosen identity. A careful and clever observer could probably tell the difference between a face which was used to outdoor life and that of a man who has spent most of his time in warm offices. Maguire hoped that this man was not so clever.

'To speak the truth I wouldn't be able to tell anyone where we are even if I wanted to. I'm a stranger round this way, and besides, you weren't taking any chances. Even I could tell that we came a very long way round.'

The man smiled an unattractive smile. 'I'll probably be in the shit for bringing you here anyway. If I'd brought you by a direct route my arse would be in a sling for a month.'

'Oh, from who?'

The other man looked at him suspiciously. 'Ask no questions . . . and you'll probably be told a pack of lies anyway.' The serious face broke into its unpleasant smile again. 'Get yourself a cup of tea. We've got a meeting starting in a quarter of an hour.'

Maguire had already noticed that more men were arriving at the hut. All were dressed in drab, working men's clothes, and all of them seemed to be poorly educated and uncouth. The man with the tattoo on his forehead who had first spoken to him was now approaching carrying two mugs of tea. He sipped from one of them and the steam from the brew mixed with the condensation of his breath. He held out the other cup for Maguire, who noticed the word LOVE tattooed across the knuckles of his left hand.

'Thanks, I could use this.' The tattooed man stood beside Maguire and they watched the room fill up while those who had arrived first unfolded chairs and put them in lines facing the dais at one end of the room.

'What do you think of our little decorations. Good aren't they?' For the first time Maguire now looked carefully at the posters lining the walls. An enormous one pinned up behind the stage was divided into two, with one side showing a huge close-up of the head and sharp features of a large brown rat, and the other a stereotyped figure of an old Jew. Maguire's first thought was that the image was rather comic and childish, reminiscent of the treatment of Fagin in the film version of *Oliver Twist*. The slogan daubed beneath the pictures was anything but funny. 'You know what to do with vermin . . .'

'It's a relief to find that someone else has the same views as I do.' Maguire tried to remain composed and took large mouthfuls from his mug of tea. 'I was beginning to think I was the odd one out.'

'Everybody thinks the same things.' The man with the tattoo was smiling broadly, showing discoloured teeth. 'You wouldn't be an Englishman if you didn't. It's just that not enough of us speak out.'

'And even fewer are prepared to act,' said Maguire, 'more's the pity. I suppose you blokes are all talk and no action, like everyone else.' He took another mouthful of tea and pretended to have little interest in the answer.

'I wouldn't be so sure about that.' The young man was still smiling broadly. 'I've got a feeling you're going to like it here.'

The chairs were all set out and most were occupied. Maguire scanned the group of men and reckoned they numbered about thirty-five. He wondered whether his friends from *Encounter* had managed to keep track of him in any way and thought that they almost certainly had not. He did not feel worried. He allowed himself a fleeting thought about Pamela and remembered how concerned she had been when he had told her of his plan. The thought that she had been gave a further boost to his confidence.

Maguire saw that two men were arranging a television set and a video player on the stage. The man

160

with greasy black hair who had introduced himself as the Sergeant stepped up to speak.

'Well as you know, brothers, it's movie night tonight; and we've got a special treat for you.' A murmur of approval came from the men in the audience and several shuffled in their seats to get a better view of the screen. 'We've had a number of very successful expeditions of late, and you'll be delighted to hear that last time out, Captain Davis permitted some video to be shot.' More approval from the audience. The man gestured for silence. 'Naturally, as you'd expect, there were plenty of volunteers when we asked for someone to shoot the niggers,' laughter from the back, 'but only Lance-Corporal Johnson was sufficiently expert on the camera, so he was the lucky one.' All eyes turned to a middle-aged man standing at one side of the hall who grinned to acknowledge his work. The expression made Maguire wonder whether Johnson might be slightly mentally inadequate. On the dais the Sergeant checked behind him to ensure that the equipment was now wired up. 'So, not too much noise now; but enjoy remembering an already memorable evening.' The man left the stage and walked across to stand next to Maguire. He whispered, 'This might interest you,' and the lights went out a few seconds before the screen was filled with an out of focus, black and white image.

As the first frames of the video flickered on to the screen Maguire noticed that two other men had entered the hall and were standing at the back of the audience. One was tall and smartly dressed in country clothes, the other was shorter and wore a heavy black coat which seemed too small for his substantial bulk. The two men were ignoring the show and talking intently. Maguire felt intrigued and was unable to draw his eyes away from them. After a while the taller of the two

161

newcomers looked around the hall and caught the attention of the man with greasy hair who had introduced himself as the Sergeant. He was beckoned to where the two men stood. The Sergeant walked across and Maguire watched as the group continued speaking in an increasingly animated manner. They completely ignored the noisy reactions of the small crowd of men, who were extravagantly enjoying the video.

Glancing back towards the three Maguire saw that the tallest of them was looking directly at him in the half-light. He could lipread the question being asked. The Sergeant turned towards him and Maguire could also lipread his answer. A new recruit; we found him today. Maguire forced himself to turn back to the screen. He watched the blurred and underexposed image of a man crouching in the darkness next to what looked like the front door of a house. The figure poured liquid from a petrol can on to a rag. He put the can on to the doorstep and began to feed the rag through the letterbox. Maguire watched and made himself join in the general laughter for a minute, before turning his attention surreptitiously to the three men. Maguire could now see a little more of the third man. He had removed the coat and was dressed in a black jacket and striped trousers. There was something else about him. He was extremely overweight. Maguire remembered what Pamela had said.

Suddenly there was a loud cheer and Maguire turned to look at the screen. It showed a group of men, each of them dressed in black, crouching in the back of a small van. The unsteadiness of the shot suggested that the vehicle was moving fast. One of the dark figures grinned at the camera and gave a Churchillian victory salute. The man next to him did the same with his hand reversed, and both men laughed silently. The audience provided the effects. Next the camera whipped from side to side as the van apparently came to a halt and the doors were opened. Maguire remained transfixed as he watched what followed, oblivious of his immediate surroundings.

Two hours later Maguire pushed his foot hard and suddenly on to the brake, and the old Citroën shuddered to a halt. The engine stalled and the car headlights flickered off. The stop was sufficiently abrupt to lunge Maguire forward, and his forehead momentarily made contact with the backs of his hands which were gripped together at the top of the steering wheel. He held his arms stiff and kept himself tightly in the same position, his bent wrists pressing into his eye-sockets as he tried hard to keep out the thoughts of the night. Despite his efforts to banish them, the ugly images swarmed around inside his head. He saw again the laughter on the faces of the men in black, again the flames spreading up the outside of the wooden door. The thoughts mingled with still fresh memories of the small body which had fallen through his arms and on to the ungiving ground at his feet, and he heard again the terrible screams of horror and the whimpers of despair. Maguire's mind reeled in revulsion at it all, and the nauseous feeling in his gut welled up into his throat and he had to swallow hard to avoid vomiting. He pressed his hands hard to his ears until the ringing in his head gave way to a more distinct sound. After moments of confusion he realized that the sound came from outside and he opened his eyes and tried to dispel his blurred vision. Someone was knocking at the window. He squinted again and now heard the voice clearly.

'Maguire? Are you all right? Can you hear me?' He looked again. It was Pamela Layfield. She was stooping beside his car in a white dressing-gown, tapping on the window. Without even properly knowing where he was going he had arrived outside her house. He reached for the doorhandle and found that it would not move. He realized that he had locked the car from the inside and now he struggled to open it. When he managed to do so, he practically tumbled out, having to steady himself with a hand on the wet pavement before getting to his feet.

'Maguire? Are you all right?'

Maguire stood up and looked at her. He saw that her eyes were full of confusion and he wondered what could be wrong.

'For God's sake say something. Are you OK?'

'Of course I'm all right.' Even as he spoke Maguire realized that he was unfamiliar with the thought that someone else cared about his welfare. He looked again at Pamela, who had linked her arm through his and was supporting him.

'Come into the house for heaven's sake.' She kicked the car door closed and guided him towards the open front door of her house. The curtains were closed and the red glow behind them looked warm and wonderfully welcoming. Even as he walked down the short path Maguire began to feel more comfortable. Once inside, he sat heavily into an armchair.

'Well, don't keep me in suspense. Are you OK? How did it go?' Pamela Layfield's face radiated curiosity and concern. In all his confusion Maguire noticed that she had not let go of his hand. He took a deep breath and tried to gather some thoughts which would express the many things he felt.

'It went fine. It went really well. These bastards. You just could not believe it. You never would believe what these bastards are doing.' Maguire could feel the anger welling up uncontrollably as he remembered. 'It's everything you suspected and worse. It's just . . . I'm just lost for words to tell you.'

'But what about you? Did anyone suspect? Did you get away with it?' Her voice was still full of anxiety.

'Terrific. It was terrific. They didn't suspect a thing. Stupid buggers. They didn't suspect anything, and they've even invited me back.'

'What do you mean, to another meeting?'

'Better than that. I expressed so much enthusiasm for their nasty attacks on blacks that they asked me if I wanted to go out on one with them. Naturally I jumped at the chance. Now all I have to do is make sure I know how to find the place again so that the lads from *Encounter* can come along and discreetly film the thing from start to finish. Then we'll have the bastards once and for all.'

'But how will you manage to have the *Encounter* people follow? Did you recognize where they took you?'

'No, and they were damned careful too. I've got to meet them at a pub called the British Bull, and they'll take me to the same meeting place. That's going to be the difficult bit. If I can just find out the location of the lock-up I went to tonight, the team would probably be able to follow a vehicle leaving it. But they've no chance of following a small group of them on foot, not without being spotted.'

Pamela looked at him hard for a moment. 'I might be able to help with that.'

'How?'

'I was watching from the school as you joined the

group outside. The man with the tattoo on his fore-head, the one who talked with you first of all. His name is Banks, Colin Banks. He was at the school a long time ago. He's an animal, but he has a younger brother who left more recently. His name is Gary.' She was obviously working out her thoughts as she spoke. 'Gary is not that bright either, but he was a more decent kid, and he did have a brief flirtation with this mob. I spoke to him about it and he was one of the few who lost interest. He told me on the quiet that he didn't like the racist stuff. He might . . . who knows, he might be willing to help.'

'If *you* asked him, you mean?'

'Yes.'

'No no. Not a chance. Too dangerous. I don't want you getting any further involved in this. When I first asked you I didn't really know quite how vile these people are.'

Pamela smiled and looked at the floor. Maguire noticed again the slight red tint to her black hair and the soft lines of her profile. At that moment she seemed extraordinarily beautiful to him.

She looked up. 'What can I get you?'

Maguire leant forward to halve the distance between his face and hers. As he did so her face came towards his, and a moment later they kissed. It was soft and cautious, their lips scarcely touching. Their hands were still clasped together, but nothing more. It was a feeling of deep warmth and pleasure which Maguire wanted to allow to circulate within him, and to be able to keep vivid and come back to. He felt his insides tighten in expectation. It had seemed so long, but now he knew. She broke away suddenly and moved backwards.

'I'll make some coffee while you have a wash.' She

turned back to him before disappearing into the kitchen and smiled a lovely smile.

In the bathroom Maguire found soap and fresh towels and proceeded to remove many cares from his face. Downstairs he could hear the bubbling sound of an old-fashioned percolator. He looked into the bathroom cupboard. He saw talc and night-cream, other simple cosmetics, but there was no sign of anything belonging to a man. Maguire wondered about Pamela Layfield's husband.

'Investigating me, Mr Reporter?' The voice behind him made him jump. He smiled, obviously caught in the act. He looked at Pamela and saw that she held a large cup of coffee in her hand and was smiling back at him. He moved towards her and took the coffee, placing it precariously on top of the laundry basket. Nothing was said. She took his hand and led him out of the bathroom towards the bedroom. A small lamp in one corner was the only light.

Maguire held her face in his hands and looked at her. Now she seemed afraid, lacking in self-confidence after so long; but the momentum swept her beyond her disquiet and she closed her eyes as they kissed, softly at first. Maguire found the cord of her dressing-gown and pulled loose the bow which fastened it. There was a moment of dismay as it seemed that the cord would form a knot, and he dared not struggle with it for fear of breaking the spell. A further gentle tug pulled the cord free. With both hands he lifted the dressing-gown from her shoulders and felt it fall around their feet. The extreme tips of his fingers touched her shoulders, stroking them very gently and briefly before travelling slowly in a meandering path down the front of her arms and on to her breasts. Her hand touched his thigh and

167

after a moment's hesitation they embraced, folding their arms around each other, holding their bodies tightly together, into the night and deep inside the closest of their secrets.

CHAPTER FOURTEEN

In the twenty years that Mrs Blake had worked for Sir John Bartholomew she had never been closer to resignation than she was today. Sir John had always been a gentleman, a perfect gentleman she might have said. Mrs Blake had shared with him in his pleasure in the many successes there had been, and had been glad too to share in the occasional crisis and disappointment in his career. There had been only a very few of them.

Master and servant had not been close, no one could ever describe their relationship as that. When Mr Blake had passed away twelve years ago Sir John, or Mr Bartholomew as he then was, had been kind and sympathetic and had sent a very nice wreath; but he had not attended the funeral. The tone of quiet concern which remained in his voice in everything he said to her for several weeks had eventually worn off and their relationship had returned once again to its strictly business footing.

At Christmas-time Sir John would always give her a gift of expensive perfume and Belgian home-made chocolates from Harrods, but he had never availed himself of the opportunity she discreetly allowed him to give her even the most innocent kiss on her cheek. They were more or less contemporaries in age if not in circumstances, and such matters always carried with them a suggestion of danger. Instead, the rather stiff man would extend a rather stiff hand and inquire whether she was visiting the family as usual. He would smile in approval at the inevitable affirmation, and then turn away to circulate with other members of the bank staff before she could ask him about his own plans.

Mrs Blake of course knew that Sir John had a house in Sevenoaks, but she had never visited it and had very little idea of what it was like. He had once described it to her as a 'modest coach-house', but she felt certain that it was something much smarter than that description implied. The only additional information she had ever received was from Hampson, the chauffeur, who brought Sir John to work each morning and took him home each night. Mrs Blake did not much like Hampson and discouraged him from becoming too familiar with her.

On the one occasion when he had said something to the effect that Sir John's home was 'quite a pad', she had wanted to nudge him a little further; but Mrs Blake did not especially want Hampson to realize that she, Sir John's private secretary for nearly twenty years, had never been invited to his home. So her inquiries could only be made in the most discursive way. For her trouble she learned that the 'modest coach-house' probably had about twenty rooms and was in five acres of grounds. She also felt sure that Hampson was aware that she had never visited, but nothing was said.

Mrs Blake knew that Sir John had never married. 'Too busy having fun and serving my country,' he had once told her in the early days. Though extremely courteous and undoubtedly distinguished, he was not an attractive man. His skin had an almost translucent quality and looked as though it would burn horribly if exposed to the sun for more than just a few minutes. His face and hands were covered in ginger freckles, and the only facial feature which had any prominence was his nose, which was slightly too long. Otherwise his mouth and eyes seemed weak, almost girlish. The greying hair had once been red and added somewhat to the overall impression of fragility and frigidity.

Mrs Blake also knew that her boss had a sister somewhere, because she had once peeped inside the single card which invariably arrived through the post on his birthday and read the emotionless message: 'Best wishes John from your sister Irene.' Once Mrs Blake's curiosity had overcome her reserve and she had asked him whether he would spend his birthday with his sister. 'Good God no,' he had seemed surprised at the question. 'I haven't seen her for thirty years.' His tone of voice had not encouraged further questions.

So, their relationship had been friendly without being familiar, and correct without being close. Today, for the first time in two decades, Sir John Bartholomew was being very inconsiderate and even downright rude to her, and Mrs Blake did not like it one little bit.

The day had begun badly when she had arrived at the office and found him already sitting at his desk. Her usual routine was to get to work at eight-thirty, which was a full hour before most of the rest of the staff. It gave her a chance to unfold his newspaper at the share-prices page, open his mail, and have his tray of tea and wholemeal toast ready as he walked in the door at nine-thirty. On the odd occasion when he intended to come to work any earlier, he would always in the past have told her, and she would catch an early train from Chiswick where she kept on the small semi in which she had lived with her husband, and still have time to get things organized for his arrival. This morning she had received no such warning, and had been upset to hear movement in his office. She had carefully opened the door to investigate, only to find him already at his desk, slitting open his mail with a gold-plated letter opener which he had kept for at least fifteen years but for which to her certain knowledge he had never had use.

'Oh Sir John. You're here.'

'Evidently Mrs Blake. Get me some tea would you?'

Like her boss, Mrs Blake did not much care for elaborate courtesies, but she knew that Sir John would have disapproved if he had heard any of his own junior staff speaking so abruptly to their secretaries. She could see no reason why he should be abrupt with her when she had done nothing to deserve it.

'Right away, Sir John.'

'Oh and Mrs Blake?' She stopped and came back in through the half-open door. 'Cancel all my appointments today. I have an important meeting here at midday and I don't want any other clutter. Organize some lunch will you?'

'Yes Sir John. May I know who and how many?'

The Chairman did not even look up from his papers. 'No to the first question and five to the second. Tea please, Mrs Blake.'

Mrs Blake had been astonished, and had deliberately not taken her usual care to close the door gently and quietly. In ordinary circumstances she would have taken in his mail and started receiving dictation by ten o'clock, but today she had neither seen nor heard a peep from Sir John by eleven forty-five. Because of his unpleasant mood she was determined not to disturb him unless he summoned her. She hoped that he would notice the uncharacteristic neglect and realize that he had been rude. She also knew in her heart that he would not give the matter a single thought. At eleven-fifty she heard footsteps in the corridor and Peter Tremayne scuttled in.

'Sir John hasn't asked for you. Do you want me to see if he wants you?'

Tremayne looked surprised. 'I think he does want to see me. He called me directly on the internal.'

Mrs Blake's tight mouth tightened still further as she pressed a button on the console on her desk. A tinny voice responded.

'Yes?'

'Peter Tremayne is here.' She doubted if the metallic machine would communicate the irritation in her voice.

'Send him in. Send him in.'

She clicked off the machine and turned to Tremayne. For the Chairman to be abrupt with her in private was one thing, but for him to be so rude in front of other staff was barely tolerable. Normally she would have opened the door and announced the visitor. Now she sat still.

'It doesn't sound as though you should keep Sir John waiting.'

Tremayne noticed the aberration and raised his eyebrows in surprise. Her expression unambiguously conveyed her mood but carried no other information. He opened the door and went in. Sir John Bartholomew was sitting on the far side of his enormous desk, apparently concentrating on piles of papers and photographs which were spread out all over it.

'Tremayne. The MD of the British Energy Corporation and the London man from American Energy Industries will be here at twelve. Davis is expected too. I put BEC in the picture last night and they're going berserk. They've completely lost their nerve and are talking about pulling out of the deal altogether – as if that would be the answer to anything, even if it were possible.' Tremayne sat down and concentrated hard. 'The Americans are being far more intelligent and realistic about it as you'd expect, and are interested in our answers and in suggesting a few of their own. That's why I asked them here today.'

'Are you going to be frank about Davis's brief?'

'That's why I called you in.' Bartholomew opened a drawer at the side of his enormous desk and took out a small tape recorder. He unloaded the cassette he had in place and put it to one side. 'I haven't put Davis in the picture, but he will quickly catch on. He understands this sort of thing completely because of our earlier work together.' His eyebrows asked Tremayne if he understood and a slight nod from the younger man indicated that he did. 'I won't need to say anything to him because he will instinctively know what to do, but I need to brief you. This business could end up being ugly, very very ugly. The rules of the game mean that if it does, everyone will run for cover – especially people like our visitors today.' Tremayne nodded again. 'They will gladly sit here and approve anything we suggest, however unpleasant or illegal, to get this situation under control. None of them, however, will want to get their own hands dirty, and if the excreta hits the ventilation system they'll be darting for cover. Which is why . . .' Bartholomew now snapped a new cassette into the machine and replaced it in the drawer, closing it with a slam. '. . . which is why I want to make sure that both of these organizations are clearly on the record.'

'By "on the record" you mean on the tape?'

'You have it. It may never be necessary for the existence of this tape to be known. It will almost certainly never come to it, but if it ever should, we will need these characters struggling alongside us to get out of the cesspit, rather than putting their size ten boots on our foreheads and shoving us under. Do you get the idea?'

'Crystal clear.'

'So when they arrive say little beyond what I ask you, and remember that we want to draw them out. Davis is an expert in these matters and I have had a bit of success in these things myself. Stay quiet and you may learn something.'

'Thank you, Sir John. I'll help all I can.' Tremayne got up and headed towards the door.

'Oh and Tremayne.'

Tremayne turned back. 'Yes sir?'

'If all this goes well – if we get over this little crisis – I may have a particular proposition to put to you. It's to do with an organization for which Mr Davis and I have a shared enthusiasm.' Tremayne's expression indicated his curiosity. 'I won't say any more for the time being, but suffice it to say that I regard nothing as being more crucial to the future security of this nation.'

A few minutes later Tremayne was back in his office. He sat at his desk with his head supported on his hands and said nothing.

'Something wrong?' Clive Hubbard spoke through the mouthful of cheese and beetroot sandwich which would tide him over in between his tea and biscuits at eleven and his lunch in an hour from now.

Tremayne did not even move his eyes in response to the question. He waited for a further moment to try to make sense of what had been said to him but recognized that he had failed adequately to do so.

'I think I've just been asked to join the Freemasons.'

After twenty minutes the intercom on Tremayne's desk clicked and Mrs Blake spoke in a taut voice.

'The Chairman's guests have arrived at the front door and Sir John wants you to go down to fetch them.'

'Right away.'

'And for some reason which no one has bothered to explain to me,' Mrs Blake was by now on the brink of losing her composure altogether, 'he has asked that you bring them up the back stairs.' The speaker clicked off.

Tremayne showed Dante Fitzwilliam from American Energy Industries and Sir Horace Beckford from the British Energy Corporation into Sir John's office without even pausing to ask Mrs Blake whether the Chairman was ready for them. Ordinarily she would never have allowed anyone to walk directly past her into the Chairman's office, but so many odd things had already happened today that she was past the point where she would question anything out of the ordinary. The door closed firmly behind them and a second later Sir John's voice crackled over the intercom.

'Tea for five please, Mrs Blake.'

'Yes sir.' She had no idea who the two newcomers were, but she could see enough with her own eyes to know this was an occasion for the best china, and no arguments.

'Sit down gentlemen.' Tremayne saw that the leather armchairs which usually stood either side of the window had been drawn forward. Sir John seemed to be very specific about the chairs he wanted his guests to sit in. 'Now we have no need to waste any time,' said the Chairman. 'We all know what the situation is – we believe it possible that there has been a breach of security and that the Lazarus file may have been compromised.'

'Heaven help us.' Sir Horace Beckford was an unusually tall man in late middle age. The slight stoop which had been a part of his bearing since adolescence remained, and was still clearly evident even as he sat in the high-backed armchair. Every aspect of the man seemed to have been elongated, so that gangly arms hung down at the sides of the chair, and thin legs extended forwards and crossed over themselves as if in an attempt to contract the overall space he occupied. 'May one ask what steps have been taken to ensure that the leak is contained?'

'And whether we've sent out scouts to get back any copies which may be floating around loose?' The American wore a dark navy-blue suit and a blue shirt with buttons at the points of the collar. His grey hair was cropped tight to his head in a style which he had scarcely altered since his time in the marines thirty years ago. Dante Fitzwilliam liked to litter his conversation with military references. It gave him the opportunity to run his hand over the back of his head and reminisce about his days in the service. Though his brief military career had begun well after the Korean war, and had ended well short of Vietnam, Fitzwilliam was one of those who believed that Kennedy had sold out the Cubans in the Bay of Pigs and that Nixon and Ford had sold out the American people in Saigon. 'Have you identified the treacherous son of a bitch who has taken the thing?'

The conversation was interrupted by a knock on the door and Mrs Blake entered with a tray of tea. Bartholomew looked up at her, obviously irritated, but his interest was immediately taken by Davis, who was following her in.

'Ah, Mr Davis.' Mrs Blake had been unaware of Davis's arrival, and Sir John's greeting took her by surprise, causing the teacups to wobble precariously on the tray. 'Put it down, Mrs Blake, do,' said Sir John.

The tray clattered on to the coffee table and Mrs Blake straightened herself.

'Will that be all, Sir John?'

'Yes, Mrs Blake. We'll have lunch in here in twenty minutes.'

Mrs Blake departed, her temper worsening at every moment. Davis pulled an upright wooden chair into the circle and placed himself heavily upon it.

'Mr Davis here has been working on this matter already, and I think it's fair to say that we have a pretty good idea who we're dealing with. What we're not certain of is the location of the offending item, or the intention of those in whose custody it may be. We also don't know to whom, if anyone, the original thief has entrusted the information, and naturally we badly need to find out the answers before taking appropriate action.'

'And then what form will this action take?' The long arm of Sir Horace extended across the table and picked up the teapot. 'Shall I be mum?'

Sir John nodded. 'Well that is very much a matter for you gentlemen. We at the bank are simple business-men, servants and functionaries, without a specific political or moral remit. Our shareholders might be ostentatiously cross if this little matter comes to light, but after a little explanation they will see very quickly and clearly the very profitable nature of our operation, and I doubt very much whether at the end of the day any heads would roll.' He leaned forward and spooned two generous helpings of sugar into his teacup and picked up the cup, stirring it absent-mindedly. 'You two gentlemen on the other hand are both in some sense representing public corporations, answerable to, and acting on behalf of, arms of your own govern-ments. The consequences for you and your respective political masters are no doubt far more undesirable.'

'Thank you for pointing that out.' Sir Horace grimaced as though the thought brought an unpleasant taste into his mouth. 'It makes me all the more grateful to Mallin Harcourt for getting us into this mess.'

'We're only too well aware that this unfortunate breach of security is our responsibility, and we realize that it is our responsibility to carry out whatever policy is agreed here today. But you gentlemen are ultimately the clients, and must give us guidance on the measures you wish to see taken. In a nutshell it's a question of what lengths you wish to go to in order to regain and then retain security for the Lazarus operation.' Sir John's eyes flickered towards Tremayne, who was watching his boss's plan unfold with barely concealed admiration.

'Well it's pretty damned clear, isn't it?' said the American. 'We've got to ensure security for the papers, and then we've got to nuke the bastards who took them, and all those who have seen them.'

'Oh I say, steady on,' said Sir Horace, hurriedly replacing his cup and saucer on the table in front of him. 'We want to get the papers back and we want to regain security, but we don't want a bloodbath.'

'Now look,' said the American, 'when these guys decided to take the papers, they joined the big league. This isn't a game, this is real life; and in real life, decisions have consequences. The consequence of meddling with the big boys is that life gets rough. They knew that. They knew what they were taking on.'

Now Davis spoke for the first time. His unexpectedly high-pitched voice seemed to cut through the fluster.

'Well it seems to me that we all share Sir Horace's distaste for unpleasantness of any type, but perhaps we would all be enlightened if we knew what Sir Horace has in mind? If he is saying that we should try to recover our property and then allow those who stole it to take the information they have gathered to the newspapers, then it would be a good idea for him to say so now so that we all know where we stand.'

'No way,' interrupted Fitzwilliam. 'Even if you limeys can't take the tough decisions, I'm prepared to. We can't afford to pussyfoot around this. It's out of the question.'

'No no, Mr Davis is right,' said Sir John. 'It's very clear where American Energy Industries stands on this, and we're grateful for the absence of any ambiguity. Now we have to know where Sir Horace and the British Energy Corporation stand. Are we going to use every means at our disposal – including potentially illegal and even violent ones – to regain our property and proper security, or aren't we? We cannot act without their authority and blessing.' Tremayne knew immediately and exactly why his chairman was spelling things out so clearly, but the specific details of what lay ahead were causing the long Englishman to bend into ever more excruciating contortions.

'Look I can't speak on behalf of the Government. I'll have to refer something like this upwards. To the Minister at least.'

'I understand how you feel, Sir Horace.' It was Davis's squeaky voice again. 'We all understand that you are merely a public servant. But the nuclear industry which you represent is a sensitive one. Sensitive secrets can be taken and can be sold to Britain's enemies. Dangerous nuclear secrets. Anyone who does that, or acts recklessly in a manner which jeopardizes or compromises the economic or military security of this nation, is a traitor, a spy. These people are enemies of the state. Surely as a senior public servant your duty is clear. Your superiors won't want to know such things, and they won't thank you for telling them. They pay people like you to take care of such matters, and not to worry them with the details. I believe it's called "need to know", which means if they don't *need* to know, don't tell them.'

Sir John had been listening carefully to Davis. Now everyone in the room turned towards the discomforted Sir Horace, and waited.

'All right then. Have it your own way. Anything goes, any measure.'

'I'm afraid it's not a question of any of us having it our way,' interrupted the Chairman, determined to push the matter to the ultimate. 'We have to be clear. You are authorizing any means, any methods, to secure the information in the Lazarus file?'

'Yes I am, God help me. I am.' Sir Horace blurted it out and stood up straight.

'Well hooray for that,' said the American, now also standing.

'Won't you gentlemen stay for lunch?'

Both declined and edged towards the exit. They were shaking hands when the door opened to reveal Mrs Blake standing with a trolley of food which she was about to wheel into the room.

'Sorry, Mrs Blake,' said Sir John. 'My guests cannot stay after all. Cancel lunch will you?'

When the two visitors had left, Peter Tremayne watched Sir John open his desk drawer and check the recording. His face indicated his satisfaction at the result, and Tremayne shared his obvious pleasure at the way things had gone. However, for the first time in the six months he had worked closely with him, there was something about Sir John's scheming which seemed slightly less than attractive to Peter Tremayne. The PA was also intrigued to see that the Chairman did not touch the recording machine or otherwise indicate to Davis that the tape had been made.

'Well, all very satisfactory,' said the Chairman smugly. 'Now, have we any other business or can we all get on with what our shareholders are paying us for?'

'There's just one thing I should report,' said Davis. The Chairman indicated that he should resume his seat. 'The old woman, Harriet Nuttall.'

'Yes, what about her?' asked Sir John.

'Something interesting. She is writing a paper for the inquiry as you know.'

'Yes yes, we know that – something about viability and suitability of the American system. Nothing very worrying as I recall.'

'Yes, that's quite right,' said the fat man. His voice rose still higher as his pleasure in conveying exciting information grew. 'Except that she has now written a letter to the Inquiry Secretary saying that she wants to change the subject of her paper.'

Sir John Bartholomew and Peter Tremayne both sat up in their chairs. 'Well, to what for heaven's sake?' The Chairman was the more impatient.

'That's just the point. The rules of the Inquiry require maximum disclosure of information beforehand so that witnesses can be cross-examined by Counsel at the hearing,' said Davis with an inappropriately wide smile. 'She told the Secretary that her paper is still in the general area of safety and economics, but that she now has some specific information she wishes to include. She says she is unable to tell him more details at the moment, but that she will do so on the day she delivers her paper at the inquiry.'

'But she's just a batty old woman,' Tremayne interrupted. 'We know that Ross is encouraging her on the basis of the work she has done before, and that everything she has done so far has always been just a harmless trip round the bay. She won't be anything to do with all this.'

'Mr Tremayne is very probably right,' said Davis, in a manner which Tremayne felt was transparently condescending, 'but I think I'd better ask one of our people to take a closer look, don't you, Sir John?'

'I do, Mr Davis. I most certainly do.'

CHAPTER FIFTEEN

'The problem is,' said Tim Walker, 'that we just cannot guarantee to stay with them. We thought we would be able to on the relatively simple exercise when Maguire joined up, and they still lost us.' The broad Australian voice was full of scepticism. 'To be perfectly frank, this sort of thing only works when the people you're interested in aren't taking much notice of what's going on around them. They've only got to take the most simple precautions like this lot do and it's practically impossible to stay close if you don't want to take the risk of alerting them. And that's especially important in circumstances like these where we've got a man in place.'

'And on an outing of the sort we're now expecting they will be even more cautious, they're bound to be.' It was Bill Tyler, the sound recordist.

'Well it's mostly a question of resources.' Peter Griffiths was leaning back precariously in a scruffy armchair with frayed arms and suspect legs. The pipe never left his mouth as he spoke and at times it was almost impossible to see him through the clouds of scented smoke which all but enveloped him. 'On that occasion we needed to stay low-key and we had just one car with three of us in it.' He removed the pipe from his mouth and tapped it on the side of his long leather boot, causing the contents to join a growing pile of ashes on the floor beside him. 'If we go ahead with the present proposal we will have to throw money and people at it. We'll need half a dozen cars with radios, several vans with cameras inside and at least a dozen people. We'll also have to consider putting a radio-mike on Maguire so that if the worst comes to the worst and we lose them, we can get clues from what's going on around him.'

'A radio-mike increases the risk,' said Tyler unhelpfully. 'These days I can get you one the size of a fountain pen, but the maximum range is a hundred yards. After that, or on the other side of a solid wall, it's as good as useless.'

Maguire had been watching and listening with increasing concern while the *Encounter* team discussed logistics. Now he felt confident enough to contribute.

'It seems to me that the big problem with a large-scale operation like that is that you're multiplying the number of cars and people about at the relevant time and place.' The young reporter had been alarmed to see how easily the group of right-wingers had been able to elude the *Encounter* team on the previous occasion, but the risks of the present proposal sounded greater and more likely to jeopardize his own position than being without back-up altogether. 'I don't suppose they tend to go ahead with these operations if the number of people about is like Piccadilly Circus on New Year's Eve.'

Griffiths looked over the piles of books, papers and laundry on the desk in front of him.

'Helpful Maguire. Very helpful. Maybe you'd like to tell us what you suggest?' He reached into his jacket pocket to produce a paper packet of tobacco and began refilling the pipe.

Maguire had expected to be challenged and had prepared his own thoughts. He knew that they were not very impressive and that they would be unpopular.

He saw his task as being as much to persuade himself as to persuade those around him.

'Well, it's all a question of intelligence.'

'Here here,' said Bill Tyler.

'Thank you, Bill – more helpful still.' Griffiths was holding his lighter upside down and puffing vigorously on the pipe. 'Go on, Maguire.'

'Well, at the moment you have to follow me from the school where they will collect me and take me to the hut because we don't know where that is; then you have to follow the van, or whatever we travel in, to the ultimate destination because we don't know where that is.' The three others indicated their impatience at these statements of the obvious. Undeterred, Maguire continued, 'If on the other hand we had some idea of where the headquarters of the operation is, or even better where the target of the raid is, you would be able to stake out the area, get yourselves properly set to get some decent shots, and reduce the risks involved in following the raiding party.'

'This is a very helpful summary of an attractive scenario,' said Griffiths pompously. 'How do you propose to get this intelligence?' Maguire returned the glare, trying hard to ignore the barely disguised contempt which was radiating across the room at him.

'The teacher.'

'The teacher?'

'Yes, the teacher. The teacher you already knew about when we first spoke. Pamela Layfield. She is very close to the kids at the school, and she has kept in touch with many who have left, including some who have flirted with the loonies. She might easily know some of those who will be planning the next raid. There's reason to think that she might be willing to have a go at finding out for us.'

186

Griffiths took the pipe from his mouth again and swept his hand back and forth several times in front of his face to clear the smoke. He sat forward in his chair and looked across at Maguire.

'Maguire? Maguire my friend. I hope you are not telling me what I think you are telling me.'

'And what's that?'

'You know bloody well what. I hope this do-gooder doesn't know about our little project already. Tell me she doesn't, Maguire. Tell me she doesn't.'

'Look, Griffiths . . .' In the face of their disappointing performance so far, Maguire's confidence in dealing with the *Encounter* people had grown. He had already considered pointing out that he had succeeded in infiltrating the group while they had lamentably failed to keep tabs on him. 'Without Pamela Layfield I wouldn't have had a sniff of this story, I wouldn't have known where to start, and I wouldn't have had the information about the anonymous notes.'

'I already had that. Remember? I had it when you came to see me in the first place.' Now Griffiths was sneering even more unpleasantly. Maguire could see how these characters got their unenviable reputation.

'Anyway, she knows, she has helped, she is entirely trustworthy and she is willing to help us some more. If she could get this information for us it would save us the embarrassment of me joining in the petrol bombing of a home for retired Jewish delicatessen owners, while you people are careering around the streets looking for me. Do you agree?'

There was a long silence as Griffiths and Maguire glared at each other through the fog and across the clutter. Eventually it was the cameraman, Tim Walker, who spoke.

'Well, I don't know much about Pamela Layfield or

anything else. All I do know is that if we can get some idea of where we're going, so that we don't have to risk following Maguire and then trying to stay with a van, it will be much better. Apart from the danger of being caught, anything you try to shoot on the hoof is bound to be unsatisfactory. If we can get advance information we can park our vehicles, or even perhaps set up in a window overlooking the scene. Then we're all much safer and we'll get our stuff in a controlled situation. It's got to be much better if it's possible.'

'Even if we just get the location of the NS headquarters it'd be a help, wouldn't it Tim?' asked Maguire.

The corners of his mouth went down. 'Sure, anything's better than what we know at the moment. They went to a lot of trouble to make sure that you didn't know where the place was, so if we're lucky that'll be the part when they are most cautious. Once the raid gets underway they might be too preoccupied with what they're doing to take much notice of whether they're being followed.'

'So I ask her to get the location of the raid if there's any chance, but at the very least the location of the headquarters?' Maguire looked all around him and then across the desk.

Griffiths stood up suddenly and picked his way towards the window. He looked out through the smog and drizzle over the landscape of bleak rooftops which stretched into the distance, and wiped away some of the grubby condensation from the window with the sleeve of his jacket. He put the still smoking pipe into his pocket.

'OK.' He paused and then turned and looked around the room, his eyes finally lighting on Maguire. 'We bring in Pamela Layfield, but God help us if her information is wrong or if she gives us away. God help us – and in particular God help you, Maguire.'

CHAPTER SIXTEEN

'Now Tibby, you stay here and be a good pussycat. That goes for you too, Miriam, and you, Dora.' Harriet Nuttall stepped very carefully around the paws of the curious cats which wanted to follow her out of the door and into her car for an outing. 'I won't be long, and when I get back I'll cook you some nice fish. There, that's a promise. Now you look after things while I'm away, do you understand?'

The repeated miaowing seemed to Harriet to confirm that her favourite cats did not understand and were as impatient as ever. Harriet was not surprised. Like herself, she reflected, they were probably too old by now to change very much. As she put on her overcoat, Harriet chuckled aloud at the thought. She was in a good mood. She tied the string of a transparent plastic rainhood under her chin.

The rain fell in a miserable drizzle on to the mushy leaves, muffling the crunch that usually accompanied her uncertain step across the gravel path. Harriet opened the car door which had never been locked these last ten years, and pulled the seat forward in order to place her wickerwork picnic basket carefully in the back. She stooped awkwardly before sinking into the driver's seat. She had to lift one leg cautiously into place, and then the other, before leaning out precariously to slam the door hard. Harriet fumbled clumsily for the seat belt and strapped herself in so tightly that she could scarcely stretch as far as the ignition. She

189

wound down the window before setting off, further to admonish her cats.

'I've only two calls to make, then I'll be back. I shan't be long. Be good.'

Harriet waited for a long time to see whether the man in the red car which was parked a little way up the road with its engine running intended to pull out in front of her. At last she decided that he did not, and she revved the tired old engine hard and loud before setting off towards Lansbury. The windscreen wipers squeaked across the rain-drenched screen, and the gearbox roared loudly in third when it should certainly have been in fourth.

Harriet Nuttall had lived in this area all her life, and as she drove through the suburbs of the small market town and back out towards the countryside, she was reminded of the time when this busy road had been just a bridle path and the houses and estates which now crowded together on either side of it had been open fields. To her it seemed only the blink of an eye since she had been a rather plain-looking little girl with unbecoming tight pigtails, playing with her brother and sister in the draughty old barn which their mother was always warning would fall down on their heads and kill all three of them. It never did, and as she had driven past it scores of times in the intervening years, she had often heard the distant echo of her mother's scolding voice calling to them across the open field to take care. All of her memories of those times, her mother, her brother James and sister Edith as children, came back to her in sepia tones. Her recall relied on faded photographs from an album which these days she hardly ever brought out. There was no one to show it to. Faces and formal expressions, formal dresses and formal poses; the large looming figure of her mother in an enormous print dress, standing uncomfortably, with an expression on her face which eloquently betrayed her discomfort. Mother had never liked having her photograph taken. Nevertheless the lined but kindly face shone brightly across the years.

Another of the crumpled pictures brought back a blurred memory of three children playing in a field of corn, with the old barn out of focus in the distance. Harriet had not actually entered the barn, which had been less than a few hundred yards from the house in which she had grown up, for the better part of twenty years; but somehow she just knew that it would still be exactly as it had been over sixty years ago when it doubled as anything from the general hospital to an aircraft hangar, depending on whether her brother or her sister had chosen the particular fantasy they were acting out that day. Harriet glanced in the driver's mirror. For once there was no queue of cars close up behind her trying to overtake. Harriet sang a very old skipping song as she drove along the narrowing roads.

Two hundred yards behind her the red Ford Sierra was causing an obstruction. The drivers of the half-dozen vehicles which were lined up behind it wondered why it was proceeding so erratically. The man in the cloth cap and country jacket would dawdle along for a quarter of a mile at twenty miles an hour, keeping at least two hundred yards of empty space between himself and the old black car in front. Then, whenever he approached a junction or blind corner, he would burst forward at great speed, only to settle down to the previous slow pace after rounding the bend. When finally the stout woman in the tweed suit driving the car behind decided to blast her horn at him, she was horrified to see the single middle finger of his left hand raised in an unfamiliar but plainly obscene gesture.

The woman braked hard and caused the car behind to come within a foot of running into her. A fresh outbreak of hooting followed, and half a mile ahead Harriet Nuttall wondered why everyone seemed so impatient and bad tempered these days, and was glad that for a change she was not the cause of the impatience.

Now Harriet was driving through country lanes which had changed very little since her childhood. These byways were as familiar to her as the rooms and passageways of her own house, and every time she came here the many small landmarks brought back teeming happy memories of little incidents which had taken place all those years ago. The ditch at the edge of the Crowsacre field into which her sister had fallen on their way to Sunday school. They had been under strict instructions to walk carefully and not to play. Edith's pretty new gingham dress had been ruined and the three children had been forced to return home, in great distress and anxiety, instead of going on to church. Their mother, who had spent many long evenings sitting in front of the kitchen range sewing the dress, was dreadfully angry to see it filthy and torn. Then she had seen the tears on the cheeks of all three of her children, and her anger had melted away; she had softened and sympathized. The gingham dress had been cleaned and mended and was finally as good as new. Somewhere Harriet still had a small and wrinkled photograph of Edith wearing it.

In another field on the other side of the lane stood a large brown farm-horse; exactly the same, it seemed to Harriet, as Ned, the gentle giant of a horse which had stood so patiently while three children were helped on to his back and had then walked steadily backwards and forwards to their endless giggling delight. Perhaps the horse standing so still and quiet in the field was one of Ned's descendants. Harriet enjoyed the thought that it might be. Her car rolled on across the landscape of her own history.

Half a mile behind her, a speck on the top of a hill overlooking the valley of her childhood, the red Ford Sierra stopped and Richard Crozier got out. Resting one elbow on the roof of his car, he steadied his newly purchased and very powerful field-glasses, and carefully focused on the back of the old Morris as it weaved its way through the narrow lanes. Crozier kept watching as the brake lights flashed on and the car slowed to a halt at a spot where a gateway made the lane slightly wider. He panned the glasses upwards and to the side, several hundred yards across the field, and a smile spread across his face. This was only a mile or so from the spot he had visited several days before. Over the brow of the next hill lay Poacher's Wood. Perhaps his recce had not been a waste of time after all.

Crozier's gaze swept back to the parked car, and as the landscape whizzed through the lens, he flashed past the figure he had been keeping so conscientiously under surveillance. She carried a basket awkwardly and was walking slowly along a narrow muddy path. Crozier took the binoculars from his eyes and squinted into the distance. Where could the old woman be going? Not on a picnic surely? From his observations so far she had seemed perhaps mildly eccentric, but not mad enough to picnic in the middle of autumn. He refocused the glasses and moved them to the left to try to see where she could be heading, following the path for three hundred yards until it came to an old and apparently derelict barn. Half of the roof was missing and there was no door. A minute later he saw Harriet Nuttall approaching.

The old woman looked around in what seemed from a distance to be a furtive manner as she entered the barn. Crozier lowered the binoculars. A distant piercing shriek made him quickly look through them again, just in time to see a large crow emerging from the roof of the building, still squawking a protest as it took to the air. Crozier looked at his watch. He would time her visit to the barn. It was the kind of attention to detail which nowadays gave him such pleasure. Nothing happened; no cars passed by. The rain was a slow drizzle, the kind of weather which feels like a light shower but soaks through all but the most resistant of clothing. Crozier had no overcoat and after three minutes of standing beside his car, he was wet through to the skin.

At last, without further warning, Harriet Nuttall emerged from the old barn and retraced her steps determinedly along the muddy path towards her car. She looked neither sideways nor back, but opened the car door and got in. She was still carrying the cane basket, but perhaps she managed it less awkwardly now. Faster than Crozier expected, the car was being deftly manoeuvred through a three-point turn and was beginning the journey back to pass him. Inside the old Morris, Harriet pressed her muddy shoes hard down on the accelerator and smiled as she wiped the drops of rain from her face. Crozier kept his eyes fixed on the approaching car, and as it rattled up the last few yards to where he stood he abruptly turned the binoculars as though following the flight of a bird across the sky. The car roared past him, and for an instant he thought he heard the muffled sound of someone singing.

* * *

George Charlton of Charlton and Cox Solicitors, High Street, Lansbury, stood at his office window watching the droplets of water chase each other down the pane. Across the road, carefully positioned so that it could be viewed at maximum advantage from his office window, was his pride and joy. A beautiful, seventeen-year-old, deep-plum coloured 4.2 litre Daimler. The solicitor had bought the car brand new direct from the manufacturers and had lavished loving care and affection upon it from that day to this. Only yesterday he had carefully washed and waxed and polished the car, so that now its perfect paintwork carelessly resisted the rain.

The weight of water landing on the sill outside caused some splashes to bounce up through the ill-fitting sash of his office window, and a few managed to penetrate and were now trickling down the inside of the glass. Along the bottom of the frame a large fly with a shiny, almost fluorescent back crawled across the peeling paint. Mr Charlton peered over his thick tortoiseshell-rimmed spectacles to see whether the fly would float away and drown. He hoped it would. He was disappointed when the fly deftly avoided the gathering puddle on the inside sill and continued on its journey. Charlton reached for a small pile of A4 papers on his desk and silently wrapped them into a roll, readying himself to swipe an almighty blow across the wooden sill which would splatter the fly into oblivion. A sharp tap on the door caught him in the middle of his moment of unfulfilled violence. He turned to see Olive, his long-suffering secretary, looking at him curiously around the door.

'Miss Nuttall here to see you, Mr Charlton.'

'Ah Miss Nuttall.' George Charlton strode across to

her, holding out the roll of paper solicitously. 'Welcome, welcome indeed. How nice to see you. How very good indeed.' His voice suggested it was a real treat. Harriet Nuttall had always liked George Charlton, but she knew that ninety per cent of what he said was entirely a waste of breath. 'Now then. Would you like some tea? Some coffee, Miss Nuttall. Can we get you . . . ?'

'Nothing, thank you Mr Charlton,' said Harriet Nuttall, settling herself comfortably on the wooden armchair which squeaked alarmingly under her slight frame. 'I'll only take up a moment of your time.'

George Charlton nodded to Olive to dismiss her and she gently closed the door. The solicitor sat and looked over his glasses, smiling in a manner which he hoped and believed was engaging. Though she was not a great source of income to him, Harriet Nuttall was one of his oldest and longest-standing clients. He had seen her into the house at Lane End; he had taken care of the sale of the goodwill in the business; he had, of course, taken care of her will which had not been changed in even the smallest particular since she had first made it perhaps twenty years ago. Although she was not likely to make him rich, Harriet Nuttall had the estimable virtue, so far as George Charlton was concerned, of predictability. She was a steady and reliable sort of person; just the sort of person the solicitor liked best. Such people were not especially good for business; but his was a country practice, and steadiness was what it was all about.

'Now then, Miss Nuttall, what can I do for you?' As he said this George Charlton glanced out of the window. His attention had been attracted by a large red car which was trying to park in a very small space on the other side of the road between his own car and

196

that belonging to the greengrocer. 'Have you thought any more about turning your bequest to that charity of yours into a legacy? It would save on tax, you know.' Charlton had not even looked at Harriet Nuttall as he spoke. His voice rose and fell as he watched the car outside edging alarmingly backwards and forwards in all too close proximity to the Daimler.

'No, Mr Charlton. That is not why I am here.' Harriet Nuttall reached into her handbag. The red car now seemed to have come to a halt without mishap, and when George Charlton managed to tear his eyes away from it, he saw that she held in her hand a large brown envelope. His head dipped forward in inquiry and the bushy eyebrows lifted above the top of his specs. He sat back in his chair and began fiddling with the old gold watchchain which stretched across the expanse of tight waistcoat.

'And what, pray, do we have here?'

'A service, Mr Charlton.'

'A service, Miss Nuttall?'

'No, Mr Charlton, I want you to do me a service.' Miss Nuttall spoke with inexhaustible patience. 'A small but important service.' Now she placed the envelope on the edge of the desk in front of her, well out of reach of the solicitor. 'This envelope,' her eyes indicated it, 'I would like this envelope kept safe, very safe. It contains some extremely important documents – important to me, that is. Not valuable, but very important. I want you to keep it safe.'

'Of course, Miss Nuttall. It's a simple enough request, and not perhaps as uncommon as you might at first imagine, but . . .'

'In a few months from now, I may come to you and ask for the envelope to be returned to me.' Harriet Nuttall was speaking slowly and precisely in a manner which left no room for misunderstanding. Suddenly George Charlton did not feel as though he should patronize Miss Nuttall any further. He paid close attention. 'If I do so, I will take the envelope away and nothing further need be said on the subject. You can forget it. I shall forget it. I will pay you a fee for your kind service. On the other hand – ' George Charlton's eyebrows would have raised themselves still further had it been physically possible for them to do so, ' – on the other hand if I do not come back, in short if something should happen to me suddenly in the next few months, then I want you to open this envelope.' Harriet stretched forward and tapped it lightly with a single finger. 'Open this envelope, Mr Charlton, and follow the instructions you will find inside it to the letter. But only,' the old woman's shiny blue eyes fixed him in position, 'only if something unexpected happens to me. Only then, open the envelope and do as I ask you to. In such an eventuality you may take your fee from my estate.'

'Oh I'm sure . . .'

'I don't think for one moment that this is likely to occur. I plan to finish what I am doing and live for a few years longer. I don't expect anything to make this service necessary. But if it should be, I want there to be no misunderstandings and no mistakes. I suppose that's simple enough, and clear?'

George Charlton was unsure how to reply. At last he leaned forward and placed his hand on the envelope as if to pick it up, but Harriet Nuttall still held it firmly against the desk.

'I was asking if that was clear to you, Mr Charlton?'

'Oh quite clear, quite clear.' She removed her hand and the solicitor picked up the envelope. 'May one ask . . . ?'

198

'No, Mr Charlton,' came the immediate response. 'Please don't ask. I have no wish to be melodramatic; for the moment suffice it to say that if and when one reaches my age, one does not wish to take chances.'

'Oh yes, yes, I quite see. Please don't worry, Miss Nuttall. You may count on me. Please count on me.'

'I will, Mr Charlton,' said Harriet Nuttall, already getting up from her seat, 'I'm relying on you completely – not to let me down, and for discretion.' Her last words carried special emphasis. Once again she was looking at him, waiting for confirmation. 'Discretion.'

'At all times, Miss Nuttall. At all times, as always.'

'Very good.'

George Charlton sat back in his chair and listened to the footsteps of Harriet Nuttall as she made her way carefully down the creaky wooden steps to the front door which led on to the street. He held the brown envelope in his hands, weighing it and wondering. He held it up to the light. It was A4 size, and there were perhaps twenty or thirty sheets of paper, folded tightly, inside. He could make out nothing through the brown paper. The message on the outside was in careful handwriting: 'This envelope and its contents are the property of Harriet Nuttall. To be opened by George Charlton, Solicitor, in the event of my death.' Steady, reliable, predictable. George Charlton mentally rehearsed all the adjectives he would previously have applied to Harriet Nuttall. Now this. He sighed. Nothing was the same any more. He looked across at the old-fashioned wall-safe and wondered what he might eventually charge for keeping the envelope secure. Very little. At least Harriet Nuttall had not broken the mould and made him rich. The solicitor was getting to his feet when he heard the sickening crunch of metal on metal. He remained still, paralysed as though trying not to accept the inevitable. When he heard raised voices in the street he forced himself to go to the window. He arrived in time to see the red car accelerating away, dragging the heavy chromium bumper from his Daimler along the street for fifty yards before it fell clear and clattered into the gutter. The solicitor involuntarily clutched at his heart with the shock of it. Then he collected himself sufficiently to race to the door and down the stairs towards the street.

Harriet Nuttall sat, utterly absorbed, over her papers. Even the gentle but persistent mewing of Dora at her ankles could not break her concentration. Many times she had read and re-read the bundle of photocopied sheets he had come to call simply 'the papers', but which were known to those who had commissioned the work by the misleadingly innocuous name 'the Lazarus file'. Now she was studying the file yet again. At first reading she had been unable to absorb properly the enormity of what it contained. Later she had been overcome with disbelief and then disgust that anyone should seriously consider what was apparently being suggested in the papers. Now she had almost become accustomed to the cynicism of the message and was concentrating instead on how best to analyse the papers, how best to exploit and expose the dreadful proposals; how to express her own revulsion, and that of any rational individual, that such a plan should even be considered.

While sharing Stephen's optimism about the potential of the papers, Miss Nuttall was astute enough to realize the present limitations of the Lazarus file for the purposes of the movement. Basically, when all of the technical and scientific jargon was filtered out, the

200

papers were a description of an opportunity; an opportunity to make money by swindling the public, and by compromising the safety of an already extraordinarily dangerous piece of machinery. But like so many documents which are prepared with a particular audience in mind, an audience with a particular viewpoint, this one needed interpretation if it was to be understood by the more general reader. Complicated sentences which turned technical shortcuts into financial margins needed to be explained as a trade-off between risk to mankind and profit. Carefully understated euphemisms had to be exploded into the language of ordinary people.

The file which had been passed to Harriet contained perhaps a hundred sheets of paper. The first bundle was an outline of the proposal to build a reactor at Ringwood. 'That would have been useful for my original work,' mused Harriet. She quickly put the thought of all her wasted effort out of her mind.

More usefully, the file contained the original brief prepared by the Mallin Harcourt Bank, in association with the British and American industries, for Professor Jacob Lazarus. The Professor had been asked *to advise on the presently available safety techniques'* and to make proposals for *'maximizing profit potential for contractors installing a wide range of safety procedures: these to cover all systems, including all high cost and high-profile mechanisms.'* Stephen Ross had described these words alone as 'dynamite . . . enough on their own to sink the bastards without trace'.

Harriet had allowed a frown to cross her face, and Ross had been unsure whether she was revealing reservations about his opinion or his method of expressing it. She had said nothing to dampen his enthusiasm; but sometimes Harriet felt that for all the

201

comparatively sheltered life she may have led, she had learned more about the ways of the world than many of those supposedly more worldly people around her. She wanted to read and study the papers carefully, to study them with the same thoroughness which had distinguished her original work from that of the majority of campaigners, some of whom sometimes allowed their enthusiasm to cloud their judgement.

Time and again at meetings of the anti-nuclear campaign Harriet had reminded her friends that their task was to persuade the unconverted. There was no point in impressing each other – activists needed no further persuasion. They had to get their message across to the widest possible audience and she believed that they would only manage to do so by reasoned debate and thorough analysis; taking the arguments point by point, fact by fact, to the proponents of nuclear expansion. Now she was employing the technique she had advocated for so long to the Lazarus file. Were the words enough to prove complicity of the bank and the industry in the Professor's concluding recommendations? Could the establishment claim to have been as astonished as anyone else would be by the Professor's scandalous proposal to fabricate elaborate safety procedures; to charge enormous sums for the installation of equipment which had public relations value but almost zero practical worth? Harriet was analysing every word of the brief carefully.

It was not, in the end, the sound of the telephone which brought her out of her concentration, but the growing nuisance of the cats which crowded around her feet. Dora remained as insistent as ever, but she had now been joined by Tibby and Clara, who organized themselves into a dance of war around her ankles. Realizing that the telephone would already have been ringing for some time, Harriet made no attempt to hurry. The caller must be someone who knew that she moved slowly; they would be patient and wait.

'Now my darlings, don't get in my way now.' Harriet picked her way carefully between the furry legs which seemed to be doing their determined best to trip her up. Though humans sometimes irritated and even angered her, she never allowed herself to become more than mildly impatient with her precious cats. Harriet cared a good deal about the future of the earth and about the future of humanity; but in her quietest moments, with her cats all around her, she knew that it was they whom she cared for more than anything or anyone else left in her life. They were her only constant friends and companions; it was they who would be there, still keeping her company, when finally she succumbed to whatever fate had destined to remove her from this world. The thought caused her no sadness. She was content.

'Hello? Harriet Nuttall speaking.'

'Hello Harriet. It's Stephen.'

'Hello Stephen, how lovely to hear from you.' There was a pause and then silence. 'Is there something I can do for you?'

'Oh no, I just wanted to ask you how things are going and check that everything's OK.'

'Yes yes, everything is fine. The work is going well. Is there any reason to think it wouldn't be?'

Again there was a pause before Stephen Ross spoke. Harriet knew him well enough by now to realize that he had something on his mind.

'No no.' It was clear to Harriet that he was trying his very best to sound confident. 'No reason at all to worry. I just thought, well you know, it's a high risk business. Some of these people are, or at least they can be, a bit unpleasant when their backs are up against the wall. I told you that when we met.'

Harriet did not feel a moment of concern. 'Oh yes, I know that; but I don't think they are going to bother an eccentric and harmless old woman.' Dora was rubbing her fur affectionately against Harriet's legs. Her attention wandered momentarily and the telephone moved a few inches from her lips. 'Anyway, my little friends here would look after me.'

'I beg your pardon?' Ross had scarcely heard her. 'Harriet? Are you still there? Did you say something? What little friends?'

Harriet recollected herself. 'Yes, I'm here. Don't worry. Anyway, no one even knows about me do they?'

'No, there's no reason to think so. Only a couple of people in our organization have an approximate idea of what you're up to, and they are entirely trustworthy. Even they have no information about the file. It's just that you cannot be too careful.'

'Oh I know that, Stephen. Don't worry about that. I've taken precautions.'

'I'm delighted to hear it, Harriet. I won't ask what they are, but knowing you I'm sure they'll be effective.'

'Don't worry, Stephen. Don't worry about me. I'll deliver one way or another. You can rely on me.'

Stephen Ross smiled. 'I don't doubt that for a single moment, Harriet. That's why I chose you. I'll call you again at the weekend. I hope you didn't mind my bothering you. Good night Harriet.'

'Good night Stephen.'

Two hundred yards away, inside the battered old transit van parked in an unlit gateway in a narrow lane, the signal came to a stop and the automatic voice-activated cutout switch clicked off. A small red digital read-out displayed the telephone number at Harriet Nuttall's house; then there was a delay and it lit up with another number. It was the telephone number at Stephen Ross's flat. A note was made in a notebook, an entry made in the log. Captain Davis would be very pleased.

CHAPTER SEVENTEEN

Pamela Layfield sat in the driver's seat of the rusting Renault and looked across, through the gloom of early evening, at the British Bull. She thought how apt was the name of the pub where the National Socialist group held some of its more social or public meetings. No doubt that was the main reason why it had been chosen; but the pub was also suitable because it was the sort of place which would not be too particular about its clientèle. It was a large detached building, covered in pebbledash which had once been white and was now defaced by masses of graffiti so various in style and content that it was very nearly impossible to sort out one message from another. There were some traditional declarations of love in coloured hearts pierced by arrows and with written confirmations that this most public form of admiration was 'true'. There were one or two rather less romantic and more explicit suggestions of how the professed admiration might be consummated. There were simple statements of the names of the artists, in huge multi-coloured letters, as though the announcement of a name in a public place provided an objective confirmation that the protagonist really existed. The predominant theme, however, was racist and it was racism of the ugliest and most offensive variety.

The teacher sat and wondered about the few hours ahead. She had no doubt that she was going to go through with her promise to Maguire to find out any details she could about the fascist group and its intentions. She was not even frightened exactly, it was more that she was simply repulsed by the thought of the people with whom she would have to deal. Not scared, but revolted. Her disgust was an involuntary reaction to the ugliness of it all. It was the meanness of spirit and even, now that she came to consider it, frequently the physical repulsiveness of the people involved in this kind of group.

Pamela thought about the matter more deeply, wondering whether she was attributing a wider range of ugly features to people whom she already knew to have ugly thoughts and feelings. She considered individuals; the pupils she had known who had left the school and had gone on to become part of this outfit. Each of those that she could bring to mind had been a loner, each a misfit in one way or another. None that she could recall had been part of a large circle of friends. They had been the sort of kids who would hang around the edges of the playground in their early months or years at the school, then they might take up with perhaps one friend, often an exceptionally weak and impressionable character. When there was an unpleasant incident in the classroom or outside, they might easily be the ones who were found to have lied to shift the blame on to a classmate. They grew up lonely and out of place, passed few or no examinations, left school and were never missed. Then for a few weeks or months the teacher or her colleagues might spot them standing with the familiar group outside the school. Sometimes they would have a newly acquired tattoo, large boots, a severe haircut.

On several occasions she had been so shocked and distressed by the sight that she had impulsively crossed the road and confronted an individual. Seldom was the youth concerned one with whom she had ever been able to strike up any kind of rapport, despite her best efforts. Now she would try again; several times she had taken a bewildered youth aside from the group, while the others stood by as onlookers, curiously unable or unwilling to intervene against her. Most often the boy would simply stare back at her, sullen and shamefaced; he would be unable to provide any coherent answer to her questions. Several times she had tried to bring one of them back inside the school to talk more easily, but she had never been successful. Her attempts were frequently met with a hostile, almost violent reaction. The kids had no wish to go back.

'What have we done to you? What have we done for you?' Pamela Layfield had asked the question of the uncomprehending child and now she asked the same question again. The system had somehow failed these youths and now they were well on the road towards prison or worse. It depressed her to think of it. Perhaps, she wondered, she was imposing this stereotype with the benefit of hindsight. It was true that many of the pupils referred to in the staffroom as 'oddballs' left the school and went their own ways. Some bloomed and surprised everybody by turning themselves into something worth while. For these few, school had been a retardant, the wrong atmosphere in which to flourish.

Gary Banks had been one of these. He had done little or nothing worth while at school. He had not managed to distinguish himself from the pack, either by achieving anything good, or by doing anything particularly bad. It had been a serious upset to Pamela when she had seen him among the group opposite the school gates. She had approached him in full view of the others and he had at first rejected her. Later, when she was back in the classroom, working late to finish some marking for the following day, he had come quietly into the school to speak with her. He had sat at his old desk near the back of the class, and she had sat at the desk next to him. At first he was ashamed, then gradually became more frank and even analytical. Former pupil and teacher had talked for longer than they had ever talked during Gary's five years at the school. He explained how he had drifted towards the National Socialist group. His older brother Colin was a member, he had nothing else to do with his spare time, and so many of the others . . . Pamela had felt desperate. If ordinary lads like Gary Banks were going to end up shouting slogans across the road at Jews and Pakistanis, then perhaps she had to ask herself whether she could ever achieve anything. She had sat patiently and talked with him for several hours, well into the darkness of late evening. The long talk gave her many insights. He had told her what little he knew about the National Socialists. It was very little. He seemed to know nothing of their full political agenda, of their allegiance to the Nazi Party of Germany, of their support for the holocaust. She had carefully explained to him everything she knew and he had been shocked and upset. He had promised that he would have nothing more to do with them and had gone silently away.

Pamela had not spoken with Gary Banks since that evening, which was three or four years ago. She had heard since that he was one of the few who had found a job, and on one evening she had seen him going into the British Bull public house with a group of friends; but there was nothing in his dress or appearance which suggested that he was still any part of the NS, and she had never again seen him among the group which assembled on the pavement opposite the school. He seemed to be one who had got away; a limited success for her, perhaps. Gary had been very much the exception in this respect. The people Pamela Layfield was now thinking of were those who would never turn into decent or well-adjusted human beings. They were misfits who at last had found something they could fit into. Looked at this way, it all seemed so sad and inevitable.

For just a moment before Pamela Layfield got out of the car, she allowed herself to think about her dead husband. She thought how horrified and astonished Tom would be if he could see her now. Firstly he would be astonished at her recklessness in even considering taking such a risk. Then he would have forbidden her to do so. Three years ago she would have obeyed him with little or no argument. Those three years had changed her practically beyond recognition. His sudden and early death had forced her to make all of her own decisions, to cope entirely on her own for the first time in her life. She was now well used to taking responsibility for herself completely, and she knew that she could never play the subservient wife again. The realization turned her thoughts to Jonathan Maguire. He was so completely different in almost every way from Tom. Maguire was not as strong a man in the traditional sense. In their love-making he had been gentler, more considerate than her husband. Despite her lack of experience, she had felt in control of him; in charge of his pleasure. Her own had been enriched by that unfamiliar extra feeling. She thought about it now and wanted him again, allowing herself to enjoy the anticipation. It was something she had rarely permitted herself in recent years because to do so had brought far more pain than pleasure. Now Pamela Layfield felt certain that whatever else the future might hold, Maguire would never impose his will on her in the way that she had allowed her husband to do. She felt proud of her independence and of what she had achieved on her own, and she knew that she would not allow anyone to take that away from her. Nevertheless, thoughts of Maguire gave her encouragement and strength, and she was glad.

She clicked open the car door and decided for once to lock it behind her. The grimness of her expression yielded slightly as she entered the stone porch of the British Bull and saw an offensive remark about her own headmaster carved into the plaster on the wall. Now that she saw it so succinctly and eloquently expressed, she thought that Mr Potter probably was indeed a wally. She smiled, and wondered which of the hundreds of former pupils who had passed through his hands and through the doors of this pub was the author of this precise observation. Pushing open one of the bright red double doors she entered the abrupt warmth and smell of the bar.

The room she found herself in was red. Dirty red. There was a worn and filthy red carpet, faded red velvet cushions and seat covers, red lampshades and red flock wallpaper. Late at night, through the cosmetic blur of intoxication, the place no doubt looked cosy and welcoming. In the early evening, with only adrenaline distorting the normal perceptions, it appeared to be exactly what it was. Pamela Layfield looked around. There were several groups of men standing at intervals along the length of the bar. Two men and a woman were sitting at a small round table with gold-painted iron legs. No one took much notice of her as she stood on the threshold allowing her eyes to adjust to the dim light. Only the barman, a downtrodden-looking youth

211

who was lethargically wiping a pint pot with a dirty cloth, fixed his eyes on her with an expression which was neither inquiry nor welcome.

She approached the bar. 'Half a pint of lager please.' Her voice sounded no more casual and relaxed than she felt. She was dismayed. Her acting would have to improve. A straight glass which was two-thirds lager and a third foam was put down on the bar in front of her, spilling the contents.

'Seventy pence.'

Pamela had to catch her tongue to prevent herself from saying 'please'. Tonight she had better leave the schoolteacher at home. She paid and went to a corner table, where she sat on a velvet-covered bench with her back to the wall and looked around. Several doors led off the bar; one of them perhaps would be to a meeting room. Which would be the one used by the fascists? She considered walking into each of the rooms, as though looking for the toilet.

Her thoughts were interrupted by the noisy arrival in the bar of several groups of four or five youths, all of them male. Everyone who came in sported the black and white paraphernalia of the local football team, and the hubbub confirmed that they had just returned from the game. The youths crowded urgently to the bar and the lethargic barman got to work filling pint glasses with frothy beer. She saw that she had been noticed by some of the young men and carefully avoided meeting their eyes, only glancing frequently up at the clock. Another group of five arrived from the football match. The clock above the dartboard indicated five-fifty.

'Evening Miss.'

Pamela looked up to see that one of the newcomers had broken away from the group and was standing across the table from her. She had to search her memory before she recognized him as the boy she had been hoping to meet. She was in luck.

'Hello Gary. It's Gary Banks isn't it?'

'Blimey Miss; you done well to remember. It must be six years since I was in your class.' He looked at the empty chair opposite her. 'You waiting for someone, Miss?'

Pamela had her plan carefully worked out and was ready. 'Yes, but I'm afraid I've turned up too early.' She put down her glass on the table and looked around. 'And to be honest, I'm not completely sure that this is the right place. This is the British Bull, isn't it?'

Banks was adjusting the chair. 'It is.' He sat down. 'But if I was taking you out on a date I wouldn't be meeting you in a dump like this.'

'I'm glad you learned something worth while when you were at school.' Banks glared across at her as though preparing a reply to a rebuke, but saw that she was smiling at him. Her eyes indicated across to the bar. 'Won't your friends miss you?'

He did not bother to turn round. 'Nah, bunch of louts that lot.'

As he talked Pamela was trying to remember more about Gary Banks. He had been a quiet and withdrawn lad, but reasonably affable and not unintelligent. He had been one of the many who had gone through the school system and had simply slipped unnoticed out of the other end of it, without it having had much effect on him, and without him having had much effect upon it. As far as the system was concerned he had vanished for ever without leaving any trace, like millions of others before him and hundreds of thousands since.

'Are you working, Gary?'

'I was. I got an apprenticeship at me Dad's place, Clarke's Engineering. But when I was eighteen they had to pay me proper money and so I got redundancy.

No redundancy pay like, just the push. Haven't been able to get anything since.'

'I'm sorry to hear that.' She looked at her watch.

'What time's your bloke expected?'

'About now.' She shook her wrist and looked again. 'It is five o'clock, isn't it?'

'No.' He turned his head and looked at the clock, 'It's five to six. Is your watch bust?' She showed it to him. 'You're slow, Miss, nearly an hour slow.'

'Oh no! Maybe I've missed him.'

'Shall I ask the barman if there's been someone waiting?'

'Oh, no thanks. We were going on somewhere else. I wasn't sure I'd be able to get here in time so I said he was to go on if I didn't turn up. I'll be off in a minute.'

'Stay and have another drink, Miss.'

'I'd like to but . . .' Pamela Layfield saw genuine disappointment on the youth's face. So far this was easier than she had expected. 'Oh all right, just a half. Then I'll have to be away.' He smiled exuberantly and took her glass to the bar. He went to stand beside his friends, none of whom was known to Pamela. She could see that several of the youths were a good deal more unpleasant-looking than Gary, and she thought that perhaps they were more likely to have the information she wanted. She was aware that she was being pointed out and commented upon. There was some laughter which, without looking, Pamela was aware that Gary was trying to discourage.

Now he was returning to her table carrying two glasses. Pamela smiled at him as she caught his eye. Though the thought had never occurred to her before, she now saw that young Gary Banks, the quiet and surly kid who had sat at the back of her class, had turned into not a bad-looking young man. His cropped hair and the earring in his left ear did little for him, but still he was quite a handsome boy. He sat down.

'As I'm here there is something you might be able to help me with.' Pamela tried to sound as casual as she could. 'Do you ever have anything to do with that group who hang around opposite the school these days?'

'Nah, not a thing. I've got better things to do with me time.' The boy took a long swallow from his drink and put it on the table. He wiped his mouth with his sleeve. 'Stupid buggers they are anyway. Me brother still hangs around with them. You remember Colin, don't you?'

'Yes I do. I've seen him there often. I've wondered about you.'

Gary seemed pleased. 'Have you, Miss? No, I took your advice; it's probably the only time I did, like.' He smiled a warm smile and she returned it. 'If I'd done so more often I'd probably be better off.'

'I doubt it, Gary,' said Pamela. 'Plenty of others did, and the truth is there's very little work for anyone whether you passed the exams or whether you didn't.' She held up her glass. 'Cheers.'

'Cheers,' said her former pupil, and half a pint vanished.

Pamela paused for a moment while deciding how to proceed. She had reached the subject before she had intended, and now she could retreat and hope to reintroduce it, or get straight to the point.

'Did you ever go to any of their meetings, Gary? The National Socialists? I need to find out where they meet.'

Banks frowned briefly but showed no sign of concern.

'Yes, before you and I talked that night. I went to a couple. Why do you want to know?'

Pamela put her glass down on the table and leaned towards him. He glanced over his shoulder and they both saw the group of youths at the bar smirking back at them. Gary ignored them and turned back to face her.

'I'm afraid I can't tell you that,' she said quietly. 'It's nothing to do with the police or anything like that. No one is going to get into that kind of trouble. It's just that I need to know where they meet.'

'I don't know about it, Miss. If it was ever to come out that I told you . . .'

'It wouldn't, Gary. I promise you it could never be traced back to you.' She fixed her eyes on him. 'You can trust me.'

'And it's nothing to do with the filth then?' he asked. 'Only me brother goes there. I don't want anything to do with them meself, but I wouldn't do nothing to get me brother into trouble.'

'It won't get your brother into trouble, and no one will ever know that you told me anything. No one will link anything to me, or to you. I promise. It'll be a secret between us.'

Gary Banks looked around the bar and saw that his friends were now engrossed in an animated discussion which involved them in a series of exaggerated flicks of the head. He concluded that they were debating the controversial last goal which had snatched victory from their team. It was a subject on which he had his own firmly held point of view. He turned back and gabbled his answer.

'It's at the back of Finches yard – in Stansham, about a mile and a half from the school. There's a courtyard of lock-up garages and only one way in. The garage in the corner looks like all the others but it's much bigger inside. There's only one access for cars and things, that's from Brewer Street.'

'And you don't know anything about what they get up to these days? Nothing about their political activities?'

Gary still spoke quickly. 'Not apart from all that calling out at the school. I don't often see Colin. He's more or less disowned me since I left the group.'

'I'm sorry to hear that.'

Having taken the plunge, the young man now seemed to relax. 'Oh don't worry. I'm not sorry. Truth is he's a bit of a stupid sod really.' He put his glass to his lips and Pamela watched his protuberant Adam's apple move up and down in large swallows. He put the empty glass noisily down on the table. 'Another?'

'No thanks.' Pamela smiled warmly at him. 'I'm grateful to you.'

The lad smiled back and wiped his mouth on his sleeve. 'Don't mention it. I reckon I owe you something. That's us quits.' She got up and began to button her coat. 'Just one thing.' She paused and looked at him. 'Next time you want to ask me anything, there's no need to make up stories about meeting your boyfriend or alter your watch. Just come and ask me.'

Pamela was about to protest but immediately decided not to bother. 'You're a bright bloke, Gary.' She reached over and brushed her hand very quickly and gently against his cheek. 'And you've turned into a good-looking one. Thanks again, and goodbye.'

When he looked up he saw the red door closing behind her. He sat still for a minute feeling the blush fade out of his face and then returned to the bar to make his contribution to the debate about that deciding goal.

CHAPTER EIGHTEEN

George Charlton threw his pencil down hard so that it bounced off his desk and on to the floor. He sat back in the creaky wooden chair, his irritation increased by the fact that the pencil had broken in two. He looked down at the paper in front of him. It was an insurance claim form and he was going through the formality of filling it in. It was just a formality. He had reached the part where he had to assess the cost of the damage. The £ sign had already been printed on the left side of the page. All the claimant had to do was to fill in the figures, 5, 50, 500, 5,000. It did not seem to matter which of these numbers George Charlton put into the gap on the form in front of him; none of them would compensate him for the damage he had suffered. No amount of cash would pay for the anger and upset he had been caused. His car, his beautiful motor car which he had bought brand new seventeen years ago and had looked after with a loving care he had never lavished on anything before in his fifty-seven years, had been wrecked. The front of this object of beauty and of affection had been ripped off, taking away the bumper and distorting the metal completely out of shape; tearing a great gash and cracking the paintwork on all sides. It was ruined. It had been his pride and his joy and it would never be the same again.

Even now George Charlton could picture the man at the car body shop shaking his head decisively when asked whether he could get a match for the particular shade of deep plum of the paintwork. They stopped making that colour in 1976 apparently; and even if he could find some of the original shade the existing paint would have faded and changed in the intervening years. It would be impossible to achieve a precise match. It further angered Charlton that this man did not seem to share, or even fully to understand, his anxiety about the match, his preoccupation with perfection. Yes, of course the metal could be welded back together and sanded down to near perfection; but would the expert be able to tell the difference? The man in the body shop was afraid so – a car this age, you know. Charlton had left instructions to spare no expense, no time or effort to get the best possible result, but in his heart he knew that his most prized possession would never again give him the pleasure which was only to be derived from something rare and perfect. George Charlton had returned to his office on the brink of tears.

Sitting alone in his office late on Friday afternoon, the solicitor stared at the brightly coloured rural view above the wall-calendar which had been a gift from the stationery shop downstairs which had taken care of printing his invoices and letter headings these last fifteen years. The 'Walsh and Sons' calendar was the only decoration on the woodchip wallpaper which had been freshly emulsioned in a different pastel shade during the two weeks of his annual holiday. Mr Charlton always spent his summer holiday touring in the Daimler. He had gone on a motor tour every year for the last sixteen, always on his own. Leaning back in his wooden chair and gazing at the country scene, Mr Charlton could easily recall the many happy days he had spent spinning through pleasant country lanes just like the one on the calendar, his perfect shiny car winning admiring glances everywhere he went.

The memory became a blur as the solicitor turned his mind back to that incident a week ago this afternoon. He recalled the shock and immediate numbness which had overcome him when he had witnessed it. It had been unreal, like something happening in slow-motion. He had wanted to reach out, through the window and across the street, and physically stop it from happening. His beautiful car, his only family and loved-one: wrecked before his eyes. And the driver of the red car; he had not even stopped, but had simply roared away, dragging the heavy chromium bumper fifty yards along the tarmac before it clattered to the side of the road, ruined and all but beyond repair. The ageing solicitor had rushed blindly into the street, but by the time he arrived there was nothing to be done. The red car had vanished. He hurried around looking for witnesses; had anyone seen anything? Did anyone get the number? No. There were shaking heads.

An old man stopped to think. 'D R something. Or was it P R something? No, I think it was D R.' The solicitor had to restrain himself from trying to throttle more information out of the old man. 'Red, yes red, definitely red. A Ford? Yes, I think so, one of those new round-shaped ones, streamlined sort of job. A Sierra? Yes, I think so, a Sierra.'

Since that dreadful afternoon seven days ago, George Charlton had seen red Ford Sierras everywhere he went. Ahead of him in traffic, darting down side-roads as he drove his modern hire car along the High Street, or parked in rows in multi-storey car-parks. Even when the registration plate bore no relation to the remembered fragment he would examine the paint-work at the rear for any tell-tale signs of a recent accident. He had had no success. The world seemed to be full of red Ford Sierra cars, but none of them, apparently, was the offending one. It was Friday, and all he had to look forward to were two long and empty days over the weekend on which he would not be looking after and riding in his wonderful Daimler.

Again the solicitor looked down distastefully at the form which decreed that everything should be reduced to mere financial value. He looked for his pencil. It was on the floor by the window. He stood up and walked towards the spot where it lay. He bent down with unusual effort and, as he straightened himself, he glanced out of the window into the street below. He had turned and was halfway back to his desk when he stopped. He remained motionless for a full ten seconds before removing his full-frame spectacles from his nose and returning to the window. Once again he looked out. He felt his legs tremble and he leaned forward and placed his head against the windowpane to steady himself. At the side of the road, just where his beautiful Daimler had been on that afternoon, was a red Ford Sierra. The car was at an angle so that he could see part of the rear number plate. E488 DRG. Even at this distance, Charlton could see that there was some superficial damage to the back of the car.

For a moment the solicitor was undecided. Should he telephone the police and take a risk that the car might vanish while he was getting through to them, or should he go down immediately and confront the driver? His secretary had gone home early to visit her sister in hospital and his partner Mr Cox was away on business. He was alone in the office. He made up his mind; he would go down and confirm the evidence. The old man hurried to the door and pulled it closed behind him as he headed down to the street.

George Charlton was very nearly killed as he stepped off the pavement without looking to cross over to where the red car still stood. A loud blast from the horn of a single-decker bus failed to move him, and a screech of brakes was followed by a torrent of abuse from the bus driver. Charlton looked back at him, apparently uncomprehending, and continued on his way.

'Senile old fool,' the driver told his passengers. They muttered in agreement and stared out of the windows at the large old man in a grey three-piece suit who was crouching on his hands and knees to get a proper look at the back of the red car. There was damage at bumper level, and there were even some traces of darker red paint adhering to the grazes in the bodywork. Damnation. The solicitor was suddenly in a frenzy of anger. The driver had not even made an attempt to disguise his crime. He obviously did not care one jot about it. George Charlton flushed with temper. Now certain that he had the right culprit, the solicitor rose to his feet and tried to bring himself under control. What should he do? He breathed deeply and made an effort to collect his thoughts. It was the end of the afternoon and all around him the shops were closing. If the driver was in one of the shops, he would soon be emerging and would drive away. He took out the notebook he habitually carried in an inside pocket and wrote down the registration number. He consulted his watch and noted the time and place. The solicitor looked around him, hopelessly trying to identify anyone who might have witnessed the earlier incident and who could now confirm that this was indeed the offending car. Nothing, he knew, could return the beloved vehicle to its pristine condition. But having carelessly, perhaps even deliberately, wrecked his treasured car, the driver had just driven off as though nothing had happened; and for that Mr George Charlton, solicitor of thirty-two years' experience, was going to get even. He must call the police at once.

Still sweating and out of breath from the excitement and his exertions, Charlton looked about him and this time waited for a gap in the traffic before crossing the road back to his office. A few yards from the entrance he saw John Walsh, who owned the stationer's shop below his office, locking up for the night.

'Evening George.'

The solicitor had no time even to return Walsh's greeting. Instead he launched himself at the wooden stairs and bounded up them like an athlete. If he could get the police before the car moved, he might be able to confront the culprit this very day. He would like nothing better. To hell with insurance and compensation; he wanted retribution. The door of his office was ajar and he burst through it and was halfway across the room when he tripped and went down heavily on the floor as though poleaxed.

Charlton lay stunned for a few seconds before recovering sufficiently to raise himself to his knees. As he did so he saw the cause of his accident. To his right, by the chair at the window, he saw two brown country brogues, knitted socks and the outstretched legs of a pair of beige tweed trousers.

'Who the devil are you?' the solicitor spluttered breathlessly. 'What in heaven's name do you think you're doing?'

The pale-grey eyes of Richard Crozier looked back at him without blinking. There was an ugly smile fixed on the thin face which did not respond to the questions. Crozier had met a great many solicitors in his time, none of them in happy circumstances, and he held the entire profession in contempt. The experience of having one of them on hands and knees in front of him gave him a curious pleasure. The solicitor struggled to his feet while Crozier made no movement. He stayed seated, carefully watching the unkempt and over-wrought figure who was trembling with exertion and anger before him. The humourless smile remained.

'Sit down, Mr Charlton.' Crozier's quiet and clipped voice seemed to allow little possibility of disobedience.

'I'm damned if I'll sit down. I want to know the meaning of this – '

The rest of his sentence was obliterated by a sudden scream from the man in the corner chair. 'Sit down!'

For the first time, George Charlton felt intimidated. He looked around him and began to assess the vulner-ability of his position. He was alone in the office; he had seen Mr Walsh putting up the shutters so he knew that the shop downstairs was closed. By this hour there would probably be no one in the offices on either side of his. He moved around his desk and sat heavily in the creaky chair.

'That's better. Now then. We need to have a little chat.'

'The only chat you'll be having is with the police.' As he spoke Charlton reached for the telephone on his desk. He had not even lifted the receiver before the newcomer moved for the first time. He leapt from his seat and moved swiftly across the room, slamming his fist down hard on the solicitor's outstretched hand. Charlton roared with pain. 'Good God man, what on earth are you – ?'

'Now shut the hell up and listen.' Richard Crozier was still squeezing the solicitor's hand on to the tele-phone, crushing the bones against the handset. His grey eyes blazed and he spoke between gritted teeth. 'Behave yourself and be a good boy and you won't be hurt. Otherwise I'll rip your bloody head off. Is that quite clear?'

Charlton nodded frantically and felt the pressure ease away from his hand. He withdrew it as soon as it was released and pulled it back into his lap, nursing the already throbbing fingers.

'That's better, that's much better.' The man returned to his seat. 'Now then, I was saying, and I don't want to have to repeat this, so listen carefully.' The man pointed a single finger at Charlton and raised his eyebrows in inquiry.

'I'm listening.'

'Last week you had a visitor, a little old lady, nice old dear name of Miss Nuttall. Mad as a hatter, but sweet with it. She came to see you last week and my guess is that she left something with you. I want it. Whatever that something was, I want it, and I want it within one minute from now.' Crozier felt very pleased with himself.

The solicitor was now sitting back in his chair. He was still nursing his hand, his eyes fixed on his assailant. He was afraid. Though this was a country practice and the overwhelming majority of his business was dull and routine, he had still dealt with a wide variety of people during his many years in the law, and he thought he recognized this kind. The recognition was not a comfort. Without moving his eyes, he simply shook his head.

'No?' The voice was once again calm, almost placatory. 'No to what? No you didn't see Miss Nuttall last week? Or no she didn't leave anything with you?'

The solicitor was trying to think quickly. The letter the man was speaking of was in the safe behind him, not three feet away. The safe was an old-fashioned type, but was still strong and reliable. Charlton had taken the elementary precaution when buying it twenty years ago of retaining the combination in his own head and entrusting it to no one else except his partner Mr Cox. Now he was glad to have done so. Though his response to this man was by now bordering on terror, he knew that nothing would persuade him to betray Miss Nuttall's secret, whatever it might be.

'No, Miss Nuttall didn't come to see me.' He tried to sound as calm as he could. His hand was still hurting. 'Miss Nuttall is a client of mine but she hasn't visited me for months.'

The pale eyes widened slightly in anger. A large hand swept back through the red hair and came to rest at the back of his neck.

'Oh dear, Mr Charlton sir. You'll have to do far better than that. You have told me a lie; and that makes me very cross. It makes me very, very cross. It would be better if you didn't make me cross.' Crozier sat forward in the chair, his elbows on his knees and his hands clasped together in front of him. 'You see, I know that she came here last week, because I saw her. I was watching her from my car, and I saw her come into your building and walk up the stairs to your office. So I'm very sorry to say that you are telling me lies.'

The solicitor was approaching panic and his thoughts became a blur of images and speculations. He considered Crozier's words. Last week, Miss Nuttall was already being watched. The car. This man had watched her arrive. He had been following her. The car had pulled away straight after she had left. All at once George Charlton was not thinking about Miss Nuttall or about the letter. He was not thinking about the painful throbbing in his hand or the imminent personal danger he faced. Suddenly he was thinking about something far more important than any of these things. His eyes widened as the realization dawned.

'So it was you?'

Crozier was still speaking. 'Now I'll try this once more and only once more. I believe Miss Nuttall left something with you . . .'

'You're the driver of the red Ford.'

'Now why don't you be a good boy and just tell me what she said and hand over whatever she left.'

'You ruined my car. You crashed into it and just drove away.'

'Then I'll be on my way and you can forget all about my little visit.'

'You. You're the driver of the red Sierra which crashed into my car.'

Now Crozier listened for the first time to what the solicitor was saying. His irritation was growing. 'Of course it was me you stupid old fool.'

'Bastard.' Without planning or thought, Charlton screamed the word at the top of his voice as he rose from his chair and launched himself across the room. So sudden were the solicitor's movements that he had reached the armchair before the younger man could react. Crozier was only halfway up when George Charlton fell bodily on to him with all his weight, flaying with his fists into the man's face.

'Bastard, bastard.'

'Get off me . . .' Crozier's voice gargled into silence as the older man caught him full in the nose with a clenched fist. The old wooden armchair collapsed and the two men fell in an awkward heap on to the floor. Charlton was still on top, and was now raining his clenched fists into the face of the stricken Crozier. At last the younger man was able to bring up his forearms to ward off the blows to his face, and as he collected his wits, he brought his knee up hard between the legs of his attacker. Immediately the solicitor's body went rigid and the air went out of him in one noisy breath. Crozier seized the moment to free himself from under the great weight, and edged to one side.

Crozier crawled a few paces on hands and knees, dabbing at his nose with his sleeve and soaking up the blood. He felt the energy draining from his body. Then he heard a movement behind him and reacted too slowly to avoid the hurtling figure of the solicitor, fists flying in all directions.

'You bastard, you bastard.' The solicitor was attacking him like a madman.

This time Crozier reacted more quickly. Instantly he was on his feet. Remembering his training in unarmed combat, he backed away a few feet and crouched, his left arm outstretched in front of him, the right held back in readiness. The fist of the left hand was clenched hard, but the two middle fingers of his right hand were withdrawn, leaving only his index and little fingers extended. The lawyer had lunged into nothingness and was now regaining his balance and looking around for Crozier. Again he threw himself anarchically at his enemy, with only hatred and fury governing his movements. Crozier steadied himself back on his right leg, took aim, and then launched forward with his right arm.

Charlton felt the sting of agony as the twin digits of Crozier's right hand simultaneously penetrated both his eyes. The roar in his ears was accompanied by immediate blackness and then an appalling squelching sound. His hands went to his face and he immediately felt the sticky wetness of blood gushing from his eyes.

'My eyes. My eyes.' They were his last words, cut

short by the sickening thud of the broken wooden chair coming down heavily across his back and neck. A moment later Crozier was sitting astride the old man's back. He leaned over and took a firm grip under the solicitor's chin and across the back of his head. With a jerk he pulled and twisted until he heard the sharp crack which confirmed that the old man was dead.

CHAPTER NINETEEN

'So Tim and Bill will be in the van. Tell them to stay outside the yard and wait for the NS transit to come out. It's a confined space and any unknown cars or vans too near the entrance to the garages are certain to be spotted.'

Pamela Layfield watched Maguire carefully as he listened to the reply. She could faintly hear the precise voice of Peter Griffiths crackling down the receiver. She had heard a great deal about Griffiths but so far had not met him. Maguire had not specifically said so, but she guessed that Griffiths disapproved of her playing any part in this matter. The fact that Maguire was now transparently ill at ease in his telephone conversation suggested a concern that Griffiths might say something that Maguire would not want her to hear. She thought she could understand why professionals like Griffiths would not like relying on outsiders whom they did not know or have any reason to trust; all the same she slightly resented it. The information she had been able to provide about the location of the NS meeting place had enabled the *Encounter* crew to go and discreetly recce the area, and to identify a spot from which they could follow the NS expedition. If all went well Maguire would be going along on the expedition and the programme would have a sensational film. Her efforts had undoubtedly made a successful outcome far more likely. Maguire was suitably impressed and grateful, but there was no message coming back from Stadium Television reflecting any pleasure there. The plan was simply continuing in a businesslike manner.

'OK. Now has any more thought been given to the radio-mike? They didn't search me last time, and I'd be quite happy to carry one. At least it'll keep you in touch with what's happening providing you're able to stay reasonably close to me. Sod's law says that if I do take one they'll frisk me, but it's a chance I'm prepared to take if you guys want me to.'

Again Pamela tried hard to hear the reply. She very much hoped that it was negative. Even though he had not been searched on his first visit, she believed that if they were going to take Maguire out on one of their raids, the NS people were quite likely to search him. If they did so and found a radio transmitter, he would be in appalling danger. She found the prospect more alarming than she would care to admit, either to Maguire or to herself. Pamela Layfield had already lost the one man in her life to whom she had given everything. Maguire had not yet filled that gap, but she felt that, given time, he might easily do so.

'Fine, if you're sure. Obviously a mike would be a great help if you did lose us; you might pick up a clue from the conversation. But if you think it's too risky, then so be it.' Maguire was looking directly into Pamela's face and could see that she was relieved. He put a hand on her arm and gently squeezed. She smiled. 'I'll be leaving here in about fifteen minutes. After that, we're all on our own. Bill's got a high-powered rifle-mike has he? Good. Well, God willing I'll see you later on tonight. Back in the office. Very good. Best of luck. Thanks.'

Maguire replaced the receiver and put his arms around Pamela Layfield's waist. She stretched her arms up over his shoulders and around his neck, and pressed her face into his jacket. For a moment she felt she wanted to exclude the *Encounter* team, the NS, and every last thing which seemed to be conspiring to destroy her newly found happiness.

'Is your London docker outfit upstairs?'

'Yes, I left it on the bed. I'll have to put it on in a minute and be away.'

'Come on.' She removed her arms from around his neck and took him by the hand. 'I'll help you.'

It was John Walsh's son Robert who first noticed a slight smell of burning in the electrical wiring of the stationer's shop late on that Saturday afternoon. He mentioned it to his father who was in the middle of dealing by telephone with a bulk order from the insurance brokers around the corner. John Walsh sniffed the air and, detecting nothing, continued to concentrate on the A4 pad in front of him which was already half filled with an order for paper clips, elastic bands, typewriter ribbons and sticky labels. Mr Walsh senior was rather irritated that the brokers should be doing their ordering by telephone on a Saturday when he had a shop full of customers; but the business was valuable and Robert was just about managing to cope with the lengthening queue.

John Walsh's irritation increased when he noticed that the fluorescent strip light directly above the counter of the old-fashioned shop was beginning to flicker. These tubes always seemed to go at the worst possible moment. He looked up from the page and spoke to the middle-aged lady who was next to be served among the growing number of customers.

'You wouldn't credit it, would you. They were replaced new a month ago. Nothing lasts.'

The comment made the woman lift her eyes to the ceiling in agreement. John Walsh noticed that she was still gazing upwards at the flickering light as he returned to writing the brokers' order.

'Six boxes of plain A4,' he scribbled. 'Two new letter openers – plastic or brass?' His words were cut short as it landed, a great blob of thick dark-red liquid on the white pad in front of him. For a moment he just looked at the page, unable to work out what could have happened. Then came the cry from the woman at the front of the queue. John Walsh looked up to see his son rushing forward to catch her as her scream subsided and she collapsed flamboyantly, both arms outstretched, against the counter. He was too late and the woman fell heavily to the floor; but instead of going to help her, all the customers in the shop were looking upwards to the flickering strip light. At the edge of the long tube on the white-painted ceiling, there was a dark-red stain of perhaps a foot across.

As Mr Walsh looked up at it, another huge blob fell, hitting his face and jacket before splashing on to the counter in front of him.

'Get the police, Robert.' The distraught look on the face of his son was reflected in every face in the shop. This time John Walsh shouted. 'Don't just stand there, Robert, get the police!'

One hour later a Detective Sergeant was standing a few inches away from where the solicitor still lay, unmoved from the spot where he had fallen, on the carpet in front of the desk. He was speaking on the telephone to George Charlton's secretary.

'And you say you left here at about 3.30 yesterday afternoon and Mr Charlton was working here alone at that time?' He paused for the repeated affirmation. All around him other officers were examining every object in the room, picking up threads from the carpet and dusting fine white powder on every surface. 'And there's no next of kin that you know of? That's fine, Mrs Lowe. There's just one more thing. The safe, yes the safe in Mr Charlton's office, is there anything of any value in it? No? Good, just papers, I see, right.' The detective was writing in his notebook and was momentarily blinded as the police photographer took what must have been his fiftieth picture of the body. 'And just finally, Mrs Lowe, the safe has been tampered with but not opened. What about the combination. Only Mr Charlton? Mr Cox too. Very good. He'll be back in a few days. Very good, we'll wait.' The detective smiled and tried to sound reassuring. 'Good night Mrs Lowe. No, there's nothing whatever you can do and there's nothing for you to be concerned about. I know it must be a great shock, Mrs Lowe. Please don't worry. Good night. Yes, Monday will be soon enough. Good night.'

As he walked through the gathering darkness along the suburban streets which led to the British Bull, Maguire tried to empty his head of all except the hours ahead. He was late and he walked as fast as he could, weaving his way determinedly through the last of the daytime shoppers who hurried home, collars upturned against the persistent drizzle. He knew that his wits would need to be at their sharpest if he was to make a success of this project, and one way or another he knew that he had a lot riding on the outcome. First there was the matter of his own safety. He had seen enough already to realize that this was a very ugly organization, full of quite ruthless people who apparently had no qualms about committing crimes. Like fanatics the world over,

234

Maguire thought, these people used an alleged cause to justify unspeakable atrocities. He knew that he needed to remind himself of their nature and what they were capable of, though the thoughts did little to comfort him.

There was also, if he was honest with himself, the question of his own professional future. He knew that what he wanted more than anything else was to join the *Encounter* team on a full-time basis. He tried to put aside his disappointment at their performance so far, and to concentrate instead on what he felt was positive. It seemed as though people like the NS fascists were beyond being stopped by the police. Maguire hoped that what could not be achieved by legal means could sometimes be achieved by the stealth and cunning of professional investigative journalists. By shining the bright light of publicity on such people, it might make them crawl back beneath the stones from which they had come out. There were many things in life which Maguire found ugly and believed should be shown up before the public. He very much wanted to be a part of making that happen.

Lastly of course there was Pamela Layfield. As he thought of her he felt slightly ashamed of his own motivation. Ambition and personal success were an undeniable part of it. Though he had at first been spurred into action by the death of the young Asian girl, he knew in his heart that it was not now merely compassion which drove him into this potentially very dangerous position. Pamela, on the other hand, had been working to improve the community for many years without the slightest hope of personal reward. She did what she did because of a commitment. He thought now of her face as they had parted, the warmth of her naked body and the unspoken appeal to come back safely and soon. Now Maguire had another reason for his determination that tonight should strike a blow at the NS organization. He wanted Pamela Layfield to feel something of the pride in him which he now felt in her.

Two hundred yards from the British Bull, Maguire realized that he had not spent enough time mentally preparing himself for the important role he was about to play: Gerry Marland, London docker, out of work and full of bitterness. He glanced down at his clothes. He wore the same donkey jacket, jeans and heavy boots he had been wearing last time. He had not shaved for several days. This time he felt slightly more confident that at least he looked the part. He coughed noisily and muttered a few sentences to himself in his south London accent before entering the pub.

Immediately inside he saw the man with the tattoo whom he now knew to be Colin Banks, and the other two men who had first spoken to him outside the school. They glanced at their watches and got to their feet straight away.

'We had just about given you up.'

'Sorry, I got held up. My sister isn't too well. I had to collect her kids . . .'

'Never mind about that now; we've got to be off. We can't afford to take the long way round to the HQ so we'll go the quickest route.' The man with the tattoo suddenly stopped and gripped Maguire's arms firmly to his sides. His dark eyes stared unblinking into Maguire's. 'It occurs to me that we are taking a big chance with you, a very big one. If it was up to me . . . I'm not sure we aren't bringing you in too soon.' He paused without faltering in his gaze. 'But it isn't up to me. What is up to me is to come after you if you mess

236

up. And believe me, Mr Marland, if you do I won't hesitate to rip your throat out.'

Even his own companions were shocked by the ferocity of the words. Maguire knew that Banks was one of the men he would most have to watch out for. He shook himself violently and forced his arms from the grip.

'There's no need to worry about me, friend. I still haven't seen any evidence that your bark isn't much worse than your bite.'

The man with the tattoo started to walk on and the others fell in behind. 'Well, you'll see enough tonight.' The raucous and ugly laugh echoed around the hallways of the blocks of flats on either side.

Amid the hustle and shouted orders which preoccupied most of the men gathered at the NS headquarters, the man known as Johnson was busy loading a video-cassette into a small portable camera. Maguire spotted him across the crowded hall and wondered whether it might ever be possible to get possession of the other tapes. He was now certain that Johnson was not quite normal. Maguire realized that he would have to be trusted a good deal more than he was at the moment to be given even a hint of where the tapes were kept. That sort of trust would be a long time coming and Maguire was very sceptical that he would be able to keep up the pretence for as long as it would take. All hope probably rested on Tim and Bill from the *Encounter* crew, either tonight or if not, some night in the very near future. They had done this sort of thing many times before and were pretty expert. Nonetheless, on the last occasion they had preferred to lose the group they were following rather than risk Maguire's cover, and he had little doubt that something similar could easily happen tonight. He resolved to wait until the end of the evening and, if all went according to expectations, to look for an opportunity to snatch the video-tape and make a run for it. It was a long-shot which he very much hoped he would not need to take.

Now it was dark outside and Maguire stood watching as a group of eight men loaded bits and pieces of equipment into the plumber's transit van which provided such good cover for the NS operation. He saw long iron wrenches, a baseball bat, and half a dozen petrol bombs going on board, and his skin crawled in dread of what lay ahead in the next few hours.

'Right, men.' It was Frank Thompson, the man known as the Sergeant. 'Board up. Your group leader knows the target and he'll tell you when you get on your way. If all goes according to plan, you should be back in an hour and a half. I've got a few crates waiting for you.' A cheer from the eight men greeted the last remark and then they seemed anxious to get going. As they climbed into the back of the van one by one, Maguire lined up with them. 'We're taking quite a chance with you, Marland. Just stay and watch tonight; don't get involved in any rough stuff. Just watch and keep out of trouble.'

Maguire climbed on board the van and the Sergeant slammed the rear door closed behind him. He shouted something to the driver and banged his fist hard twice on the metal. Maguire peered into the gloom and pulled a section of the large tarpaulin sheet over his body and up to his neck. All around him the other men were almost completely hidden in the same way, with only their faces showing. Maguire saw that the man with the tattoo had a number of ski masks which he was now silently handing around. He felt the van reverse out of the garage and into the yard.

As the van began to move forwards Maguire felt a

238

deep sense of unease about the next few hours. Until now he had been preoccupied with the logistics and the personal risks of becoming involved in this project. Abruptly there came the realization that for the first time in his life he was on the point of witnessing, and even becoming involved with, something of pure evil. At that moment, huddled in among these desperate and inadequate people, on his way to be a part of some unspeakable act, Maguire felt himself in crisis. He had strict instructions from the *Encounter* team not to commit any criminal act, no matter how hard he was pressed. If he found himself in a position where to do so was inevitable, he must as a last resort leave the scene by whatever means available. On no account must he put himself into a position where he could be accused of performing as an *agent provocateur*. That principle was a great comfort to Maguire, though he was worried about what he would do if directly called upon to act. He found himself suddenly in turmoil, struggling with confused and conflicting emotions. Luckily, his time for dwelling on the crisis was limited.

The van was now edging out of the yard, to a spot where it would be visible to Tim and Bill, when he heard a shout outside and raised voices. For a moment Maguire imagined that the camera crew had been discovered. In that case it would take just a few seconds for the NS to realize that he must be a part of a trap. He tensed himself for escape. The van came to a halt and both rear doors were flung open. Maguire was steadying himself to make a break for it when he heard an unfamiliar high-pitched voice.

'There's been a change of plan.' It was the fat man, known to the group as the Captain, and next to him in the darkness stood the other man whom Maguire had seen in conversation with the Sergeant on his first visit.

'I'm very sorry, men,' the Captain was saying, 'I know you were looking forward to some nigger-bashing tonight, but I'm afraid I'm going to have to disappoint you.' A loud groan came from beneath the cover and the men shuffled in their places. 'Unfortunately we have an emergency situation which has been brought about by an unfortunate incident involving Lieutenant Crozier. I need not go into details now, but for reasons I don't expect you to ask, we need a small contingent to effect a house-breaking. Not exactly our usual MO, but unfortunately very necessary. At least three volunteers please.'

Maguire immediately realized that his chance of remaining a part of the expedition was now very slim. He wondered how to react. Then he saw that the Sergeant had walked away and was at some distance, talking to other members of the group. It occurred to him that in the darkness the Captain and what must be Lieutenant Crozier might not realize that he was a new recruit. House-breaking was unfamiliar territory to the men in the group and so none had yet indicated that they wished to volunteer. Seizing the opportunity, Maguire was the first to stick up a hand, and as he did so he saw two other men follow suit. Maguire recognized Johnson, who still had the video-camera over his shoulder, and Colin Banks, the man with the tattoo.

'Good men. Lieutenant Crozier and I will be coming with you. Let's be off as soon as possible shall we?'

The men who were being left behind moved reluctantly to get out of the van and once again the doors were closed on Maguire and the rest. At the front of the vehicle a discussion was going on, and Maguire saw that the driver was changing places with Crozier, and the fat man was getting into the passenger seat beside him. Then the van was once again heading off into the darkness, and at a signal from one of the men with him, Maguire lowered his head beneath the tarpaulin and was left alone with his thoughts.

When the sudden jolt came Maguire was uncertain whether he might even have been briefly asleep. He was unsure, but felt as though the vehicle might have been travelling for about half an hour and he was stiff and cold, huddled uncomfortably on the steel floor. When he became aware of it, he realized that the van was being driven very quickly and was swinging around corners, the tyres squealing at each bend in the road. He poked his head from the cover and saw several of the other men looking out.

'What's happening?'

'Crozier thinks we might be being followed.' It was Johnson speaking.

'Where the hell are we going?'

'Don't ask.'

'Is it the police?'

'Crozier doesn't know. He's trying to check whether it is a tail before we decide what to do.'

The van screamed forwards at what seemed a reckless speed for several more minutes before gradually slowing down.

'What do you think, Captain?' Banks shouted the question to the two men in the front. The fat man did not answer. Now the van was in what seemed to be a dark and narrow lane. It was travelling at no more than fifteen miles an hour and both men were looking intently in the driver's mirror. Maguire raised his head to peer out of the rear window. All he could see was pitch blackness.

'I think we either lost them or they weren't following us in the first place.' It was Crozier's voice.

'Which do you think?' asked the fat man.

'Maybe they weren't following us,' said Crozier.

There was a long pause as the van cruised along the lane. There were no lights in any direction.

'OK, we'll take a chance. Head on towards the house.'

CHAPTER TWENTY

Ever since her retirement from business Harriet Nuttall had made a particular point of not being a creature of habit. She liked her life to be organized and without too many surprises, but she tried to avoid getting into routines or arranging regular engagements. Dr Frank Castle and his wife Elizabeth were among the very few people with whom Harriet felt totally at her ease. As a result she always accepted their invitations to dinner, but it was many years before it occurred to her that this was a regular occasion which took place on the first Thursday of every month. She had first seen the pattern to their meetings twenty years ago, but in all that time neither the Doctor's wife nor she had ever referred to it.

'Are you OK for dinner on Thursday?' Mrs Castle's invitation would usually be issued casually at a chance meeting while shopping, or it would be contained in a note popped through her letterbox, or given via a telephone call. Harriet automatically kept the first Thursday of every month free, but was never presumptuous enough even to pencil in her dinner engagement on her calendar until the invitation had been issued.

'Oh Thursday?' she would answer as though surprised. 'Yes, that would be very nice, Elizabeth. About seven-thirty?'

Harriet would always take a small gift for her friends. Perhaps a small bunch of sweet-peas if it was high summer. Out of season she might take a jar of home-made jam and always a bottle of fortified wine. Harriet was never completely sure whether the Doctor and his wife actually enjoyed the fortified wine she brought them. She herself had not touched an alcoholic beverage since her sister's wedding more than fifty years ago, and the wine she took to the Doctor's house was never opened while she was there. Occasionally Harriet wondered whether the Castles might be too embarrassed after all this time to tell her that they did not like the stuff, and had been storing it away in a cellar for the past twenty years. Elizabeth was always so effusive in her gratitude that Harriet thought it would seem ungracious to stop bringing the wine altogether, and in her more mischievous moments it rather amused Harriet to reflect that if her suspicions were correct, then the Doctor would have a very impressive store of fortified wine indeed.

By the first Monday of November, the invitation for dinner on the Thursday had not been issued. This was unusual. Harriet began to think that perhaps the occasion would be missed. If so it would be quite literally the first such omission in twenty-five years. Her disappointment was only tempered by the fact that she had an enormous amount of work still to get through in preparing her paper for the inquiry, and she would use the evening profitably enough. Nonetheless, she could not help but feel concerned. The lapse made her wonder whether her friend Elizabeth or her husband was unwell; so on Tuesday morning she telephoned the Doctor's house. No, there was nothing wrong, Elizabeth told her. Frank had been feeling a little under the weather but was now fully recovered. Elizabeth had been meaning to drop a note in. Could Harriet come to dinner on Thursday evening?

'That's very nice. I'd like to. You're quite sure Frank is feeling well enough? I wouldn't want to intrude.'

244

Elizabeth had been fulsomely reassuring that she was not intruding and the engagement was made for 7.30 as usual. Harriet smiled as she wrote the appointment on the calendar which she always kept on a noticeboard in her kitchen. Despite the enormous amount of work she had still to do, she would not have liked to miss her regular outing; and anyway, at her age any change increasingly seemed unwelcome.

At seven o'clock on Thursday, 5 November Harriet Nuttall left her house and locked the door behind her. She got into her Morris car and set off to drive the twelve miles to Dr and Mrs Castle's house at the foot of the Hersham hills on the outskirts of Lansbury. There was no moon and the night was pitch dark. The old car revved noisily to make the hazardous hill-start out of the drive. As it emerged into the blackness, just over the brow of the hill so that only the roof would have been visible even if anyone had been looking for it, a battered white transit van pulled up and parked at the side of the road. The lights were extinguished and Miss Nuttall had no reason to notice the vehicle as she turned her car in the opposite direction.

'Right on cue,' muttered the Captain, only just loud enough for Crozier to hear. Crozier smiled in satisfaction. 'Wait five minutes and we'll go. We'll take two of the men. You're sure you know what we're looking for?'

'I know, and if in doubt I'll lift it anyway.'

'Remember, though, if we have to do any damage, or take anything substantial, it must be made to look like a burglary. Make sure the men know that. If we find what we're after, their job will be to keep a look-out and to lift any valuables they can find.'

'I'll make sure they've got the picture. I'll go first

245

and get in. Tell the others to follow me at one-minute intervals.'

Five minutes later Richard Crozier was putting to use some of the knowledge he had gained from his many years in prison. He walked quietly up the gravel drive leading to the dark old detached house and slipped a long steel crowbar from inside the sleeve of his jacket. The ancient sash window of the kitchen was open within a few seconds and Crozier climbed up silently into the house, standing quite still once inside to adjust his eyes to the complete darkness.

There was no sound from anywhere in the house and Crozier prepared to summon the others; then he stopped. From somewhere ahead of him he could hear a strange muted cry like that of a very small baby. His insides froze as he strained to make out what the noise was. Now he seemed to be able to hear it more clearly and it was quite distinct. It was a baby, wailing as though abandoned. Crozier frowned. He flicked a pencil torch from his pocket and shone a strong beam directly ahead. The torch immediately picked out in spotlight two bright blue and yellow eyes which glowed back at him through the murk. Then, beneath the bright eyes, the lips curled again and emitted the uncannily human-sounding wail. The cat was approaching him, mewing loudly all the time. Now that Crozier had the explanation to the mystery he felt more relaxed, and as the cat reached him he put out his hand towards it. The cat reacted as though it was being grabbed by a hostile stranger and it spat at him and dug sharp claws deeply into the back of Crozier's hand.

The mixture of shock and sudden pain made Crozier shout aloud and pull away, but as he did so another reflex enabled him to make contact with one leg of the escaping cat. Instinctively his powerful hand closed and gripped the animal, which now flailed out of control in the air, hoisted up by a single back paw. The alarmed miaowing from the cat filled every corner of the house.

The knowledge that he had captured his attacker took Crozier's mind from his own pain, and it was channelled instead into a blind hatred for the thing which had attacked him. Still reacting without thought, Crozier swung the cat violently around his head, spinning and spinning in several complete revolutions until it gained great momentum, and then he let the animal go. Dora's deranged squeal ended abruptly as she was splattered against the kitchen wall, instantly falling dead like a stone on to the ground.

'What in God's name is happening?' The voice came from the Captain whose fat shape filled the open window. Crozier looked up from nursing his damaged hand and could see that the large figure was flanked by the three other men. One of them, Johnson, was aiming the video camera into the room.

'Christ, there was a bloody monster in here.' There was something like a sob rising in his voice as he continued to press his hands hard together to ease the pain.

The Captain swung the beam of his torch around the room and swiftly alighted on the dead bundle of grey fur lying quite still on the floor. He moved the beam up the wall to see the blood splashed liberally across it.

'It's just a poor little cat.' The Captain did not try to disguise his contempt. 'You've probably woken the whole neighbourhood with your effeminate screaming. Let's get on with it; as fast as possible.' The four men climbed in through the window.

* * *

Harriet Nuttall had driven for three of the twelve miles of the journey to Dr Castle's house when she realized that she had left the bottle of fortified wine on her kitchen table. She was angry with herself. This sort of thing was uncharacteristic, and she was impatient with the thought that it might be a sign of her increasing age. She slowed down and looked at her watch. It was only just after ten minutes past seven and she probably had time to return to get the gift without making herself late. She looked carefully in her rear-view mirror to ensure that there was no other vehicle behind her, and then cautiously manoeuvred a slow but perfectly executed three-point turn in the narrow country road.

Confused and anxious about the turn of events, Maguire decided simply to play along with whatever was going on. He had expected to travel to a city suburb and witness some sort of attack on members of the Asian or West Indian community; perhaps a house or a nightclub, something of the sort. Instead they had come to what seemed to be a small town he did not recognize, and for the time being it appeared as though the expedition was a simple burglary. What was more, the decorations, books, photographs and furniture told him unambiguously that the house belonged to an old person who was almost certainly as straightforwardly Anglo-Saxon as it was possible to be; not a West Indian, not an Asian, and probably not even a Jew. Maguire had been sickened and disgusted by what had happened to the cat, but even as he considered it, he realized that it was no more than he had half-expected would happen to some innocent mother or child. The apparently pointless cruelty to a dumb animal made him feel sick, but he was managing with increasing difficulty to maintain his act. Just at the moment he felt as though his life probably depended on his ability to do so.

Maguire had been sent upstairs with the instruction to look for valuables and to take as much as he could. As he wandered around in the darkened rooms, being particularly careful not to touch anything, he considered the possible explanations for what was going on. If the NS needed money there were far more lucrative targets than an old rundown house like this one, and much nearer too. He also had no idea whether the *Encounter* team had managed to stay with the NS van, and whether they were filming at this moment. If not, then he was on his own. If that were the case he shuddered to think of the consequences for him of being caught, either by the NS people or by the police. He had resolved simply to carry out instructions and get out as fast as possible when he heard the crunch of gravel as the old Morris car pulled into the driveway.

From downstairs he heard an abrupt whistling note which the Captain had said would be the alarm signal if anything went wrong. In such a case, the group were to remain exactly where they were and not move. Maguire had no difficulty in remaining still; he was paralysed with fear. It was the police for certain. They would soon discover his true identity and his name would be in the newspapers as a member of an extreme right-wing organization which had been caught burgling the house of an old-age pensioner. Even if he was able to convince the police or the courts of his true role, there were still his colleagues. He could easily imagine the faces of the people in the newsroom when they learned how his first expedition at the behest of the high and mighty *Encounter* team had been so comprehensively bungled. It was humiliating, but at this moment his greatest emotion was plain fear.

As he waited for whatever would follow, the loudest sound Maguire could hear was his own heartbeat. At last he distinctly heard the front door opening and a few seconds later he heard footsteps and the unnaturally loud miaowing of a cat; then came the puzzled voice of an old woman.

'Now then, Tibby, what's the matter? It's only me. Did you think it was someone else?' Maguire could sense that the person was walking down the hallway as she spoke. A light went on and cast eerie shadows of the banisters up to the landing. 'I just forgot my present for Mrs Castle. Now what's the matter, Tibby, this isn't like you to be . . .' Maguire was in dreadful suspense as he waited for what would inevitably follow. There was a second or two of silence, then the cry. It was a strained wail of horror which came from frail and weak lungs, but filled the house with the old woman's sudden agony. Maguire felt his flesh go cold, and then he heard a further shout and was once again overwhelmed by fear. 'Who's there?' The old woman's voice was suddenly transformed from being laden with pain to being filled with defiance and anger. 'I know there's someone here. Come out, you coward. Come out now.'

Maguire pressed himself against the wall behind the door of the old woman's bedroom and silently prayed that she would not enter. Her step was in the hall and then it stopped. 'I know you're here, you coward. Come out and show yourself. I'm not afraid.' Maguire thought the sound of his heart would shake the house. He heard her step-fall on the stairs. He closed his eyes and searched his thoughts for a course of action. The old woman was now halfway up the stairs, her head level with the landing, and only just a few feet from where he stood. 'Are you up here? I know you're here somewhere.' The voice was determined and courageous. The sound of more footsteps followed. 'Let's see if you are just as brave with an old woman as you are with a defenceless cat.' Now Maguire could hear the woman's panting breath just outside the bedroom door. He determined that if he was discovered he would rush past her and try to get out of the house. It was completely dark in the room where he stood and the light from the landing now filtered through the crack in the door. He held his breath as he saw the slight shape of the old woman pass the tiny gap between the door and the wall. When she next spoke she was just a few inches from him. 'You're in here, aren't you? Come out and let me see what a brave man you are to kill a defenceless cat.' The old woman was taunting. 'Let me see you.'

Harriet Nuttall walked through the dark room directly across to the table by the side of her bed and switched on the lamp. She turned as the weak bulb illuminated the room. The light and the sudden gaze from her sad eyes fixed Maguire to the spot where he stood. The old woman stood still for several moments, saying nothing, her eyes full of reproach which spoke eloquently. Maguire wanted to say something. He felt he could not bear her blame. He was about to speak when without warning a dark figure dashed into the room from the landing. Everything then happened faster than Maguire could see or understand. He was aware that a hand was raised and the old woman put up an arm in self-protection. The hand flashed downwards. Maguire saw a glint of metal and heard a dreadful thud as the weapon landed on Harriet Nuttall's head. In the same movement as the descending weapon, the old woman's knees gave way and she collapsed in a heap on the floor.

'Don't, for Christ's sake don't.' Maguire rushed across the room and grabbed at the raised iron bar just in time to prevent it from coming down a second time on to the woman's head. The two men struggled for ascendancy over the weapon until their battle was halted by a barked order from behind them in the doorway.

'Stop that, now!' The tone of the voice allowed no possibility of disobedience. Maguire relaxed his grip on the attacker's arm and turned enough to see that it was the Captain who had spoken. Behind him the lunatic Johnson was pointing the video camera at them all. Maguire released his hold altogether and saw that the man he had been fighting was Crozier.

'You stupid bastard,' Crozier snarled.

'That's enough.' The Captain was unambiguously in charge. 'We've got a job to do. Let's finish what we came for. You take the woman downstairs, and don't damage her any more.' Maguire looked at Crozier and saw that he was about to protest. 'She might have information we want.' The Captain seemed exasperated. 'Now that she's discovered us, at least we can find out what she knows before . . .' He failed to finish the sentence, turning instead back towards the landing and speaking over his shoulder as he went. 'Get her downstairs carefully and try to bring her round.'

Crozier reached under the old woman's arms and hoisted her awkwardly on to her feet. A faint groan from deep in her throat confirmed that she was alive. As he carried her towards the door, Crozier turned to Maguire with an angry snarl.

'You and I will sort this out later.'

'I'll be ready,' said Maguire. At that moment his

detestation overcame his better sense and he felt he could hardly wait.

As the initial shock began to sink slowly in, Maguire tried desperately to think of a way out of what was by now an appalling and wholly unexpected situation. He was instructed to continue the hunt for valuables, and bag whatever he could find. He grabbed some small candlesticks which could have been silver from the dressing-table, and an oil painting which could have been an original from the wall. He wrapped them in a pillow case from the old woman's bed. All the while his mind was turning over the question of what to do. His first priority must be to ensure that the old woman was not hurt any further and to get her to some medical attention. He wondered whether he could in some way alert the *Encounter* crew who might still be in the area, and regretted the fact that they had decided not to give him a radio-microphone. Ten minutes passed and Maguire heard the other men go downstairs. He fell in behind them and headed for the kitchen.

Someone had brought a small lamp from another room and placed it in one corner. A teatowel was spread over it to allow just a little light through. Maguire saw that the old woman was sitting in a chair. She looked surprisingly upright and Maguire could see that her expression was alert. The Captain and Crozier were speaking to her in whispers, but her replies were loud and clear.

'I don't have the remotest idea what you are talking about. Certainly I am preparing a paper for the Ringwood inquiry, but it's a straightforward appraisal of economics and management. It's all based on publicly available information.' To Maguire's astonishment the woman was obviously not at all intimidated by the experience. 'You can get it from the library.'

The Captain's reply was inaudible from where Maguire was standing, but enough light fell on the face of the old woman to confirm that her determination was growing rather than diminishing. Her tone of voice carried rising indignation.

'I don't know anything about any secret papers. If you want me to help you you'll have to be more straightforward. At this moment I have not the slightest idea what you are talking about.'

If the old woman was confused, so was Maguire. None of this was what he had expected. He was relieved to see that the old woman appeared not to have suffered too much injury, but still his thoughts concentrated on how to get her, and himself, out of danger.

'What about the trips to the barn and to the lawyer last week? That was all just routine too I suppose?' It was the louder and rougher voice of Crozier.

'The first was a plan for a picnic which was not fulfilled because the weather was not as nice as I had hoped. The second, a discussion about my will with Mr Charlton who has been my solicitor for twenty years. You're welcome to know every detail of my will if you wish to.'

'Miss Nuttall, did you know that your nice Mr Charlton is dead?' It was the first thing the Captain had said which Maguire could properly hear. Still he had not the slightest idea what this could be about. He wondered again about the *Encounter* crew and then saw to his amazement that Johnson was taking video pictures of the events in the kitchen from the doorway. He looked back at the old woman and could see she was genuinely dismayed. 'Did you know that, Miss Nuttall? And did you know that he died protecting whatever you had told him or given him to keep? Did

you know that? I hope it was worth it, Miss Nuttall.'
His voice was quiet and very threatening. He repeated
himself. 'I hope it was worth it.'

'Well you can kill me too if you like, it won't make
any difference to what I'm telling you, because I'm
telling you the truth.' Now for the first time the old
woman's voice seemed to be trembling. Maguire
glanced at Johnson and noticed that his hand was
moving the zoom bar to get a close-up of the woman's
frightened face. He wanted to smash the camera from
his hands. When she spoke again, the old woman
sounded distinctly bolder. 'Kill me now if you're going
to, but I'm not saying anything more.'

'Oh I think you are, Miss Nuttall,' said the Captain.
'Marland.' Maguire was too absorbed in his thoughts
to recognize his own alias and for a moment he failed
to move. 'Marland!' The voice was more abrupt and
Maguire pulled himself together and stepped forward.
'Bring me that rather ugly cat.'

If anything Crozier seemed disappointed that he did
not actually have to do any damage to Miss Nuttall's
favourite cat, the one she referred to as Tibby. It had
been a masterstroke. As soon as it became obvious to
her that these men really did intend to torture the
animal until she told them everything she knew, she
hesitated no longer. She seemed to resign herself to
the inevitable, and told them straight away about the
copy of the papers she had hidden in the barn. Crozier
said that he had searched the barn earlier, but she
assured him that he would never find her hiding place
without her help. Even under this duress she stuck to
her story that the visit to the solicitor was to alter her

255

will, so the Captain and Crozier were convinced that at least this part of her earlier story must have been true.

'You killed the solicitor for nothing then,' said the Captain.

Crozier shrugged his shoulders. 'The old fella was crackers anyway.' He spoke without a trace of irony. 'What I did was practically self-defence.'

Crozier and the Captain told the three other men to watch the old woman and went into the next room to discuss how to proceed. Increasingly desperate, Maguire took the opportunity to try out his only idea.

'I don't know about you fellas but I didn't join this bunch to beat up old ladies – not white ones anyway.' Neither of the other men spoke, but Johnson, who was still recording, swung the camera on to him and waited for his next words. It unsettled him still further but Maguire knew that this might be his only chance. 'If the old woman dies, we'll be murderers. I don't mind that if it's a stinking Jew we're talking about, or a black. But I don't fancy going to jail for the rest of my life for killing a harmless old British lady. She's the sort I joined the NS to protect.' The other two men simply looked back at him, saying nothing. Maguire continued. 'I say we get her out of here and to a doctor before something even worse happens. What do you blokes say?'

'Why don't you shut the hell up, Marland?' Banks replied with an ugly look. 'You've been a real let down so far, so do yourself a favour and don't make it any worse.' At that moment the Captain and Crozier came back into the kitchen. The Captain was the first to speak.

'Crozier, Johnson and Marland will take the old woman to the barn so that she can show us where she's hidden the papers. I'll stay here and collect the stuff we're interested in and confuse the trail a bit. Meanwhile Banks will go back to the others to make sure they know that they're our alibi for tonight.' Maguire was slightly relieved; one down, three to deal with. 'We'll meet at Poacher's Wood which Crozier has recceed.' The Captain looked at his watch. 'Say two-thirty.'

Harriet Nuttall was tied up and a handkerchief was shoved roughly into her mouth. Crozier told Maguire to help him carry her to her own car and he did so as gently as he could. The old woman was propped up in the passenger seat and Maguire and Johnson were told to crouch down in the cramped back seat while Crozier drove the car out into the countryside.

At the house, the enlarged figure of Davis sat over the desk at which Harriet Nuttall did her work and began carefully sorting through her papers. He knew precisely what he was looking for. His intention was to identify and remove anything that referred to the Lazarus material, but to leave all other papers apparently undisturbed. Tonight's experience reassured him that Harriet Nuttall was unlikely to have told anyone else about it. If that were the case, and only material relating to her original paper was left, no one would guess that the papers had been touched at all.

After an hour and a half Davis was satisfied that he had looked through every paper he could find and had collected the ones relating to the Lazarus file. He began to wonder about the rest of the scene. It was as difficult a problem as he had ever encountered. Why would anyone abduct an old woman like Harriet Nuttall? Why would an ordinary burglar even harm her, let alone take her from the house? Davis wondered and searched his memory for some help in his training. His blubbery face grimaced into a smile of pleasure but no happiness. He had an idea. Only a lunatic would do such a thing. A particular kind of lunatic.

Davis walked slowly up the stairs and entered Harriet Nuttall's bedroom. The pencil thin torchbeam immediately picked out the dressing-table and he crossed the room to it and opened a top drawer. He was still smiling as he grabbed handfuls of the old woman's underwear and threw them around the room, stopping only when he found exactly what he was looking for. A vile laugh came up from deep in his throat as he took the linen garment in his hand and went to the bed. In the pitch darkness of the lonely old house, the fat man sat on the edge of Harriet Nuttall's bed and undid the zip of his trousers.

CHAPTER TWENTY-ONE

'What? Not a thing?' Pamela Layfield was trying to keep control of herself so that her voice would not convey the desperation that she felt. She had heard nothing from Maguire and at last had telephoned Stadium Television. The relaxed and upper-class voice on the other end of the telephone was that of Peter Griffiths.

'Nothing. They lost them I'm afraid, that is to say more properly that *we* lost them. It was always a risk; we suspected that they had spotted us so we pulled back. It was better to do that than to take a chance of compromising Maguire.' There was a long pause during which Pamela wondered whether Griffiths was trying to convince her or himself. He continued. 'At least this will give him a chance to get the lie of the land. We'll know whether we can risk a radio-mike next time for instance. If they didn't search him tonight then it's an option for next time. There's also the fact that they're also much more likely to trust him after he's been on one outing.'

'I suppose that's right, but I thought he would have been back by now. He's been with them for five hours. How long before you inform the police?'

Griffiths had not even considered doing so and the idea that this schoolteacher should be thinking such thoughts alarmed him.

'Oh, there's no need to think about that for a long while yet. If anything happened to Maguire my guess is we would hear sooner rather than later. We've plenty of experience of this sort of thing. Believe me, he's all right. He's probably joining in the celebrations and consolidating. He's a good lad, Mrs Layfield. Don't you worry.'

Pamela Layfield knew that she was being patronized. She was already very much aware that Griffiths regarded her as an outsider to be tolerated only on sufferance, and that she was being kept decidedly at arm's length. She was in their view very much an amateur among professionals. Pamela considered asking why all this experience had led to the *Encounter* crew failing to stay with Maguire on two consecutive operations, but decided not to increase the hostility against herself; if she heard nothing in the next few hours she would very badly want to keep in touch, and so for the moment at least she must remain on good terms with Griffiths. On the other hand she felt she had far more at stake than he did, and she strongly believed that his confidence was misplaced. She thought for a moment longer and then spoke decisively.

'If we haven't seen or heard from him by six in the morning I'm going to call the police.' She heard Griffiths begin his protest as the telephone receiver was on the way to the cradle. At his office in Stadium Television, Griffiths spoke for a few seconds into the dead line before replacing the receiver. He turned to Tim Walker and Bill.

'Hysterical bloody woman.'

'We've got what we came for. Why don't we leave the old woman here? Let's get out while the going's good.'

'We've got orders, that's why. Take her to Poacher's Wood. You heard the Captain.'

Maguire was now taking every opportunity to speak to Johnson while Crozier was out of earshot. This was his third attempt and he had made no discernible progress.

'What are you whispering about again? Are you two in love or something?' Once again Crozier interrupted them. Maguire was relieved that Johnson made no effort to tell Crozier what had passed. In the absence of much to be happy about, he thought it an encouraging sign.

Maguire looked into the pale face of the old woman. With the earlier violence and rough-handling she had received, Harriet Nuttall was now only semi-conscious. All colour seemed to have drained from her cheeks and even with his complete lack of experience in such matters it was clear to Maguire that unless he could get her to some medical attention within the very near future, it would be too late and she would be dead. In that case he would be an accessory to murder. The whole episode seemed increasingly like a nightmare and for the first time he felt bitterly that he had been abandoned by the *Encounter* people. So much for the professionals, he thought.

They had recovered a package full of papers from the old disused barn which Crozier had spoken about, and Crozier seemed pleased to have done so. They would soon be rejoining the Captain, so the time for him to do something was running out. It was increasingly clear to Maguire that Johnson was simple-minded; he had been taking video footage of events all through the evening and even now he was intermittently taking pictures. Maguire thought that perhaps he would respond to whoever put the greatest pressure on him at any one time. He also hoped that at the very least Johnson might remain passive, and would not interfere if Maguire insisted on getting some help for the woman. That, however, would have to be done before the Captain returned.

Crozier on the other hand was a completely different prospect. As he had manhandled the old woman from one location to the next, he had been humming and singing as though on a Sunday afternoon outing. Apart from being completely devoid of compassion, he also appeared to be quite oblivious to the possible consequences for all of them of the death of the old woman. Maguire felt quite certain that Crozier was deranged.

Maguire and Johnson returned to the back seat of the car and Crozier put the old woman back in the passenger seat. Even as he walked round the front of the car to get into the driver's seat Maguire took the opportunity to speak to Johnson.

'She's not going to last another hour if we don't get her to a hospital. Then we'll all be murderers. That's all right for Crozier, he's already killed the solicitor. He's nothing to lose, but we have.'

It was all Maguire had time to say before Crozier opened the door and got into the front seat. As he started the engine Johnson spoke in a nervous but excited voice.

'Hey Crozier, Marland here reckons you're a killer. But he says we aren't so far, so maybe we should get the old woman to a hospital before she snuffs it.' Maguire felt a surge of alarm. He was trapped in the back seat of the car and could not escape. Crozier switched off the engine and slowly turned around, his left elbow resting on the back of his seat.

'Oh does he now?' He smiled broadly at Johnson. Johnson returned the smile and added a short burst of hysterical giggling. 'That's all Mr Marland knows, isn't it Johnson?' He turned directly to Johnson. 'What's your count of young niggers now, Johnson? Five or six

262

is it?' Maguire looked at Johnson and saw that he was now nodding vigorously and practically losing control in his growing excitement. Maguire suddenly felt very cold and now he thought how pathetically he and the others had underestimated what they were getting themselves into. Crozier turned again to Maguire. 'So you see, Mr Marland, if that's your name,' Maguire felt a further chill through him, 'you're in good hands. Relax, don't worry. We'll be talking to you a bit later.' Crozier faced forwards and started the engine. The car set off towards Poacher's Wood.

No one spoke during the short journey along the narrow country roads. Maguire stared out into the moonless night, lost in his own thoughts. They were travelling along a narrow lane with no room for two cars to pass, but with occasional wider places where gates led into the fields which lay at either side. They drove on steadily until Crozier suddenly yanked the steering wheel and the car skidded into a ditch on the right-hand side of the road. 'The old woman isn't a very good driver, is she.' Crozier laughed at his own joke. The unexpected movement threw Maguire sideways so that he was resting against Johnson and at the same moment the old woman slumped against Crozier. Maguire saw him roughly push her back into her own seat so that she was propped up against the door. The car was now at a thirty-degree angle and Crozier was revving the engine hard. The smell of burning rubber confirmed that the wheels were spinning in the mud.

Crozier switched off the engine and got out of the car. He walked around the front and opened the passenger door. The old woman immediately slumped into his arms and Crozier lifted her bodily out of the car and put one of her arms around his neck. Without looking around at the other two men he set off across the road and through a gate which led into an open field.

Maguire decided that there was no further point in trying to deal with Johnson. This was his chance to get away and perhaps to raise the alarm; but he had no idea how far it was to the nearest telephone or house and he felt sure that if they saw that he had gone, Crozier would just kill the woman immediately and make a getaway. His only course must be to stay with her and try to prevent the worst. He got out of the car and began to follow Crozier across the field. As he looked to his right he saw that Johnson was walking a few feet away from him carrying the video camera. Maguire's caution and his patience were nearing exhaustion.

'Gentle Jesus, Johnson, if I see you pointing that camera at me again I'll make you eat it.' Johnson did not respond but continued to point the camera at Maguire as he walked.

Maguire and Johnson soon caught up with Crozier and the old woman. Maguire saw that her legs were being dragged through the heavy mud. The group had walked two hundred yards when Maguire noticed a flashlight in the trees ahead. Crozier turned to Johnson. 'That's the Captain.'

The group had to cross a narrow ditch to get into the woods. When they were still a few feet away from the light Maguire heard the familiar high-pitched voice. 'Did you get the papers?'

'We got them,' said Crozier.

'Excellent. How's the old woman?'

'She's nearly dead.' Maguire was desperate and increasingly felt that he had nothing more to lose. 'We should get her to a hospital.'

The Captain looked at Maguire uncomprehendingly and then at Crozier.

'He's been talking like this all night. We've got a problem with this one.'

'We brought him in too soon.' It was Johnson. 'That's my opinion if you want it – sir.'

Maguire saw the Captain's face flicker from confusion to anger. 'You don't mean that this is the new man? Not the man the Sergeant brought back a week ago?' Johnson nodded. Maguire stood still and prepared to make a run for it. 'For Christ's sake, how was he allowed to come out on this?' The Captain was clearly incredulous. 'We never allow this. Never.' He looked at Maguire. 'You'd better just shut up now and behave yourself. There's going to be an enormous row about this come what may, so don't make it worse for yourself. I hope you've seen enough tonight to know that we aren't joking.'

'Oh I've seen enough all right,' said Maguire. 'Now what are you going to do with the old woman?'

The Captain ignored Maguire and spoke to Crozier. 'Naturally we've got to kill her. And what is more I think our new recruit should do it. Just to show his commitment you know.' From the corner of his eye Maguire could see that Johnson had begun running the video again. He was glad that at least one of them was preoccupied. He knew that the critical moment was approaching and his heart was pumping blood hard around his body and into his brain. The scene swam in front of his eyes as he fought to retain control of himself.

'I joined this group because I don't like blacks and Jews, not to kill old ladies.'

'This is a military operation.' The Captain's reply

was abrupt and angry. 'You don't ask questions, you just carry out orders. Superior officers decide what is for the good of the cause. Your job is to do as you are told. Now then?'

Maguire knew that he was on the brink of a personal crisis in which he would be unable to act at all unless he did so immediately. There were three of them and one of him. He had no real hope of overcoming all of them but he had to try. The alternative was to leave the old woman to certain death. He had no idea of a strategy but tried to take a deep breath to clear his brain. Crozier was obviously by far the most dangerous and would need to be immobilized first. The two men were looking directly at him, as though challenging him to defy the Captain. In an instant he brought up his right foot and kicked Crozier between the legs as hard as he could. The man let out an unrestrained scream which took the Captain's attention long enough for Maguire to lash out at him with his fist. He caught the small fat man full in the nose and felt the crunch as the gristle smashed into the bones of his bloated face.

Maguire looked around wildly. Crozier was immobilized for the moment and the Captain was clutching at his face. Johnson was putting down the video camera and coming at him. Maguire leapt on to him from one side and pulled him to the ground. The two men fell heavily and Johnson began to struggle. Maguire sought to hold the man's head still for long enough to enable him to land a decisive punch. The fight lasted several seconds before Maguire heard from behind him the nauseating crash of shattering bone. The sickening sound made both men momentarily pause. Maguire looked over his shoulder and saw that the Captain was leaning over the old woman who was slumped in a shallow ditch next to a large tree. In his hand he held what looked like a long truncheon. He raised it again above his head.

'No!' Maguire's desperate scream seemed to tear apart the air and to fill the small wood before carrying on into the night. It hung long in the branches of the tall trees and echoed in his own head before abruptly ending as the truncheon came down once again on the already broken skull. Several seconds of stillness passed as the hot and heavy breath from the lips of three men turned to mist in the cold night air. No breath was visible from the lips of Harriet Nuttall.

As the dreadful reality dawned on Maguire he saw that he must act immediately. Abruptly he turned and landed a last punch which Johnson was able to ward off with his elbow as Maguire leapt to his feet.

'Stop him. Stop him.' The Captain's high-pitched voice seemed unexpectedly controlled, but no one was able to obey as Maguire started running. Within moments he was through the trees and thrashing across an open field surrounded by the enormous darkness. Back in Poacher's Wood the three men nursed their wounds and were impatient of those sustained by the others. At last they were all on their feet and ready to return to the van.

'We'll need to get out of here before that bastard raises the alarm.'

'He won't do that,' said the Captain calmly. 'What would he tell the police?' He allowed a small rumble of grim laughter. 'He's in this up to his neck.' The other two men walked a few steps before the Captain stopped them. 'Just a minute,' he said quietly. 'Take the old woman's underwear.'

267

CHAPTER TWENTY-TWO

Maguire was scarcely able to breathe as he half stumbled and half ran the last few yards to Pamela Layfield's house. After the fight he had covered a distance of some five miles on foot and had never been in any doubt of where he was headed. It was three-thirty in the morning and at her upstairs bedroom window, Pamela Layfield had all but given up any expectation that Maguire would arrive safe and well. Nonetheless, ever since the telephone conversation with Peter Griffiths two hours before, she had remained staring trance-like into the empty street.

When at last she saw Maguire approaching through the dark and mist, Pamela ran down the stairs and reached her front door at the same moment he did. He stumbled into the house and directly into her living-room where he flopped, exhausted, into a chair. He covered his face with his hands as though in an effort to blot out the events of the previous hours.

Pamela went to him and kneeled in front of him, gently holding his wrists. She felt the tension in them as he pressed hard into his face. She waited for several minutes hoping that he would speak first. Then, when no words came, at last she could stand it no longer.

'Just tell me. Are *you* all right? I don't want to know anything else until you're ready. Just tell me that: are *you* all right?'

Maguire did not move. Then his head began to move steadily, nodding slowly up and down, in what at first seemed to Pamela to be affirmation and then, when it continued, caused her still greater alarm.

'You're saying you *are* all right? Maguire, tell me for Christ's sake.'

'Yes.' The word was muffled by his hands which were still held tightly to his face. 'Yes, I'm all right. I'm all right.'

'Thank God for that at least.' Pamela leaned forward and laid her head sideways so that it rested in his lap. She felt one of his hands touch the side of her face and her neck.

'You just would not believe it.' The murmur was barely audible. 'You just would not believe what I have seen tonight. I just simply cannot begin to tell you the horror of it.' Maguire's mind was full of a mixture of anger and disbelief as even now he struggled to be sure that it had all happened as he thought it had.

'Don't tell me now if you don't want to. I knew it would be dreadful.'

'You have no idea. I promise you, you just have no idea.' There was a long silence as both sat and tried to sort through their own thoughts. Maguire took his hand from Pamela's neck and once again pressed his fingers hard into his face, causing the blood to drain from the surrounding skin.

'Have you spoken to the *Encounter* people?'

'No,' said Maguire. 'I came directly here. The NS spotted a van following them at one point and tried to lose it. I don't know whether they managed or not. I just hope and pray they got some footage. If there's no independent evidence of what I've seen and been involved with tonight then I, all of us, are deeply in trouble. I promise you, you cannot begin to imagine it.' Pamela did not know how or what to reply. 'Pamela?' There was a pause as she waited to try to find the words. 'You haven't spoken to them have you?' He lifted her head so that he could look into her face. He held his hands on her cheeks and asked her directly. 'Have you? Do you know what happened?'

She covered his hands in hers and held his fingers tightly, looking at him, her heart breaking for him. 'I have spoken to Griffiths. I'm afraid it's not good news.'

Peter Tremayne stood on the steps of the Mallin Harcourt Bank at the end of the day, waiting for two cars to arrive. It was raining hard and from the vantage point of the stairs leading to the entrance, he looked down on a billowing and bobbing sea of black umbrellas. Investment managers, analysts, brokers and bankers hurried like scampering animals into the little holes in the ground and thence to the tube trains which hurtled them out to their homes in the suburbs.

Tremayne had not been told why Sir John Bartholomew had asked Sir Horace Beckford of the British Energy Corporation and Dante Fitzwilliam of American Nuclear Industries to see him this evening. Without warning, he had simply been instructed to issue the summons; and it was clear that the Chairman anticipated no reply other than immediate acquiescence. Tremayne had been told to speak directly to the two men and under no circumstances to leave a message with a secretary or anyone else. When he had eventually managed to speak to each man personally, both had been disconcerted by the invitation and had sought details on the telephone. Tremayne had learned enough in the past week to realize that even had he known anything he would have been unable to pass it on over an open telephone line. To his surprise both men had agreed to come at once.

Now he was waiting on the edge of the downpour for the cars to arrive, with specific instructions to shepherd the two guests straight through the bank's normal reception procedure and in to the Chairman without anyone seeking their names or business. Normally Mrs Blake would have been asked to undertake so tiresome a job, but Tremayne had noted that even she had been scrupulously excluded from knowledge of this operation. He had noticed too how Mrs Blake's anger at the Chairman's recent behaviour had been growing in scale and visibility as she had been more and more excluded, while he had been asked to undertake so much which would normally have been her preserve. In such circumstances Tremayne was glad to have been taken into his master's confidence, but all the same he felt a growing sense of disquiet about the matter now at hand. He was ambitious, few people more so; but the affair they were now involved with was very far removed from the kind of business he expected to be transacting when he joined the world of merchant banking. He had known that it would be hard work and that sometimes unpleasant decisions which affected people's livelihoods had to be made. He knew too that in such matters even a degree of ruthlessness would be required. But even the few details he knew of this present business left little doubt that it fell outside that sphere; very far outside. It involved a very nasty subject and some very nasty people, the kind of people whom Tremayne would normally have gone to considerable trouble to avoid. He would be glad when it was all happily resolved and he could get back to some of the many more pleasant aspects of his chosen career.

For the rest of the bank's staff it was unusual to say the least for so exalted a figure as the Chairman's Personal Assistant to be waiting for so long at the front door. As Tremayne peered out of the entrance porch into the rain Roberts, the long-serving doorman, sought to avail himself of this all too rare opportunity to address a member of the bank's senior management at greater length than the usual morning greetings.

Sir John Bartholomew was right enough, it seemed, but the old Chairman, now there was a real gentleman; one of the old school. He was always especially courteous, even when speaking to the most menial of the bank's staff. He would make a point of remembering their names and those of their wives. Tremayne reflected that the present chairman could scarcely be troubled to remember his secretary's name, let alone that of the doorman.

The traffic was heavy, made worse by the dreadful weather. Tremayne remained at the door for long enough to hear Roberts's views on the ever growing commuter chaos of London and the difficulty caused for the ordinary working man by rising property prices. The young man made several vague efforts to respond sensibly to the smalltalk, and was at last mightily relieved to see the large black limousine which he recognized as belonging to Dante Fitzwilliam, and not far behind it came the maroon Rolls-Royce which conveyed Sir Horace Beckford. Tremayne put up his umbrella and rushed into the rain to escort the American into the bank. The man in the Burberry raincoat stepped out of the limousine and into the bank's entrance. Tremayne asked him to remain where he was while he performed the same service for Sir Horace. Tremayne had to hold the umbrella high in the air to clear the head of the long lanky figure from the British Energy Corporation. By the time both men had weaved between the waves of commuters to reach the steps of the bank, Tremayne was thoroughly wet.

In the outer office of the Chairman's suite, Mrs Blake took great pains to study her papers carefully and not even to look up as Tremayne walked the two men directly past her. Without pausing to be announced, Tremayne knocked on the great wooden doors twice and entered the Chairman's room. Sir John Bartholomew stood up hurriedly and walked around the desk to meet the two men.

'Sit down, gentlemen. Sorry to have brought you here at such short notice, but there have been developments.' Tremayne thought the Chairman seemed breathless. He had no idea what Bartholomew's news was, but he could see that he was excited about it. 'There are developments and I think there will shortly be more. I need to keep you up to date, abreast of things we might say. You need to know what's going on, and what's likely to follow.'

Tremayne noticed that the chairs had been arranged in the same pattern as they had been on these men's last visit when his boss had been at pains to record their conversation. He had little doubt that the same exercise was being repeated and he made up his mind that he would speak as little as possible.

'Mr Davis has had some measure of success in tracking down and recovering the Lazarus material. I will give you details of that in a moment when he arrives.' Bartholomew looked at his watch. His face seemed pink and flushed. Tremayne wondered whether he was completely well. He seemed to have lost his composure, to have been affected by excitement or even pleasure. 'I'm expecting him at any time. I'd prefer not to begin without him if you can wait a few moments.' Tremayne now noticed for the first time the glass tumbler and the small golden pill-box standing open on the desk next to the Chairman's writing-pad.

Sir John took out two tiny white tablets into the palm of his hand and swallowed them with a mouthful of water.

'Is everything secure now? Is that why you've called us here? Are we celebrating?' The American was obviously confused by Bartholomew's manner, unable to decide from it whether the news was good or bad.

'Not yet,' answered the Chairman, 'but as I say we have experienced some measure of success. When I have described it to you I will outline for your approval what I propose as phase two of our operation. If that is successful then I think, gentlemen, we can hope that most of our problems are over.' He smiled a wide smile and sat down in the large leather-covered chair. 'Then we can get on with what we're all much better at – making money.' The smiles were interrupted by a buzz on the intercom and Bartholomew flicked the switch.

'Mr Davis is here, Sir John.' It was the clipped voice of Mrs Blake.

'Send him in directly.' The intercom clicked closed and Sir John sat up straight in his chair, his hands clasped together on the desk in front of him, and still smiling broadly. Without speaking, Mrs Blake let Davis in and closed the door behind him. The fat man sat in the only empty chair. Everyone immediately noticed the swollen and blackened eyes but no one made any remark.

'Good evening gentlemen.' He clasped a package wrapped in brown paper to his chest and sat waiting.

'Well gentlemen,' the Chairman sat back once again, 'Mr Davis has some information for us, and some pictures I believe?' His eyebrows asked the question and Davis affirmed. 'Well then, why don't I leave it to you. We'll want to use the video. Tremayne?'

Peter Tremayne held out his hand to Davis who

274

seemed reluctant to part with the package he clasped to his fat frame. After a momentary pause Davis handed it across, and Tremayne went to one corner of the office and opened the doors of a wooden cabinet which was fitted into the wall. He pulled a handle to reveal a platform which supported a large television set and video-player. Tremayne had to struggle to unwrap the cassette from the masses of thick paper, and at last as the tape was being loaded, Davis began speaking.

'My operatives and I gained some intelligence that Stephen Ross had handed the Lazarus papers to an old spinster called Harriet Nuttall for some analysis of their content. Further inquiries and surveillance suggested that Miss Nuttall was planning to reveal details of their contents at the public inquiry into the Ringwood project.' There was an audible gasp from the two industrialists and Davis paused for his information to sink in. 'You will appreciate that in such circumstances our main task was to recover the papers from the old woman before she could pass them on to anyone else, or of course prepare her new paper.' Davis looked around at his attentive audience. He was beginning to enjoy himself. 'Secondly we had to try to discover whether Ross has passed on this information to anyone else. It has always been our intention to move in on Mr Ross last so that we could confirm with him that we had identified all people who had gained knowledge of our file. You will appreciate that if he was eliminated in the beginning we would have no eventual backcheck as to whether we had neutralized all potential sources of the information.'

'Oh I say.' Horace Beckford's expletive suggested that he was hearing news he did not wish to hear.

'Some problem, Horace?' asked the Chairman. 'Tremayne, get Sir Horace a glass of water will you?'

'Is it absolutely necessary that we should know all this? Can't we just rely – ?' He was not allowed to finish the sentence.

'Absolutely essential I'm afraid, old man,' said the Chairman. 'I told you at the beginning that although the bank acknowledges immediate responsibility for this leak and therefore for undertaking whatever is necessary to resolve the difficulties caused, we are at the end of the day only acting as agents for our clients, and that in this instance is yourself and Mr Fitzwilliam here.'

'Damn right,' said the American, banging the wooden arm of his chair with his clenched fist. 'I for one want to be told everything so that my organization can be sure exactly where we stand in all this. We want to be certain that we have total security. Let's get on with it for pete's sake can't we?' The reproach was directed unambiguously at Sir Horace who shrugged his languid shoulders and sat back in his chair. Tremayne handed him a tumbler of sparkling water and he gulped at it eagerly.

'Perhaps we should see the video?' suggested the Chairman.

Davis struggled to get out of the armchair and waddled gracelessly over to the television. He flicked a switch which dimmed the centre light in the office and the screen lit up. Davis took up the narrative.

'My operatives went to the house of the old woman in Lansbury and proceeded to gain entry. Our monitoring of her telephone calls told us that she was away for the evening so we knew we had time to effect a proper search.' The television showed unsteady pictures of the approach to a large and isolated old house. The camera went to a window and panned around to reveal the shape of a man standing in the shadows. Davis ignored the question everyone present wanted answered and continued to talk. 'Our priority was to find any trace of the Lazarus papers and any clues as to whether they had been circulated more widely. We also, of course, had to make the whole episode appear like a burglary.' As Davis spoke the camera was tracking into the house through the open window. Tremayne remembered how anxious Davis had been at their first meeting when he had attempted to take notes. He wondered whether Davis knew that he was being tape recorded as he spoke and tried to imagine what his reaction would be if he found out. He guessed that the unpredictable fat man would not be pleased.

He looked at the Chairman and saw that he was totally immersed in the video pictures. While the other two businessmen were clearly involved in this extraordinary episode only because circumstances had forced them into it, Sir John Bartholomew looked as though he was enjoying himself. His face looked unusually flushed with excitement, yet dark shadows underlined his eyes, providing a combination which gave the Chairman an almost macabre appearance. For the first time since he had known him, Tremayne thought the Chairman looked a very sick man. Now, for a moment, Peter Tremayne tried to stand back from the situation and look at it from the outside. It seemed scarcely credible; before him was the Chairman of an internationally famous merchant bank and two members of the senior management of two international industries with close links to government, watching the video of a burglary which they had authorized on the house of an old woman. Tremayne allowed himself to imagine for just a moment what a journalist would make of the scene he was presently witnessing. The thought brought a flicker of a smile to his face as he concentrated once again on Davis's narrative and the video. The pictures had zoomed in on what looked like a small grey blanket bundled against a wall. Tremayne could not make out what it was but thought he saw a splash of dark red. Again Davis did not refer to it and no one asked.

The four men sat silently and listened to the alarming story of Harriet Nuttall's surprise return from her dinner engagement, her initial defiance and then finally her compliance with the interrogation. There was a mass of dark and confusing images on the screen, and the sound was kept low as Davis continued his commentary. The old woman had eventually admitted, he told them, that she had hidden one copy of the Lazarus file. This copy they had subsequently recovered. She had assured them that Ross had given it to no one else, and they had reason to believe her. Towards the end of Davis's account, Tremayne became increasingly anxious to hear news of the old woman's present condition. She sounded, from the story, as though she was rather an eccentric and endearing old person. Tremayne was concerned. The video showed scarcely discernible images of the inside of a car, which was hurtling through the darkness, while the outline shape of Miss Nuttall could be seen slumped in the passenger seat. The tape was stopped.

Davis announced that all documents and evidence relating to the Lazarus material which Stephen Ross had dispersed to Harriet Nuttall had been recovered and were secure. He said no more. Since no one else was going to ask the obvious question, Tremayne decided to do so.

'How is the old lady now, Mr Davis?'

Davis did not react, but the Chairman and the American looked up at Tremayne in apparent surprise,

278

while Sir Horace Beckford seemed simply embarrassed and remained staring at his elongated fingers.

'I'm sorry, have I said something wrong? I was just wondering where she is now. Have I missed something, or isn't there a risk that she will tell all when she recovers from this?'

Davis stood up and walked towards the window. He glanced out into the street below and then turned abruptly. 'It's probably just as well that Tremayne has asked, because we don't want these gentlemen to feel that anything has been kept from them.' He glanced around the room and saw that Sir John was slowly nodding in agreement. He walked back to the corner of the room and restarted the tape. The camera was now in a wood, and the screen was filled by the awful shape of a twisted body lying among the leaves. Davis resumed his commentary. 'Harriet Nuttall is dead. We eliminated her as a security measure. We made it look like a burglary and then a sex attack. This was two days ago now, and as far as we know her body has not yet been found.' Once again the tape was clicked off and the group of men remained staring at the snow-storm of static on the silent screen. Davis addressed them in the darkness. 'All that remains, gentlemen, is for you to give us permission to perform something similar in relation to the original thief, Mr Stephen Ross, and we can all put the unfortunate episode behind us.'

'Lock up when you go, will you Peter? I have to discuss some further details with Mr Davis later on tonight but you needn't be involved in that. I'll see you in the morning.'

'Right, Sir John.' In a final triumph of determination

over nature Peter Tremayne managed an apparently warm smile at his boss before he closed the outer door of the Chairman's suite. In the last half-hour he had been very close to losing his struggle to maintain composure in the face of what he had seen and heard. He stood for a moment, staring blankly at the heavy mahogany door, before turning suddenly and walking across the room to another smaller door at one side of the office. He threw it open just in time to reach the handbasin before he was wretchedly sick.

CHAPTER TWENTY-THREE

'We've got to go to the police, for God's sake. There's been a bloody murder and I've been a part of it.' Jonathan Maguire sat with his head in his hands, running his fingers through his hair, his elbows resting on his knees. 'I shouldn't even have waited this long.'

'And I say we've got to wait and think.' Peter Griffiths tipped back in his chair, puffing on his pipe in a way which might have been calculated to infuriate Maguire still further. He removed the pipe from his mouth and tapped it on the heel of his shoe. 'Our position in this is very sensitive. We're a long way exposed, and we've got our reputation to think of.'

'Your reputation?' Maguire's shout filled the room and echoed down the empty corridor. Griffiths grimaced at Maguire and allowed his chair to fall forward. He walked over towards the door and stretched out his foot to close it with a bang. Maguire took the point. When he continued his words were measured and his voice more controlled.

'Look, Griffiths, let me see if I can get this across to you. An old lady is dead; battered to death by a maniac. I, Jonathan Maguire of Stadium Television, witnessed it, and some might even choose to allege that I took part in it. I know who the killers are. I can identify them; have them brought to justice.' He stood up and walked to the window and looked out into the empty early-morning gloom. 'That was four days ago and the old lady's body is still in that wood. Those people are still out there, and the police are hunting them. For all I know they may kill again, they may already have killed again. If they have or if they do, and I could have stopped them,' now Maguire turned around sharply to speak to the back of Griffiths' head, 'what do you think that is going to do for your precious reputation?'

Griffiths was refilling his pipe. He waited a few seconds before speaking. The digital clock on the wall peeped. It was 5 a.m.

'But, my dear Maguire, no one knows that you were a witness, do they? And those that do think you are Marland or Maitland or whatever it was you told them. They think you are an out-of-work docker who lost his nerve when the going got rough, and that you are in it as deeply as they are and therefore extremely unlikely to go to the police.' The reporter's whispered words were heavily laden with irony. 'As yet, no one knows that the *Encounter* programme, famous as it is for its care and expertise in such matters, has become involved with an ugly gang of raving maniacs, has buggered up its surveillance, has failed to acquire any footage, and has ended up being a party to the murder of a defenceless old woman. And Maguire – ' now his voice fell still further so that it was barely audible even to Maguire a few feet away; nonetheless the words lost none of their import, ' – I've spent too much time building up the reputation of this programme to stand by and watch a fresh-faced young reporter with an overworked conscience flush it down the john in an instant without even taking a few hours to work out whether there's any way of salvaging the situation.' Griffiths turned around and fixed his eyes on Maguire. 'Got the picture?'

* * *

On another side of the quiet city, Peter Tremayne lay awake in his bed and stared at the ceiling. He closed his eyes tightly and pressed the tips of his fingers into his eyelids. The image came back more vividly still; the dark and twisted shape of an old woman lying dead among dead leaves.

In one movement the young man sat up and swung his feet out on to the rug beside his bed. He shook his head and opened his eyes, looking around his tiny bachelor apartment. It seemed even smaller than usual. The whitewashed walls were exactly as they had been when he had moved in two years earlier, except for the addition of the poster featuring an erotic pink silhouette of a half-dressed ballerina. The usual disarray surrounded him: a rowing machine in one corner, an expensive hi-fi stacked up where he had removed it from the boxes, with the wire to the stereo headphones snaking across a pile of compact discs strewn over the floor. A damp dressing-gown lay half on the edge of the bed and half on the floor. The dim glow from yellow streetlamps showed faintly through the blinds, casting spooky shadows across the room. Peter Tremayne had spent the last ten hours struggling with crowding thoughts, and still he could not decide what to do. Whatever it might be, he knew that he would think more clearly in the office. He began to dress.

The usually frenzied city streets were quite empty in the twilight of early morning. Despite his best efforts at stealth, Tremayne's steel-tipped heels seemed to strike the damp city pavements with an alarming resonance. It was a four-mile walk to the office and Tremayne had timed his journey so that he would arrive just before Roberts. He knew that the ageing commissionaire got to the bank at six o'clock to open the doors for the cleaning staff. Tremayne waited on a corner in front of a sandwich shop several hundred yards away, from which he had a clear view of the front door of the bank. At exactly two minutes to six he saw an old man wearing a flat cap and khaki overcoat dismount from his bicycle as he emerged round a corner from the opposite direction, and scoot the last few yards towards the steps leading to the large double-doors. He watched the man look carefully about him before taking the heavy keys from his pocket. Tremayne pushed his hands hard into his coat pockets and walked briskly towards the old stone building.

'Morning Roberts.'

'God bless my soul.' The old man turned around abruptly and put his hand to his chest. The front wheel of the bicycle turned sharply and Tremayne had to step back to prevent it falling on him. His brief moment of concern for Roberts's welfare was unnecessary. 'You gave me the shock of my life, sir.' He leaned his bike against the wall.

'Sorry Roberts. I didn't mean to frighten you. I've got to make an early start on some papers for the Chairman. He wants them as soon as he comes in.'

The commissionaire stood back politely. 'You go right in, sir. I'll have to switch off the upstairs alarm.' The two men entered the bank and Tremayne waited while Roberts fumbled with the keys to lock the great heavy doors behind him. Then the old man went into his lodge behind the bank's reception and opened a panelled cupboard. He glanced over his shoulder at Tremayne, who deliberately turned his head to reassure the commissionaire that he had no intention of trying to see the alarm procedure. The moment brought Tremayne his first smile for many hours.

'You can go up now if you like, sir. I'll be making a cup of tea presently if you'd like one?'

'No thanks, Roberts. I've taken tea this morning.

I've quite a bit to do so I'd be glad of some peace and quiet.'

'Right you are, sir.' The old man pushed his cap back from his forehead.

Tremayne bounded up the stairs towards his own office. Once inside he quickly found his keys and quietly entered Sir John Bartholomew's room. The chairs were set out just as they had been left last night and Tremayne now sat heavily in the one which had been occupied by Davis. He closed his eyes. The walk had cleared his head and he began to think quite coherently.

Almost immediately Tremayne found himself wondering how he could have been so stupid as not to have realized that this or something like it was the inevitable result of the plot he had seen unfolding before him. There had been a murder, a brutal and merciless killing of a defenceless old woman and he, Peter Tremayne, Oxford double-first and high-flier, was indirectly a party to it. He stood up and walked briskly around the room, grinding the knuckles of one hand into the palm of the other. His mind began to overflow once again with a confusion of thoughts and images; the lifelong promise and now confident expectation of success turning into tatters; the public scandal, the humiliation, even the hopes of his parents. Suddenly all of his fears were those of a small boy in trouble, and he wanted a way out.

The door of the Chairman's private bathroom was ajar and he went in, sniffing the air to reassure himself that there was no lingering smell of his own vomit from the night before. He glanced in the mirror at his raw and unshaven face, and for the first time in his life he looked and felt old. He looked more closely and pulled down the skin of his cheeks further to reveal his pink and bloodshot eyes, then ran the cold tap and splashed water liberally across his face and held the towel against himself for a long time. How could things have come to this, he asked himself, how could he have let all this happen without doing something to stop it? Why had things gone so terribly wrong in a life during which everything had always gone so satisfyingly right?

Tremayne was on the edge of despair. He was deeply in trouble. He thought of his father, and then of his old school and wondered what guidance it would offer him now. He thought of his former headmaster, and in a moment he was a small boy again standing before the great man and listening across the mists of memory. The right thing; always do the right thing. In your heart you always know what it is, and you must have the courage to do it. That is what distinguishes us from the rest; that is the tradition you inherit. Tremayne thought about the advice. He knew what the right thing was, and now he marvelled at how long it had been since this had been the parameter by which he had judged his own actions. The morality of the market-place was very different.

The right thing was to go immediately to the local police station and tell them everything he knew. Yet even as he entertained the idea he realized that if he did so he would be immediately finished at the Mallin Harcourt Merchant Bank, and would probably never be able to work in business again. Loyalty was another prized virtue, and in the unforgiving clique of the City of London, loyalty was valued above all other virtues, including legality.

Tremayne walked out into the office and closed the bathroom door behind him. He noticed the television set which had not yet been pushed back into the cupboard. He walked across and was beginning to put the equipment away when he wondered about the cassette. He glanced around and then remembered that he had seen Bartholomew put it away in the top drawer of his desk. He walked across and sat in the large leather chair. The drawer was locked. He pulled harder but it remained firmly shut.

Tremayne sat and thought for a few further moments. He got to his feet and went to the door, opening it a few inches. There was no sound. He went back to the desk and began looking for something suitable. The gold-plated letter opener. He picked it up and began to try to open the drawer. The point entered the keyhole and Tremayne manoeuvred it around, trying to turn the lock. He struggled for several seconds before the blade slipped out of the hole and skidded noisily across the front of the drawer, making a slight scratch in the lacquer. Tremayne licked a finger and rubbed at the scratch. Immediately its vividness faded and almost disappeared. Once again Tremayne pushed the letter opener into the keyhole and twisted it around. There was a sharp click which seemed to reverberate around the room. The drawer slid open and the cassette lay there. Tremayne grabbed it and returned to the video player.

The tape was only three-quarters of the way through its run. Tremayne switched on the television and pressed the *play* button on the video. He stood back a few feet and once again he saw the shape of the dead body of the old woman lying in the leaves, her limbs splayed out in the grass next to the exposed roots of an enormous dark tree. There was a flickering of static at the end of the picture and gradually another scene began to emerge. The pictures of the burglary had obviously been placed over an old recording. Tremayne stepped further back and sat on the arm of a large leather chair behind him and fixed his eyes on the screen. He remained transfixed, almost hypnotized as he saw the flames, a house on fire, and the indistinct shapes of many fire engines. He reached across and turned up the volume. He found it difficult to comprehend what was happening. In the distance there was the pandemonium of fire-fighting, but in the foreground he could hear the sound of the laughter of several men. He wondered who could be laughing while a house was burning. Then a familiar high-pitched voice broke through the mêlée.

'That's one fewer family of niggers round this way.'

Tremayne continued to watch as the camera panned away from the distant flames and found the red and fat face of Davis laughing extravagantly into the lens. The face was close enough to the camera so that when the pudgy hand came out it was able to push the lens back so that it pointed towards the flames.

'Bugger off Johnson. It's time we were away. Let's get moving.'

Now Tremayne could hear the screams from the distance. The men in the picture heard them too and paused. Someone was crying. He could not make out what was being said. The voice was distant and the accent foreign. He reached forward and once again turned up the volume and the words came through loud and clear.

'My children. My children.' Tremayne sat stunned.

Again the camera panned away to find Davis and several other men. By the time it found them they had turned and were walking away. Once again they were laughing loudly. Tremayne stood up and switched the video player off. He pressed the *eject* switch, lifted out the cassette, and sat in the unusual quiet, listening to the faraway sounds of the cleaners going about their morning tasks. He was still holding the tape in his hand. He cast his mind back over what it showed,

288

gradually putting pieces together, taking it all in, analysing as he had been taught to do. Now he had all but made up his mind. It would not be enough on its own. Then he remembered the Chairman's audio tape-recording.

Tremayne returned to his boss's desk and once again sat in the enormous chair. It was a chair he had very much hoped one day to occupy. If he followed the course on which he had now embarked, he would not have the slightest chance of ever occupying this chair. If on the other hand he kept silent, recent events had made his chance of becoming Chairman of the Mallin Harcourt Merchant Bank very good indeed. He looked at the drawer where Sir John kept the secret cassette recorder and pondered. Perhaps thirty seconds passed as Tremayne tried to consider all the many implications of the act he felt sure he was about to undertake. The consequences were clear and drastic. He thought once again of the old school which had expected so much; the headmaster who had spoken of the right thing; the old school tie.

Abruptly Tremayne pulled open the tiny drawer and flicked the sound tape from the recorder. He walked back to the cupboard by the television and took a blank video cassette and an audio tape. He returned again to the desk and placed the blank videotape in the drawer which had been locked, and the new sound-tape into the recorder. He closed both drawers and went out into Mrs Blake's office to look for an envelope. He sat at her desk and wrote an address in large clear letters. He put the two tapes into the envelope without pausing and sealed the flap. On his way out of the building, Tremayne stopped off in his own office to pick up some of his personal belongings.

CHAPTER TWENTY-FOUR

Stephen Ross looked around at the huddle of mourners who stood close together at the edge of the newly dug grave in the windswept churchyard. There were perhaps twenty people present and it struck him that they represented a very wide variety of types. It was odd. To many, Harriet Nuttall must have seemed a conservative old spinster who had led a sheltered life, seldom travelling far or experiencing much outside her immediate environment. Yet the range of people who turned out to mourn her sudden death was testimony to the extraordinary breadth of her experience and concerns. There were a number of women who looked rather like Harriet herself. Dark hats with narrow brims, secured in place by mother-of-pearl studded hatpins. Dark coats and sensible walking shoes. Mingled indiscriminately among them were friends from the many environmentalist groups to which Harriet had belonged. It seemed that some of Harriet's older friends had known nothing of her enthusiasm for environmental issues, and were now surprised to discover this other part of her essentially very private life. As the mourners had waited for the hearse to arrive, Stephen Ross watched the different friends chatting, crossing the generation gap as Harriet had herself. He wondered what she would have made of this gathering of all her different realms of interest. Now, as the coffin was gently lowered into the dark grave between them, Stephen Ross felt as though perhaps in some real way she was here.

Incongruous among the mourners were two men in

light raincoats and trilby hats. Stephen Ross recognized them immediately as the police. Next to them was a group wearing more expensive but shabbier raincoats. These were the journalists who had for the last week been running sensational stories of the violent death of the much loved old spinster – a phrase widely used of her since her death. The police were in no doubt that they were looking for a burglar, but a burglar of a particular type. This man, they had said, would be sure to have previous convictions for some sexual offence. Clearly he was a pervert of some kind, and they were scrupulously examining criminal records for any trace of a man with such a *modus operandi*. All over Britain men with such records had been routinely taken in for questioning by the local police. For each of them it was a familiar routine every time this type of crime took place. The police had no sympathy. It was part of the price these men knew they had to pay for their special crime.

The public had been particularly anxious to help. This was the type of crime that society could be unanimous about. A defenceless old woman disturbs a burglar who should, according to all the familiar rules of criminal behaviour, immediately flee the house. Instead this one confronts the old woman, brutally kills one of her cats, probably to force her to reveal the whereabouts of non-existent valuables. Then, filled with anger and frustration at being unable to find any treasure, the burglar beats up the old woman, abducts her from the house, takes her to a lonely wood where he assaults her afresh and caves in her head with a blunt instrument. The public was anxious to assist the police and could scarcely have been more helpful. There had been scores of reported sightings of the black Morris car with a man driving and a woman apparently asleep inside, slumped against the door. There were other clues, sightings of strange men seen running in one direction and another. There were dozens of cars unaccounted for, and police officers manning an incident room which had been set up at the local police station were assiduously sifting through every scrap of information from the public, no matter how insignificant it might seem.

Stephen Ross looked around and felt a deep sense of dismay at the pointlessness of it all. Harriet had been an exceptional woman. He had felt frustrated by his inability to get this across to the police in any way which they would have begun to understand; and when they learned that he had actually met her on only one occasion, they more or less lost interest in him. He had begun to talk about nuclear matters, but it was clear that the police had no enthusiasm for such things. They were interested in evidence, and in this case the evidence was clear and unambiguous. They did not suppose that Mr Ross could be suggesting that nuclear spies, or whatever fantastic creatures he was envisaging, went into the bedrooms of old ladies and masturbated in their underwear. No? Of course not. Well then. They were looking for a burglar who was also a pervert, that much was clear. Could he take a look through Miss Nuttall's papers? They saw no objection. They just had to wait for the coroner's report to be finalized and for the executors of the estate to give permission. They would be in touch.

Stephen Ross joined the single file of mourners as they walked past the open grave and prepared to leave the cemetery. There was to be no other gathering. No one, it seemed, felt that they knew her well enough to take the initiative. He was about to get into his car when he felt a gentle tap on his shoulder and looked around to see a man in his sixties with grey hair and a dark suit. The man's face looked ravaged by exhaustion and grief.

'Excuse me, are you Mr Ross?'

'I am.'

'May I introduce myself. My name is Cox. I'm a solicitor, late of Charlton and Cox. My practice represented Harriet Nuttall. May I have a word with you?'

'We had a burglary several nights ago. As a matter of fact it was just a few days before the night that the police believe poor Miss Nuttall was killed.' The solicitor lifted the delicate china teacup to his lips and replaced it on the desk which had belonged to George Charlton. 'My partner, George Charlton, was killed more or less at the spot where your feet are now.'

Ross shuffled awkwardly and looked around him. 'What were the burglars after? You don't ordinarily keep much in the way of valuables in solicitor's offices, do you?' Stephen Ross glanced at the small old-fashioned safe in the corner.

'Nothing was taken,' said Mr Cox. 'They couldn't get the safe open; but the police believe that the unfortunate Mr Charlton interrupted them in the attempt and paid for it with his life.'

'I'm very sorry.' Stephen Ross took a sip of his tea. 'You'll forgive me for asking, but you'll understand that I'm wondering why you've asked me here. What has this to do with me?'

The grey old man smiled patiently. 'You've been very kind in coming here and bearing with me so far. I'm grateful.' He stood up slowly and began pacing around the room, as though trying to make up his mind how to express what he had to say. 'You see, Mr Ross,

I am in some difficulty. In law my duty is quite clear. I have a letter in my possession which is addressed to you. By rights I am obliged simply to hand it over to you and allow you to leave this office without making any further inquiry.'

Now Stephen Ross leaned forward, concentrating hard on what was coming next. 'But in this case I am intimately involved because the only reason that it is I who am delivering this letter to you and not my partner Mr Charlton,' the solicitor now had his back to Stephen Ross and there was a slight tremor of emotion in his voice as he spoke, 'is because my partner was killed in this very office, and I believe the reason he was killed is that he refused to hand over a letter which was entrusted to him by one of our oldest and dearest clients.'

Already Stephen Ross knew what was coming. He remembered Harriet's words. 'I've taken precautions. I'll deliver one way or the other. You can rely on me.'

'That client was the person from whose funeral we have just returned, Miss Harriet Nuttall. The burglary and my partner's death took place less than one week after Harriet Nuttall visited him and, according to our practice log, gave him a letter.' Now he turned back to face Stephen Ross. He seemed to have composed himself. 'That letter was to be opened in the event of her untimely death. As executor in the absence of Mr Charlton, I have opened the letter. Inside it was a bundle of papers which are marked to be handed to you.' Now Mr Cox tapped his jacket in the area of his heart which seemed to indicate that the papers were in an inside pocket. 'You see, Mr Ross, I believe that inside these papers are clues which will shed light not only on the death of Harriet Nuttall, but also on the death of my partner. You must understand, Mr Ross,' now the old man fixed Ross with watery grey eyes but spoke firmly, 'you must understand that George Charlton was my partner of twenty-eight years' standing; he was also my friend, my trusted and much loved friend. And whoever killed him will be brought to justice if it is the last thing I ever manage to achieve.'

Stephen Ross took a moment to absorb what was being said to him and then told the solicitor that he understood completely. The two men opened the envelope containing a long letter addressed to Stephen and a bundle of papers. The letter contained information about an open window and a footprint on a window-ledge, a description of a man at a bus-stop and of a man who appeared to be a bird-watcher who drove a red car. Ten minutes later both were on their way to a disused barn five minutes away from the spot where Harriet Nuttall had been found murdered. Their journey was fruitless, but now Stephen Ross knew everything he needed to know.

As he paid the taxi-driver outside the studios of Stadium Television, Stephen did not look up to notice the battered white van which had just come to a stop across the road. The fat man at the wheel had experienced growing concern as he had followed the taxi all the way from Stephen Ross's house. Now his suspicions were confirmed. He and his operatives had been watching Ross almost constantly since the meeting with Bartholomew. The orders had been to move in at the first secure opportunity, but Ross had been taking unusual precautions; staying with friends for most of the time, and having constant meetings with people at his home on his occasional visits there. Now he was going to Stadium Television and that looked very bad indeed.

The fat man was wondering what to do when his eye was caught by something else. An old black Citroën car had pulled up at the kerbside directly in front of his van and an attractive woman emerged from the passenger door. Moments later the driver's door opened and for a few seconds Davis could not believe what his eyes told him. The man who got out of the car was immediately confronted on the pavement by several other people who appeared to know him. The group exchanged conversation while the attractive woman waited on the other side of the car. It gave Davis the opportunity to be sure that he was right. There could be no doubt. He was dressed quite differently, he had shaved and had a completely different hairstyle, but there was no mistake. It was the man he knew as Marland.

Davis watched as the couple crossed the road towards the Stadium Television building. They walked directly towards Ross, who was waiting on the pavement, and appeared to introduce themselves. The group shook hands and then entered the building. They remained within Davis's sight for long enough for him to see the man known as Marland wave a friendly greeting to the commissionaire, who waved back in return. The fat man remained still, staring into the blur through the windscreen. The conclusion was inescapable. Marland worked for Stadium Television. He had infiltrated their organization. He knew everything. Slowly the fat man turned the key in the ignition and set off along the road for half a mile until he came to a telephone booth. Davis's mind was still turning over fast as he dialled the number of the Mallin Harcourt Bank.

'Sir John Bartholomew please.'

'One moment, I'll put you through.'

'Hello. Chairman's office.'

'May I speak to Sir John please?'

'Who is calling?'

'Tell him it's Davis.'

There was a slight pause before the familiar voice came on the line.

'Hello Davis. Davis?' The fat man was silent, his mind still preoccupied with the implications of his discovery. Now he had only one instinct working and that was for self-preservation. 'Hello. Are you there, Davis? Is that you?' The fat man heard the voice more faintly. 'What the devil is going on? Mrs Blake, did you say that Mr Davis was on this line? Well he's not here; no one's here.' The fat man held the receiver away from his ear as he reached his final decision. 'Davis? Are you there, man? Say something for goodness sake.' Slowly, the pudgy hand replaced the receiver on the cradle. The next number it dialled was that of the South African Embassy. He asked for the visa department.

Inside the Stadium Television building Maguire took Ross directly to Peter Griffiths' office. The four sat down among the debris and Griffiths completed the introductions.

'Stephen Ross is the man who originally sent us the material which was the basis for our programme about the attempts by American companies in complicity with some British banks, including Mallin Harcourt where Mr Ross formerly worked, to circumvent the nuclear proliferation treaty. He telephoned me yesterday to tell me that he has now got some more information relating to this area.' Griffiths was self-consciously behaving like a detective who has gathered together all the suspects at the end of the story to work out the culprit before an appreciative audience. 'Mr Ross mentioned a name in which we already have an interest through Mr Maguire and Mrs Layfield here,' he turned deferentially to Maguire and Pamela, 'which is why I have invited you two to join us.'

Over the next hour Stephen Ross explained about the Lazarus file.

'I took a number of papers, some of them at random, when I left Mallin Harcourt. The ones relating to the NPT were the first ones I analysed and understood the importance of. I gave them to you, Peter, and was very pleased with the programme you made.' Griffiths nodded smugly. 'But when I discovered the Lazarus information, I realized that we in the anti-nuclear movement could make such an impact with it that I just could not resist handling it myself.' He looked around, expecting dissent, but none came. 'You're kind enough not to say it, but that was obviously my biggest mistake, because it cost poor Harriet Nuttall her life.'

'So the National Socialist people we have been interested in are also the people employed by the nuclear industry to get back their papers?' said Pamela.

'Apparently. But the problem now is, how do we prove it?'

The group sat in silence for some while. Maguire was still struggling with his feelings of disbelief and horror at what he had witnessed on that night, and also of confusion about what he ought to do next. Despite his own disquiet and that of Pamela, he had so far heeded Griffiths' instructions to remain silent. More than anything else he had wanted to understand why the NS group had raided the old lady's house and what papers

298

it was that they were looking for. Now at last he understood why Harriet Nuttall had died.

There was a loud knock on the door. 'Enter.' Griffiths' voice sounded irritated and abrupt. Maguire was finding it increasingly difficult to like him. Pamela had already made up her mind that she would never be able to do so. A secretary walked timidly into the room.

'This arrived for you half an hour ago. Someone delivered it by hand at the front desk and insisted that you got it straight away.' The woman put the packet down on the desk and left the room. Griffiths allowed his chair to fall forward on to four legs and thrust himself forward to pick up the packet. As he did so Stephen Ross glanced at the brown envelope and something about it caught his attention.

'May I see that?' Griffiths handed it to him. Ross took it and turned it over. 'I thought so.' He pointed to the print on the edge of the flap. 'This is from someone at the Mallin Harcourt Merchant Bank.'

'Fascinating.' Griffiths spoke with obvious pleasure. He ripped open the packaging as he spoke. 'How very interesting.' He held up the two tapes between finger and thumb. 'How very, very interesting.'

CHAPTER TWENTY-FIVE

Sir John Bartholomew sat at his desk and looked around him. His surroundings represented some of the trappings of influence and wealth which went with his position. Within his power he had the ability to guarantee success or failure for enormous industries and businesses in Britain and abroad. By deciding when and where to invest the huge resources at the command of the bank, he could make or break great men and great companies almost at a whim. He could, if he chose, have a chauffeur-driven car at the door within seconds, travel first class to any part of the globe, register in any hotel in the world, and if he did not like the service, he could buy it. Only a very few eyebrows would be raised about the Chairman's little indulgence and such questions as there were would be of little significance. The speed at which decisions in the international money markets had to be made meant that in large areas of the bank's business, the Chairman could act without reference to others, merely reporting more significant matters to the board in due course. The Chairman of so important and influential a bank had instant access to mandarins and ministers, to foreign governments and heads of state. From a pinnacle of respectability and influence in the City of London, the Mallin Harcourt Merchant Bank and its Chairman Sir John Bartholomew were entitled to feel practically invincible.

Yet, the Chairman reflected, how fragile a thing is power. Sir John Bartholomew looked at the palms of his smooth hands. He turned them over and placed them flat on the desk, then raised them again and took a tight grip on thin air. How elusive a thing it all was. Hundreds of judgements could be made in a day; some would be right, some would be wrong, the consequences of either were most often slight, the difference between them marginal. Thousands of decisions would go by without comment, without anyone even noticing the results be they either good or bad. Then one time, just one of those thousands of judgements could be dreadfully and hopelessly mistaken. It would disappear amid the chaos of other matters coming and going across his desk in the central heart of the mass of banking business. Then one day it would return to his in-tray, and sit there like a grenade, waiting to explode in his hands; and at this moment there was nothing, with all the enormous power and influence at his command, there was absolutely nothing he could do to prevent it.

Sir John Bartholomew blinked through the haze of his thoughts and wondered about the Lazarus file. The decision to commission it had seemed so uncomplicated, even uncontroversial at the time; he could not even remember exactly when he had done so. The decision to implement the recommendations had seemed an easy one; it was an enormous venture, a measured risk, and there would be a substantial profit for his shareholders. It was straightforward just like the vast majority of the bank's business, just like so many other banking decisions.

What had been his failing? Sir John Bartholomew sat in the seat of power and asked himself what he had done wrong. It must be that he had insufficiently considered the consequences of a breach of security.

For a moment he imagined the feelings of a multi-millionaire gambler who had staked everything he owned on a proposition which would net only a few pounds if it came up successfully, but would ruin him if it failed. It was a stupid gamble to have taken, he could see that now. He regretted having done so. Even if the situation was remediable, the eventual return would not have been worth the time and trouble it had already taken to put it right.

At no time even now did it occur to Sir John Bartholomew that it was wrong to have considered the Lazarus proposals simply because they were dishonest. Nor did the Chairman consider the morality of increasing the risk to the public by installing safety systems which did not properly function. The only disaster which concerned Sir John was the potential problem for himself and his bank. Having briefly chastised himself for his imprudence, the Chairman wondered about the chance of that disaster occurring. Was that simple wrong decision waiting in his in-tray to explode in his hands, or could he even now keep matters within his powerful grip?

The Chairman visibly jumped as the loud buzz of the intercom broke the silence. The twinge of pain in the area just above his heart made him reach, almost as a reflex, for the small box in his waistcoat pocket. As he put the tiny tablet on to his tongue, Sir John reached with his other hand for the switch and clicked it open. It was Mrs Blake.

'Sir John? I have Stadium Television on the telephone for you.'

His eyes flickered towards the speaker and a frown crossed his brow. The receding pain in his chest made a momentary comeback before fading again almost as suddenly.

'Stadium Television? Who from Stadium Television?'

'The man says his name is Peter Griffiths, sir.'

Bartholomew thought quickly. He felt a keen interest to know what the television people wanted, but he was extremely reluctant to speak to them himself.

'Has Tremayne come in yet?'

'No sir, there's been no word from him yesterday or today. Mr Hubbard says Mr Tremayne had said something early last week about his father being unwell, but I'm afraid there's been no specific message from him.'

'Keep telephoning his flat. And we've still heard nothing from Mr Davis?'

'No sir, not since we were cut off from speaking to him yesterday. He hasn't been back on the telephone. What shall I tell the television people, Sir John? They're hanging on.'

'Put the call through.'

'Sir John Bartholomew?' The Chairman recognized the voice of the man who had so often been the scourge of the City.

'This is he. How may I help?'

'I work for the *Encounter* programme on Stadium Television. I don't suppose you ever see it, we go out on a Saturday night.'

'I've seen your programme once or twice, Mr Griffiths.' Bartholomew was taking unusual care to be polite and patient. 'How can I help?'

'We're doing a programme tomorrow night about the City of London's response to the Chancellor's autumn budget statement. We'll be showing a short film we've made about the Stock Exchange reaction both here and in New York; and we're also gathering together a group of eminent bankers and investment managers for a studio discussion.'

303

Bartholomew was immediately suspicious. He interrupted. 'Who else have you asked to take part?'

Griffiths had anticipated the question and was well prepared. 'We've asked Sir Geoffrey Tate from Marsh Hamilton, Roger Kyle from Manchester Royal Life and the junior minister Mr Sawdon. The first two have agreed and the minister is trying to postpone another engagement in order to be able to come.'

'Hold one moment.' The Chairman flicked a switch on the side of his telephone and then reached for the intercom. 'Mrs Blake, call Geoffrey Tate, Roger Kyle and Arthur Sawdon at the Treasury. Ask them if they've agreed to participate in a Stadium Television programme tomorrow night about the Chancellor's budget statement.' He clicked off without waiting for a reply and returned to the telephone. 'As you know I rarely do television programmes, Mr Griffiths. May I ask why you have invited me on this occasion?'

Once again, Griffiths had done his homework and was ready. 'Because as you know, following the recent EEC decisions on encouraging aid for the developing world, the Chancellor is expected to say something about further tax concessions for investment in third world economies. We know that your bank has substantial investments in Namibia and certain other African countries, and we're told that this is an area you have strong views on.'

'I have indeed. Successive governments have for many years been discouraging investment in some African countries simply because they don't like the political complexion of the regimes there. We have maintained for many years that investment is good for the black man and ought therefore to be encouraged.'

'Quite so, Sir John. But you'll accept that this is a

controversial area and we think it's important that the views you outline should be given an airing.'

'When would this be, Mr Griffiths?'

'Tomorrow night. The programme goes out live at nine-thirty so we would want you at our studios by nine o'clock at the latest.'

The Chairman's mind raced. Like a butterfly compelled to fly near to the flame of a candle, he felt an almost irresistible need to get close to his potential antagonists. In normal circumstances he would have instantly refused, but Roger Kyle was a persuasive campaigner against investment by British companies in some African countries. Mallin Harcourt had a crucial interest in opposing that line of argument. He told himself that this was the reason why he was tempted.

'My secretary will call you back within half an hour with my answer. Leave a number with her, will you?'

Bartholomew replaced the receiver and began to turn over every possible aspect of the present situation. Analysis, that was what he now needed; a cool analysis of the potential benefits and the downside of flirting with people who could perhaps do him such mortal damage. Perhaps he could use the occasion to find out what was going on; perhaps he would take Tremayne with him and the sharp young man could poke around asking questions while he appeared on the programme. Then another unpleasant thought flickered through his mind and he reached into his pocket for the small brass key on the end of a gold chain which was fixed to his waistcoat. He placed the key in the lock on his desk drawer and tried the lock. It would not turn. Momentarily confused, the Chairman turned the key in the other direction and tried the drawer. Now it was locked. He turned it once more and again it turned. He pulled the drawer open a few inches. Had it been unlocked before? He could not now be sure and tried to remember whether he had locked the drawer as usual on the previous evening. He could not picture himself doing so. The Chairman opened the drawer fully and the sight of the video cassette instantly brought a feeling of relief. He took it out and turned it over. Then he opened the left-hand drawer and flicked the audio-cassette out of the tape recorder. He replaced both tapes in the right-hand drawer and locked it, pulling firmly at the handle to ensure that he had done so before replacing the small key safely in his pocket. Twenty minutes later Bartholomew called in Mrs Blake.

'Sir Geoffrey Tate and Roger Kyle both confirm that they have been invited to appear on the *Encounter* programme to talk about the budget statement and the third world issue. Both have accepted. I've been through to Arthur Sawdon's office in the Treasury but he's away in his constituency at the moment. Nobody there knows about it but they say it is possible he has agreed to do the programme without telling them. Shall I keep trying?'

'No, Mrs Blake, that's all right. Call Mr Griffiths back and tell him I'll be at his studios at nine tomorrow night. Tell them my fee will be two hundred pounds plus expenses and will be non-negotiable. Say that I will be donating it to the ex-servicemen's charity. That will be all.' She was writing in her notebook as she retreated. 'Just one moment, Mrs Blake. Have you been ringing Tremayne's flat?'

'Yes, Sir John. I'm afraid there's no reply.'

'Well keep trying.' Bartholomew's irritation at the behaviour of his personal assistant was spilling over on to Mrs Blake, but she was rapidly getting past the point where she cared. 'And keep trying Mr Davis.'

* * *

Jonathan Maguire and Pamela Layfield sat opposite each other in the foyer of Stadium Television and waited. For the first time in many days, Maguire felt at ease. Plans had been laid, and something like justice was soon to be done. Pamela stared at him for a long time, her eyes conveying some of the warmth that she increasingly felt for him. She had been wondering when to raise the subject which had been on her mind for several days, and decided that this seemed an opportune moment.

'You do know that Mr Griffiths and his like are a prime cartload of bastards, don't you?'

A pained expression crossed Maguire's face and he carefully avoided her gaze while considering the remark. He was becoming increasingly familiar with the way she seemed to articulate bluntly but precisely his own more remote feelings. Now her words expressed a little of the deep sense of disappointment he had already been feeling for several days.

'Yes, I know. I didn't think they would be, but they are.' He looked up at her again. 'Maybe they have to be. Maybe that's the only way to get this particular type of job done.'

'It can't be the only way. You're just making excuses for them. Griffiths is just an incredibly selfish bastard.' Pamela knew that she was more exasperated than the situation justified, but she had been suppressing these thoughts, and now that she had begun to give them expression she was becoming more and more angry. 'None of them really gives a damn about Miss Nuttall, or you, or even getting justice. All they care about is their damned programme.'

'But maybe that's the key to success.' Maguire felt he was struggling with himself as well as with her. 'Maybe Griffiths has got to remain obsessed with his

307

programme; otherwise it will just be like the others, no different from the competition.'

'That's just an excuse for being a natural born-again bastard; and anyway, if that's what's involved in making these damned programmes I don't want any part of it. It's sick, and I don't want you to have anything to do with it either.' She was calmer now. They exchanged a half-hearted smile. 'Do you?'

Maguire thought for a while. 'I believed that I did. I've wanted it for a very long time. Now that I've seen it up close I can see that I don't.' Pamela stood up and moved across to sit beside him. She put her arms around his neck. 'But these guys are the top of the profession, and if I can't work with them, I don't think I want to be in it at all.' Pamela squeezed him more tightly and kissed him on the cheek.

'Don't worry, I'm a rich widow. I'll support you until you find something else.' Maguire pulled back a few inches to look at her. His expression asked the question and she answered. 'I'll tell you all about it – after this last programme.'

At precisely 9 p.m. the two-tone beige Rolls-Royce glided to a halt outside the studios. Maguire and Pamela had been too busy during the last thirty-six hours to think very much about the actual confrontation with Sir John Bartholomew, and now that everything was prepared the realization of what lay ahead in the next hour began to dawn. The worry about what would happen if the Chairman of the bank did not show up, or if something went wrong with the tightly worked-out plan, dissolved as they saw the man with the greying auburn hair and pale skin emerge from his car and completely ignore the courtesy of the Stadium Television commissionaire who had rushed out to open the door for him.

'Miserable sod.' Maguire's lips scarcely moved as he spoke.

'Not as miserable as he will be shortly.' Pamela and Maguire gave each other a last nervous smile before the bank Chairman was in the foyer and Maguire walked across to greet him. Behind him a harassed-looking middle-aged woman scuttled along in an effort to keep up. Bartholomew said she was his secretary but did not mention her name. Maguire was aware that the Chairman of the bank seemed to be paying particular attention to him.

'Don't I know you? Surely you have interviewed me before some time?'

'No Sir John,' Maguire answered with complete confidence. 'I'm quite positive that I would remember.'

'That's odd,' said Sir John. 'I'm usually very good with faces, and I feel as though I've seen you somewhere recently.'

'I'm afraid there's no chance of that, Sir John. I've been completely preoccupied with another project for several months.'

The Chairman shrugged off the matter and Maguire delivered him to Peggy, the programme's PA, who would take him to make-up. The secretary was to be taken directly to the green room. As he disappeared down the corridor to the make-up department Maguire heard him asking whether 'the others' had arrived.

'Yes I think so,' said the PA, 'they'll be upstairs. I'll take you there shortly.'

Maguire and Pamela went to the *Encounter* offices to make sure that last-minute arrangements were going well. Though only very few people were directly involved in the programme, half a dozen of the other journalists were around because they had heard that things might get interesting. Griffiths was being made up in his own office.

'He's here,' said Maguire.

'Is he in make-up?'

'Yes.'

'Does Peggy know to keep him there until we give the word?'

'She knows.'

'You wait as late as possible and then bring him to the green room. Then stall him until the last possible moment.'

'I know that, Griffiths. We've been over it a dozen times.'

Griffiths smiled a rare smile. 'I'm sorry.' He paused. 'I'm nervous, for Christ's sake.' Maguire and Pamela were surprised by the unusual glimpse into Griffiths' personality. Neither had expected to find a chink in his usually impermeable shell. 'Have we stood down Geoffrey Tate from Marsh Hamilton and Roger Kyle from the MRL?' Maguire confirmed that he had done so just twenty minutes earlier. 'What did you tell them?'

'I said we had a last-minute change of programme; an important news story had just come in. I told them to watch the programme.'

'And we never got a "yes" from Sawdon anyway?'

'No, he never got back to us.'

'And what about the other two, are they here?'

Pamela answered, 'Yes, they arrived fifteen minutes ago. They're as happy as little sandboys, getting ready to respond to a list they've been given of under-researched and naïve questions about pollution from nuclear installations into the North Sea.'

'Terrific.' Griffiths seemed to have exhausted things to worry about. Then he remembered another. 'Is the video ready?'

'*Everything* is ready,' said Maguire. 'Now stop worrying and think about your part. You've got the most difficult job of all.'

'Thanks for reminding me. That makes me feel much better.'

'Let's leave him to it,' said Pamela.

Ten minutes passed before Peggy telephoned the green room and said that Sir John Bartholomew was getting restless and wanted to talk to the other guests before the programme started. It was now 9.15 and Maguire knew that he had to prevent the banker from becoming suspicious for another fifteen minutes. It would not be easy. Maguire took Pamela to one side.

'You go down and bring him up to the green room. Say you're new here, which won't be a lie, and get lost on your way back. If he asks about tonight, tell him you haven't been working on the programme about the budget – which also won't be a lie – so you can't tell him anything about it. Try to get him to the green room just before nine twenty-five.'

'Fine. Leave him to me.' Pamela set off to the make-up department. By the time she got there Sir John Bartholomew was on the brink of losing his temper.

'Where's Mrs Blake? Where are the other guests? We're on in ten minutes and I haven't been given a clue what the questions will be about. Is this the way you people usually do things? If so I won't be appearing on any of your programmes again.'

Pamela apologized very politely and proceeded to guide him down apparently endless corridors. As they walked she was aware that the bank chairman was fumbling in his waistcoat pocket, and eventually she saw him produce a tiny golden box. He removed the lid as he walked and stuffed two small pills into his mouth. He sucked in his cheeks as though trying to draw hard on them. The pair walked for three minutes before she stopped a commissionaire and asked the way to the green room. She looked over her shoulder at Bartholomew. 'Sorry, I'm afraid I'm new here.'

'Good God.' Sir John Bartholomew raised his eyes to the ceiling and stood while the commissionaire gave detailed directions. The Chairman was breathing heavily.

In the green room upstairs Mrs Blake sat in a chair in one corner and wondered how her boss would get on in this rare appearance on television. Though she had worked for Sir John Bartholomew for twenty years she could not help hoping that he would perform badly. Until now she had always been loyal to him, but she would never forget or forgive the intolerable way in which hc had treated her in the last few weeks. He had been rude, inconsiderate, and she very much thought it was about time someone took him down a peg or two. She even suspected that Peter Tremayne had walked out in a bad temper because of the way they had all been treated, and Sir John was just too insensitive even to have realized it. Now, in Tremayne's absence, he expected her to turn out for him on a Saturday night, without even an apology.

Mrs Blake sat quietly as two smart-looking gentlemen she recognized as recent visitors to Sir John's office were shown into the room. She had not been introduced to them but she assumed that these were Geoffrey Tate and Roger Kyle whose offices she had telephoned yesterday for confirmation that they were also appearing on the programme. In ordinary circumstances she would have introduced herself to them, but so aggrieved did she feel by all the recent secrecy that she decided she would simply sit quietly and stay in the background until all this present unpleasantness blew

312

over. The two men talked to a programme researcher for several moments and were then told that they were required for make-up before going into the studio. Moments later the woman who had been introduced as Pamela came into the green room followed by Sir John Bartholomew. Mrs Blake got quite a shock to see him wearing studio make-up, which had failed to conceal the unusually deep shadows which underlined his eyes. She thought he looked rather unwell and also rather ridiculous.

'Where are the others? I thought they were up here.'

'I thought they were,' said Pamela. 'Take a seat and I'll go and see.' She walked out of the room and closed the door.

'Have you seen the other guests?' Sir John asked his secretary.

'Yes, two gentlemen you know. They were here a moment ago, they've been taken to make-up I think.'

'What a shambles.' The Chairman snarled the remark to no one in particular and sat down heavily in a chair. A minute passed in silence before Maguire came into the room.

'Could you come to the studio now, Sir John? We're on in two minutes. The others have been held up in make-up and will meet you on the set. You'll have a chance to talk while the introductory film is running.' The banker was about to protest when Pamela returned.

'Sorry Maguire,' she said, 'Sir John is wanted right now. This moment, the director says. Straight away.'

'Tell him we're coming. This way, Sir John.' The Chairman was still complaining loudly as he was escorted out of the door towards the studio. A blaze of bright lights greeted him and he saw the familiar *Encounter* set against a background of black drapes. In front of it there were four chairs, one set apart and a group of three. A man wearing headphones urged Bartholomew towards one of the three chairs, then shouted, 'Thirty seconds to on-air, standby everybody.'

As he spoke Peter Griffiths came on to the set, acknowledged Sir John and sat in the single chair facing a camera. Over to his right Sir John Bartholomew noticed two other cameras were pointing at him. Scores of bright lights seemed to be shining directly into his eyes and beads of sweat began to roll down his face. He called across the studio to Griffiths.

'I'll be complaining about all this to your Chairman directly after the programme. I've never been treated this way in my life.'

'Sorry, Sir John. Just bear with us,' Griffiths called back over his shoulder, 'it'll all be over in half an hour.'

At one side of the studio Pamela Layfield stood with Maguire and gripped his hand. She glanced at a floor-monitor close by which showed the shot from the camera that was trying to focus precisely on Sir John Bartholomew. The very tight close-up emphasized the unusually heavy perspiration and deep dark lines beneath his eyes. Pamela was shocked by his appearance. She tugged on Maguire's hand.

'Look at Bartholomew. He's ill.'

Maguire looked at the monitor and shrugged his shoulders. 'If I was in his position I'd be feeling ill.'

'No, I mean he's really ill. Look at him.'

As Maguire turned to the monitor the camera had panned away and was pointing at the cardboard caption of the Stadium Television logo. Pamela spoke again but her voice was drowned out by the booming shout from the floor manager.

'Ten seconds to on-air. Standby grams, standby vtr, standby studio.'

Sir John Bartholomew looked at the empty chairs and then up at Peter Griffiths. As he did so he saw that two other men were being escorted on to the set. He blinked through the perspiration which was now streaming down his face and for a moment could not believe the evidence of his own eyes. The two men now sitting down next to him were Sir Horace Beckford and Dante Fitzwilliam. The surprise on their faces turned rapidly into alarm. Sir John looked around in a moment of panic and saw the man wearing headphones crouching underneath the main camera and counting down from five with his fingers. At one, he swept the air with his hand and in the distance the signature music of the *Encounter* programme could be heard. Sir John was about to get to his feet. He looked across at a monitor in one corner and saw that the titles were running out, and that the programme had begun with a wide shot which included himself and the other two men. He heard Peter Griffiths begin to speak.

'Good evening. In *Encounter* tonight we hear why these three men, two eminent industrialists and one of Britain's leading international bankers, authorized a criminal burglary of a private house which led to the tragic and violent death of a respected old woman from Lansbury.'

Sir John Bartholomew felt the life drain out of him. As he fixed his eyes on the studio monitor he saw a tight close-up of himself, the sweat now running down his face. The studio lights seemed to bear down upon him oppressively, and the tight feeling like a thick belt across his chest which had been becoming more acute all afternoon was now making it difficult for him to breathe. He gasped in the air.

'And we show conclusive video evidence and hear

audio-tapes which prove that this man, Sir John Bartholomew of the Mallin Harcourt Merchant Bank in the City of London, embarked on a plan to defraud the British taxpayer of millions of pounds. He planned to do so by introducing safety procedures into a proposed nuclear installation which would not have worked, and would potentially have put thousands of lives at risk.'

The banker watched, quite helpless, as the camera shot went back to include all three men. He glanced across at the industrialists and saw that like himself, they appeared to have become paralysed in their seats.

'And having been responsible for the death of one defenceless old woman who discovered their plan, these three men went on to authorize the death of the man Stephen Ross who had originally learned of it. Our reporter successfully managed to infiltrate the extreme right-wing group which carried out these atrocities on behalf of the three men and their organizations, and we also have exclusive footage of their racist crimes and a tape-recording of their private plans. At the end of this report, we'll be interviewing the three men here, live in our studio.'

Still unable to move, Sir John Bartholomew watched the monitor and saw the pictures he had last seen on the video in his office flicker on to the screen. He glimpsed a man who had been one of the raiding party and who had just now guided him to his seat in the studio. He heard Maguire's voice on the commentary, and finally he knew what had happened. A moment later he regained some control of himself and realized that the studio was no longer live. He sat forward and was about to try to stand. He felt a hand on his shoulder, and looked up to see a uniformed policeman with a good deal of gold braid on the peak of his cap.

'I am David Williamson, Chief Constable of Rosminster police. I arrest you on a charge of conspiracy to murder.' The policeman looked at his watch. 'Uniformed officers and members of Special Branch are attending the weekly meeting of your little club at the garage at this moment.' The banker felt his vision begin to blur as though from intoxication, and the rest of the policeman's words boomed incomprehensibly around his head. 'In return for that information, and conclusive evidence against you provided to us by the gentlemen of the media, we have agreed that we'll be taking you into custody at precisely ten o'clock. In the meantime,' the harsh grip from the gloved hand pushed Bartholomew firmly back into his seat, 'stay right where you are and answer the nice man's questions.'

As Maguire's report began, everyone in the studio became transfixed by the scenes unfolding on the monitors. So extraordinary were the pictures that the programme director, vision-mixer, cameraman and floor-manager became immersed in them. On the floor of the studio, only Pamela Layfield paid any attention to what was going on around her, and her mind had become immovably focused on Sir John Bartholomew as he gazed, unblinking, at the screen. At last the video report was coming to an end and the PA was counting out of the recording. In the studio gallery the director returned her attention to the monitors and told the cameramen to stand-by.

'Counting out of video, five, four, three, two, one.'

As the report came to an end, Maguire's recorded voice betrayed just a trace of the triumph he felt. 'This is Jonathan Maguire reporting for *Encounter*.'

At the edge of the studio Maguire squeezed Pamela's hand as though to share his moment of pleasure with her, but her attention was now completely elsewhere.

'What is it, what's the matter?' he asked. His question was interrupted by the voice of Peter Griffiths echoing across the studio.

'And now we turn to the three men who are intimately associated with the events described in that report, and first of all to Sir John Bartholomew, Chairman of the Mallin Harcourt Merchant Bank. Sir John . . .' There was a pause. The studio director had taken a close-up of the bank Chairman, whose face remained turned towards the studio monitors, his eyes unblinking, the shock and hatred now replaced by emptiness.

'Sir John?'

Still there was no answer and no movement. In the gallery, realization dawned first on the studio director.

'Oh my God.'

'Sir John, are you all right?' Peter Griffiths' voice indicated his growing concern but still he did not quite understand. 'Sir John?'

'Oh Christ,' said Maguire in sudden horror, 'what have we done.'

Pamela knew the answer. 'We've killed him. That's what we've done. We've killed him.'

A large crowd had gathered in the television room of the departure lounge at Heathrow when word of what was on the *Encounter* programme spread among those waiting for their flights. It was unusual to say the least to hear a promise of conclusive proof of murder against men sitting in a live television studio. Among those taking a particular interest in the opening scenes was one man who had some difficulty lifting himself sufficiently from his seat to look over the heads of those who crowded in front. The fat man had listened carefully to the opening, and now showed no reaction to the close-up shots of Sir John Bartholomew sitting so still in the studio.

As the chaos grew in the television studio, the picture cut away from the silent and unmoving Sir John, back to Peter Griffiths, who appeared to have lost control of himself and was fumbling to find any sensible words to say. As he looked helplessly around the studio for advice or relief, the television sound from the departure lounge loudspeakers was dipped for a flight departure announcement.

'Flight BA 169 to Johannesburg is now boarding at gate number 19. All passengers for flight BA 169 to Johannesburg, please board now at gate 19.'

'Fascinating programme, eh buddy?' The American voice next to the fat man sounded genuinely enthusiastic.

'Quite so,' came the high-pitched reply. 'I wish I could watch more of it, but I'm afraid that's my flight.'

Fontana Paperbacks: Fiction

Fontana is a leading paperback publisher of fiction. Below are some recent titles.

- [ ] CABAL Clive Barker £2.95
- [ ] DALLAS DOWN Richard Moran £2.95
- [ ] SHARPE'S RIFLES Bernard Cornwell £3.50
- [ ] A MAN RIDES THROUGH Stephen Donaldson £4.95
- [ ] HOLD MY HAND I'M DYING John Gordon Davis £3.95
- [ ] ROYAL FLASH George MacDonald Fraser £3.50
- [ ] FLASH FOR FREEDOM! George MacDonald Fraser £3.50
- [ ] THE HONEY ANT Duncan Kyle £2.95
- [ ] FAREWELL TO THE KING Pierre Schoendoerffer £2.95
- [ ] MONKEY SHINES Michael Stewart £2.95

You can buy Fontana paperbacks at your local bookshop or newsagent. Or you can order them from Fontana Paperbacks, Cash Sales Department, Box 29, Douglas, Isle of Man. Please send a cheque, postal or money order (not currency) worth the purchase price plus 22p per book for postage (maximum postage required is £3.00 for orders within the UK).

NAME (Block letters) _____

ADDRESS _____

_____